Tamer

Tamer

Jill Farr

For my family.

Both consanguineous and chosen.

1

She found, to her surprise, that the door was open. She walked into the parlor, and everything looked so strange that she thought, "Oh my God, why am I so afraid?"
Jacob and William Grimm, "Little Red Cap"

If there was anything Jane hated more than driving in the dark, it was driving in the snow.

And now, as she squinted through the falling flakes noisily being sloughed side to side by her largely useless windshield wipers, and peered into blackness, Jane also realized that she hated being miles from civilization, especially with a dead phone.

She also needed to piss. "Fuck," she whispered. Cooi whined from the back seat as if in agreement.

"I know, boy" Jane muttered. Right on cue the low gaslight pinged on, adding to the prickle of anxiety spreading through her chest. She glanced out, as if doing so would make a gas station materialize, but the isolation seemed complete. It had been two hours since sunset, six since they had left Boise.

The directions from Richard said they would see the sign three miles past the town center. Her phone was long dead, cord missing, and Jane knew the spare charger in one of the four garbage bags stuffed into her back seat wasn't a car charger. She would have to find someplace open to power up her phone and contact Richard.

What am I going to do? She was panicked, but the overwhelming feeling was defeat. Self-loathing began to swirl into the anxiety and its voice grew loud enough to hamper the decision matrix her rational mind was trying to compose.

Normal adults have credit cards or partners stable lives savings that let them do things like drive cross country without it being a life threatening situation why can I not get my shit together?

Tears stung her eyes. She blinked them away–no time for that right now. Maybe later, when she was trying to fall asleep. A little low self-esteem nightcap.

It felt like the car's engine sputtered–*don't you dare die, you piece of shit*–and she leaned forward, blinking into the night. The car lights shone so halfheartedly they only illuminated the road for a few feet ahead.

In a moment of ridiculously misplaced regret, she felt guilty for cursing the car whose only sin was not being able to overcome her neglect. Car maintenance was one of those things, like building a grown-up wardrobe, starting a 401k, taking time off of work to visit the kids, that Jane always had on the mental list of things to do When She Got Some Money Together. *I'm sorry I'm sorry justmakeitjustmakeit* PLEASE *I'll give you an oil change the minute I get paid I swear...*

You said that 6 months ago, she imagined the car moaning in reply.

She shrieked, way too loudly, as the snow on the road caused the tires to skid. It was getting more and more packed on the road, making it indistinguishable from the bank. Cooi whined again, the high pitch indicating he desperately needed a rest stop.

Jane shushed him aggressively, then sucked in her breath when her slight movement caused another skid.

"Fucking hell...this is it; this is how I die. Stupidly."

The wind had picked up and the snow became a white sheet, blowing almost horizontally it seemed.

Jane felt the cold air seeping through the worn rubber on the tops of the door windows, and on her feet, from beneath the car.

Is it time to stop? Is it time to just give up and wait for daylight? I can barely see.

Wait...

Jane narrowed her eyes and gasped. *Oh my God, it's real...*

There it was. A blinking red light up ahead in the distance.

Thank you thank you thank you...it had been years since she had given up the Christmas and Easter church-attending Catholicism pretense for the grandfather who raised her. But she still felt the impulse to thank something, somewhere. God, The Universe...whatever.

Fighting the urge to gun the gas, she sat up straighter and fixed her eyes on the blinking red point.

It got closer until she was at what was ostensibly an intersection when it wasn't covered with snow. Looking at both sides of the road, she saw a signpost on one corner and the letters were just visible–Route 7. Jane leaned over and reached down into the passenger-side floorboard, scrambling through the general detritus until she found it; the envelope with the directions Richard had given her on the phone. When her phone died, it became the sole guidance for getting to the cabin where Kimmy had lived with her boyfriend, Richard, and his father, Abe.

Her eyes went to the second to last line, the point where they finally were, the last turn she started to think they had passed. There it was...Route 7.

"YES!" she screamed as she turned, causing Cooi to yip and the tires to skid in a reminder that it wasn't over yet. Jane read and reread the last piece of information on the envelope; *about two miles down on the left.*

Relief flooded over her. Two miles. At the worst, they could hike two miles.

It was probably only a few moments, but it felt like an age. The car creeping ahead, slipping now and then, Jane scanning the horizon for any sign, any light, any movement. Cooi whined again and Jane didn't even bother to shush him.

Finally–finally there it was...a pinprick of light on the left. Left. Her heart pounding with excitement, as well as relief, Jane resisted the urge to mash the gas pedal. The road curved slightly and it came into view more clearly. The light was coming through a set of two windows and as they got closer, Jane could see that it was a cabin.

"We're here, Cooi," Jane sighed.

The cabin was quite a way from the road and the windows were barely visible through the trees. As they crept closer, finally sliding to a stop parallel to the lights, Jane could see they were at the bottom of a hill that led up to the cabin.

She threw it into park and turned off the ignition. As eager as she had been to arrive, now that the imminent danger had passed, there was a different uncertainty. These were strangers. People she had never met in person and only knew through her Aunt Kimmy.

And she was only here because Aunt Kimmy was gone.

Kimmy had helped her father, Jane's grandfather, to raise Jane, after Jane's mother—Kimmy's twin—died in a car accident. The very same way

Kimmy was killed, the week before. A coincidence so cruel that Jane had asked a distraught Richard three times to verify she had heard correctly.

Kimmy had been aunt, sister, mother, and best friend to her, and grandmother to Jane's three children, now adults, all of whom had been devastated by the news. Unable to take off from their jobs without penalty, they were unable to join her in the trek to the Pacific Northwest for the memorial.

They had also sounded almost angry—at Jane? At God? At what?—after the initial explosion of grief when they heard the news.

Lucas had not cried, but had asked questions she didn't know the answers to. How did it happen? Where had she been going? Jane felt dumb, as she often did when questioned by her oldest son, and he had hung up the phone with an "I love you" that sounded almost grudging.

Anne Marie had sobbed so long and hard she couldn't talk, and had said she would call back later…and never did.

The periods of time that went between phone calls with Jane and her second born had grown longer and longer, and the conversations they did have always seemed to come back to some reference to

Jane's insensitivity, or shortcomings. She asked too many questions, she was oversharing, she was too much this, too much that.

Just...too much. In general.

Robin had taken the phone from Anne Marie and said the "I love you" and "Goodbye," with little to no emotion, a textbook Robin response, but Jane knew it was a hard loss, and it was Robin that she actually worried about the most.

Thinking about the kids had taken her mind off of her grief for a moment, but now, it returned, accompanied by a disbelief at the dark fact that both her biological mother and her adopted one had died while driving.

Why had she never visited? It was a question that haunted her now. In every moment when Kimmy had asked her to (moments that had increased in the last year) Jane thought to herself, "I'll go when I get my shit together."

As she sat looking at her hands on the steering wheel, Jane thought, ruefully,

"Well, I should have known that would never happen."

A glance in the rear-view mirror also reminded her that she had, almost on a whim, packed up not just the things she would need for the three or four days Richard had convinced her they would need to settle Kimmy's estate, but her entire life.

It was the latest "Jane Move" as Kimmy had called them. The most recent whirlwind decision to leave a place–and a man–and start completely from scratch.

Like a snake, shedding its skin, once again, Kimmy used to laugh.

Only Kimmy found it funny, because, well, that was how Kimmy had lived her life too.

Until three-and-a-half years ago, when she came north to Oregon for a job, studying wolves, and met Richard.

"I don't know how to explain it well enough over the phone," Kimmy would say, "But this is the last stop for me. This is my forever home, my forever person. Or at least "forever" how long it lasts," then she would laugh the Kimmy laugh, and tell Jane, "You have to come up for a visit."

Jane never had.

The plan she made as she packed up the car and left, three days before, zipping out of the still-balmy Ft. Worth winter, was to get through Kimmy's wake, and then after that... well, after that there was no plan.

Grief and decision-making had kept her mind occupied for the days and the nights of the drive. But now that the drive was finished, and her objective reached, the realization that she had nowhere to go, no money and no prospects threw the shadow over her thoughts again.

Cooi's *I need to pee now* yelp brought her back to the present. "Okay, okay, I know...", Jane was unbuckling her seatbelt when suddenly Cooi's yelp turned to a low growl.

"Just a second, Cooi, Jesus--" a sudden rap on the window caused her to jump and scream, and Cooi began to bark. A man, shrouded in both darkness and a large scarf was standing next to the car. For the briefest of moments Jane felt a primal urge to fight, to run, but the bundled man leaned towards her and said, "You are Jane, aren't you?" She nodded, and he patted his chest. "I'm Abe." He gestured for her to open the door. "The snow is picking up...let's get you inside!"

Suddenly, Jane was acutely aware of her feet.

The Vans she had slipped onto her sockless feet in Ft. Worth were woefully inadequate. Glancing around the front seat, she quickly grabbed (and dumped) the two plastic bags that had housed her breakfast and lunch. Slipping them over her feet, she reached up and pulled off the scrunchies from her braid, slipping them over her ankles.

Jane could see Abe smile as she shoved the door open and stepped out. Cooi bounded out, cavorting for a moment before pissing on a mini snowdrift dangerously close to Abe's feet. After relieving himself for what seemed like an eternity, he capered again like a mini Lipizzaner stallion and headed toward the cabin like he'd lived there forever.

Abe gestured toward her dog with his head. "He's got the right idea. Let's get your feet out of this snow."

As they trudged, Jane felt what she could only describe as comfort, although she didn't know why. Growing up in Texas, Oklahoma, and the surrounding southwest states, she could count on one hand the number of times she'd experienced snow in volume like this. The gusts of wind had passed, and once again the giant flakes were falling silently, no longer representing a threat. They made a carpet around them that crunched as they walked, and once they were standing on a cleared path that led directly to the cabin's door, she could see that it was covering the home like a coat.

Before following Abe into the now open door, lit from within with a glow only a fire could provide, Jane glanced all around her.

What had seemed dark and bleak moments before from the car, now seemed light and happy. The moon shone onto the snow, illuminating the trees, the cabin and Abe like stage lighting. Jane felt like she had stepped into an alternate reality.

She looked up at the sky. A breathtaking number of stars sparkled above, diamonds in a pillowy ceiling of night air, clustered here and there, spread across the expanse.

Pure, unadulterated, childlike wonder flooded over her, and for just a moment, in the face of her amazement and joy, there was no space for grief.

She was remembering once again–like she had so many times when she had the good fortune to be where the sky was clear enough to see more than just a handful of the stars–that she didn't feel awkward, or tired, or worried, or unworthy when she looked at them.

She felt like everything was in order. Even if it wasn't.

Abe said nothing, just let her stare, until her quickly chilling feet prompted her to follow Cooi up the path.

Jane stepped onto the stone steps and into the open door, almost instantly dropping everything she was carrying from her overextended hands.

Richard, the man her Aunt Kimmy had lived with for the past few years, stepped towards her, tears in his eyes and a smile on his face. His son, Abe, bent to retrieve her wallet and keys from the floor after patting her awkwardly on the arm. When he stood, she could see that there were tears in his eyes as well, and without thinking, Jane reached out and touched his cheek. Never in her life could she remember touching a complete stranger with such familiarity. She looked back to Richard, who had stopped about a foot away from her, and reached out her hand. He took it, and the three of them were suddenly sobbing.

After a moment, the spell was broken and Jane again felt like the woman who was stepping into the home of two strangers. Shyly, she stepped back onto the mat that stood just inside the door and tried to awkwardly remove the plastic bags from her feet.

"I'm sorry," she said, "I wasn't really prepared for snow."

"No need to apologize," Richard's voice was a soothing baritone, and Jane was surprised to hear a faint accent that she couldn't quite place. He bent to help her wrestle the truck stop bags and Vans from her feet. Richard pointed at the legs of her thin jeans, soaked around the ankles.

"I'll grab you a pair of sweats."

Abe hung his coat, and stepping out of his boots, took long steps across the cabin's entryway into a small kitchen at the back and grabbed a couple of towels. He tossed one in front of the fireplace, and after whistling Cooi to his side, wiped the dog's feet with the other.

For the briefest of seconds, Jane began to protest, years of self-training on how not to burden others and muscle memory of offering apologies kicking in, but their movements were so natural, and the feeling of the process so familiar, as if this was a habit they had developed over years, that for once, she let someone else care for her and her dog without apology. It was as if Richard's words had contained some kind of magic.

"Get by the fire and sit down," Richard gestured towards an area created around a rough stone hearth that took up fully half the room. Three loveseats of varying heights, covered with various fabrics, and two overstuffed leather chairs created a half-moon around the flames, and Cooi sat in the center on the towel Abe had placed on the thick rug, looking like a scruffy king waiting to be surrounded by his court.

Jane moved to the floral loveseat directly in the center and it occurred to her as she was sinking onto it–an inkling supported as she saw Abe and Richard's faces–that she was drawn to it because it was so obviously in this rugged mancave because of Kimmy. Richard returned from a back room with a pair of women's sweatpants, and from the fond way he looked at them before handing them to her, Jane knew whose they were. He indicated a mudroom to the side of their small kitchen.

"Get out of those and we'll put them by the fire."

Jane padded to the mudroom, closing the wooden door. She pulled off her jeans, quickly pulling on the sweats, deciding not to think about the fact that Kimmy may have worn them only a few days before.

As she came out, she saw Richard in the kitchen, a tiny section of the room that held an old refrigerator, cast-iron stove, sink and a few cabinets.

"Can I make you some tea, Jane? We have green, black, and an herbal mix that–" his abrupt, choked halt told her that it was an Aunt Kimmy blend. Tears stung her eyes as she remembered the countless times Kimmy–the eternal hippie witch doctor, Jane had always called her–had forced her to swallow some bitter herbal concoction for a sore throat or upset stomach. Grief coursed through her. *How can she be gone?*

"I'll have the herbal tea. Thank you."

Abe still stood by the door. "I'm going to get more wood." He turned back to the snowy dark and Jane heard the door shut behind him. Cooi was looking towards the door and actually whined. Jane smiled and patted his head. "Have you found a friend, boy?"

As Richard put the kettle on and bustled around–Jane heard the clink of cups and all the noises of tea-making–she looked again at the giant mantel.

The cabin was not large, but it also wasn't small. It appeared to be rectangular, stretching back farther than it was wide, with a narrow hall leading back beyond the kitchen area, and the room they were in held quite a lot, even though it appeared sparsely furnished.

The stones of the fireplace reached all the way to the ceiling, and from the wood panels of the kitchen almost to the wall that held the door. The stones themselves were of every imaginable size, and of varying colors and finishes. Some black, or reddish, some as smooth as marble, still others, variegated and rough. On the top were shelves that held framed drawings and photos, as well as knick-knacks such as small statues, or simply other rocks. A single slab of granite made up the mantelpiece, and its twin lay on the ground as a hearthstone. They were rough, pale, and each was the size of two tall men laid end to end. With the heel of her hand at the bottom edge, Jane's fingers barely touched the top.

"This fireplace is magnificent," she said quietly, turning to Richard as he came up beside her, holding a steaming cup. She smiled and took it back to the loveseat and sat down. "Did you build this place?"

"We did!" Now that they were sitting, Jane took a moment to examine her aunt's partner. He had always been in the background of Kimmy's phone and Zoom calls, waving or asking polite questions, and Jane thought he seemed like a mild, attractive older man who matched her aunt's physical energy, if not her peppy personality.

But she could see that he had a craggy, careworn face–even more so with what she knew were lines of grief etching it further, and dark circles under his bloodshot, but still striking light blue eyes. He was tall, muscular, wiry, with salt-and-pepper hair that was cut close. It was impossible to guess his age. He could have been a haggard 40, or a very well-preserved 65.

Again, the accent had surprised her, and she could hear it even more as they talked, with Richard asking about the roads and her downplaying her level of unpreparedness in her replies. Kimmy had never mentioned that he was from anywhere other than the United States.

Abe came in from outside. He carefully laid down one armful of newly split logs on the hearth and walked the other one to the metal tub beside the stove in the kitchen. Jane suddenly remembered only weeks ago that Kimmy sent her a picture of burnt eggs in a cast iron pan, Richard grinning in the background. *Perils of cooking on an antique, FOR an antique. :D*

Jane heard Abe running water and placing the kettle back on the stove.

Blowing into her cup, she tested her tea and found it cool enough to drink. It had hints of chamomile and lavender. Closing her eyes, she let it do its soothing work, knowing calm was the herbs' purpose, thanks to her aunt's tutelage. How would it be possible for this grief to abate, when every other thought had Kimmy or her influence in it? Jane squeezed her eyes shut, fighting the guilt that had plagued her for the last few days…knowing that her last, in-person visit with her aunt had been years ago, despite Kimmy asking her regularly to come north.

When she opened her eyes again, they went once more to the fireplace, admiring the mantel and stonework. Jane glanced over all of the jutting shelves again. The pop and crackle of the fire was the only sound, aside from Cooi's snoring and the clink of the kettle against a cup as Abe poured his own cup of tea.

She stood and went to the fireplace.

"The mantel and hearthstone both came all the way from Finland," she heard Richard say. *Maybe that's the accent*–she realized–*slightly Finnish.*

Looking at each photograph on the shelves in turn, she could see they were Richard's family–there was a marked resemblance. A man who looked like a much younger version of Abe, in front of a cabin that could

have been a diminutive cousin of this one, and the faded handwriting across the bottom– the scrawl so common in old texts, with a distinct European flavor to it–read, *Abraham Ulfsson, 1850.*

"The family resemblance is amazing–he looks just like Abraham," She chuckled, "This has to be your forebear, correct?"

"Something like that." Richard's voice was soft. Jane thought that seemed like an odd answer.

Some of the shelves contained pebbles, small rocks, mid-sized rocks–smooth, rough, everything in between–and on one, a few oblong stones that on closer inspection, were actually chess pieces. Small, rough-hewn, made from a light stone, gathered together as if for a family portrait. Glancing to the side, she could see their dark compatriots, gleaming ebony in the flickering firelight, and the flat stone propped just below her elbow, with rows of divots inlaid with alternating dark and light stones she recognized as the board.

"These are gorgeous! Are they old?" She was reaching to pick one up when Richard's answer made her draw back.

"They are, indeed. Very old." He laughed. "Go ahead and take a closer look. They're made of walrus tusk and obsidian. You can't hurt them. Besides," his voice seemed thick with emotion. "This is not a museum. These things are special, but they're meant to be appreciated. Touched."

Jane lifted the scowling King from his perch amid the other pieces. It felt cool, sleek...and it was as if the history held within it sent a charge through her hands. The carving was exquisite, the expressions on all the faces exaggerated, and minutely detailed.

"How did you...where..." Jane shook her head and replaced the piece carefully. Her brief attempt at community college had first been directed at following in Kimmy's footsteps–wildlife biology–but before flunking out, she had grabbed at another major that held interest for her; art history.

She hadn't retained much book knowledge from that time, but her instincts were asking why something this old wasn't in a museum.

"They're family heirlooms."

There was another photo within her eyeline, and as Jane examined it, an odd feeling came over her. Again, a man so like Abraham it was uncanny, standing with his foot on the running board of a very old car, smiling, with his arm around a woman.

She looked either Native American, or Hispanic, dark glasses indicating she was perhaps blind, and the little boy standing in front of the two of them was unmistakably a blend of the two.

Black hair like his mother, with her wide cheekbones, prominent nose, and his father's clear, light eyes. The inscription at the bottom of this one read, "Abraham, Creirwy, och Rikaarti Ulfsson, 1915". There was something nibbling at the back of Jane's mind.

"Is this...?" She waited for Richard to fill in the blanks with a specific title. All he said, quietly was,

"Another forebear."

"Is Rikaarti a version of Richard?" Jane's eyes continued to roam over the shelves.

"It's Finnish. The mother of that...Abraham was Finnish.. We still have family in Finland, in fact, I spent most of my early life there."

Accent, explained, Jane thought.

"Should I get any more bags out of the car?" Abe had come to the small sitting area. It occurred to Jane that he did not seem comfortable with sitting; he had barely stopped moving since they'd come in. Abe was always in the background of her aunt's calls as well, but she smiled now

to realize he never sat still long enough for her to engage as much as she had with Richard.

He wordlessly asked again about her bags, indicating the door with his head. Jane had grabbed her duffel when she left the car.

Evidently Abe had seen the trash bags in the back. Jane blushed with embarrassment.

"Um, I think I have enough for a couple of days in my duffel." She said, "I don't want to be a both–" She stopped abruptly.

Her gaze had followed Abe's, and as she looked at the door now–Jane could see that there were what could only be giant, deep claw marks down almost the whole length of the painted red door. For a moment there was only the crackle of the fire. Both men began to speak at the same time, but Abe held up his hand and Richard became quiet.

"Jane," Abe's voice was calm and soothing. A thought flashed through Jane's mind, *"He sounds like someone trying to keep an animal from running."*

"Jane," she looked at him after the second time. His eyes were kind. "What's wrong?" She saw him trace the path of her sight and he nodded. "Yes…you know we foster wolf hybrids, don't you?"

Jane shook her head. He nodded.

"You do know about your aunt's work, at the preserve, though, correct?"

This time it was Jane that nodded. As a nature biologist, Kimmy had always worked with endangered species, and her work with a wolf preserve was what had brought her to Yellowstone, then Idaho, and then Oregon. The details had not been as plentiful after her move to the mountains, and her relationship with Richard, but Jane knew they worked together, and tracking packs across the Cascades was the most recent project.

"It was an unexpected outcome of the tracking project," Abe gestured for her to sit down, and she did, but her heart was beating now. She didn't know why, but something about the deep marks had shaken her.

"It's not, strictly speaking, legal to own wolf hybrids in this county," Richard chimed in. "When we find them, we ensure that they're socialized to humans and adopt them out to other experienced individuals or send them to special reserves."

Richard gestured towards the door. "Sometimes we underestimate our guests'…domesticity, let's say." Abe chuckled, and sipped his tea. But Jane could hear something in that chuckle. Her grandfather had always told her that she knew more about men than she realized, and if something felt off, to listen to that *knowing* instead of her mind. Or other people.

Her mind wasn't sure what to think. Her *knowing* told her that both were hiding something–and they didn't seem like men who liked hiding things–but it also felt like they meant her no harm. That they wouldn't let harm come to her.

Jane picked up her tea, trying to keep her hands steady. Kimmy had never mentioned fostering hybrids. It seemed as if something were off about the explanation, but nothing she could imagine would explain why they would lie about such a thing, or why it should even make her so uneasy.

But there was something else going on.

"As I was saying," Abe sounded as if he was trying to be lighthearted and change the subject. "I can go get your other…bags if you'd like."

"I…that stuff can stay. I'm…" They both looked at her unexpectedly and Jane sighed, no energy for subterfuge.

"I actually just left my boyfriend. We broke up not too long ago, were trying again to work it out and…it didn't. Those garbage bags in the back…that's all of my stuff. Like, in the world. I brought in a bag for tonight, and I'll be out of your hair after the wake tomorrow. I don't want to be a bother."

The two of them looked at each other, their expressions unreadable. *Man, I never want to play poker with these guys,* Jane thought.

"Was that an overshare?" Jane laughed. It felt good to say something true and to be vulnerable. Even if it was only because she had no strength left to pretend everything was okay.

"There's no such thing as that with us," Abe said softly. "We're family." As soon as he said it, he seemed embarrassed, and shrugged. "I mean, *we* consider *you* family."

"You know," Richard's voice was careful, and Jane thought it still sounded as if he was calmly approaching a frightened rabbit. "You could always stay here for a while. If you don't have somewhere specific you want to go right away."

Somewhere specific that she wanted to go? There were a million specific places Jane wanted to go.

"Or if you need time to save money, to get you somewhere specific." It was as if Abe could read her mind. He blinked at her, almost like he had gotten caught. "I mean, you can work from anywhere, right? Aren't you a freelance journalist?"

"A copywriter," Jane said softly.

*Sure you are, when you actually turn in **copy**, that you've **written**,* she could almost hear Mitchell (or any of the agency managers she worked with) saying. "I mean, I do some journalism as well, but it's been a while." Her tea had gotten cold. She finished it anyway. "But to answer your question, yes, I can work from anywhere there's Wi-Fi."

Abe gestured to the ceiling. "It may be hard to believe, but we do have Wi-Fi. Other than that, we're cavemen."

Jane hesitated. Years of covering her tracks, making sure that she wasn't asking too much, taking too much, or being a burden moved her lips. The phrases and actions were automatic at this point.

"I don't want to be any trouble. I hope you don't think I was telling you guys that so that you'd pity me, or offer–"

Richard held up a hand, leaned forward. "Sweetheart, your aunt knew you were struggling." The invocation of Kimmy and her loving concern brought the grief which had temporarily been dispelled from the room crashing back.

"We discussed asking you to come here. We wanted you to. Abe is right–we may not have ever met, but we feel like we know you. Kimmy spoke so..." His own despair got the better of him for a moment and Jane could see it, the depth of his loss and pain written on his face. He composed himself. "Kimmy spoke so often of you, and loved you so much." He shrugged. "We love you too. I know you don't know us, and it might seem odd, but it's true."

It was true. Jane could feel their love and the genuineness of their offer in the air. It effused out from them almost like scent, and the realization of it was almost...like a high. Jane could never, in the few seconds that she spent searching her mind, remember a time, in any kind of relationship—with her family, children, lovers—where she had ever felt—no, not felt, *known*—so clearly that she was loved. That she could trust the words of the person expressing them so completely. For a few otherworldly seconds, she sat and just felt it. And appreciated it.

"Thank you," she whispered.

Abe cleared his throat. "So. If you want me to, I can get your things. We made up the loft for you—I can haul them up before I turn in."

Richard was standing. "You're welcome to stay up for a while, if you'd like—"

"No," Jane rose, shaking her head. "I'm exhausted. I'll turn in too. I know I kept you up, waiting for me." She nodded as Abe, who had gone over to her coat, pointed at her pocket for permission to get her keys. Once again, the deep claw marks made a faint drum sound in her instinct. *It's just a primal reaction*, she told herself. *I've evolved to see wolf—or wolf hybrid, whatever— claw marks and run the other way.*

Abe went out into the cold.

Richard had walked over to a heretofore invisible trapdoor in the ceiling.

Jane watched him flick out a latch that laid flush against the door and pull, bringing down the stepladder that led up to the attic hideaway. The steps were wide enough that Cooi was able to ascend, at Richard's encouragement, and with his hands supporting him. "I would just watch him, when the stepladder is down," Richard explained, and then pointed to a handle sticking out, halfway up. "Once you're up, pull on that to bring the stairs."

He kept his gaze up looking at Cooi as he peered down, and faintly chuckled.

"You're a lot like Kimmy." He indicated Cooi with his head. "Not many people have the patience for coy-dogs —or want the legal risk of getting caught with one in the wrong state— and not many of them are as well socialized as he is. That's a testament to you."

"I hope so," Jane said quietly. "I was hiking a friend's property and followed a creek onto his neighbor's. This one and the rest of his litter had been bagged up and thrown in. Somehow, he made it out, I guess the bag got torn on the rocks, and...I just couldn't leave him. Or take him to Animal Control." She shrugged. "One of the few good decisions I've made in my life." Richard's smile was so genuine, so full of emotion, that it felt like the most natural thing in the world to move towards him and hug him, almost at the same time he was opening his arms. "I'm so glad you're both here."

"I'm so glad we are too."

Once up in the loft, Jane looked around, and immediately thought of her favorite book from childhood. *This must be what Heidi's little loft room in the Alps looked like*, Jane chuckled. Abe's head poked through the opening of the trapdoor stepladder. "Hey, there, bags coming through!" One by one, the four trash bags containing Jane's worldly goods were carefully placed on the floor.

Wow! Did I just move in with my uncle and cousin that I've never met before tonight? Jane chuckled out loud at the absurdity of it all, and it turned into a giggle when Abe joined her laughter, without knowing why.

"I put the bag with Cooi's food in it in the kitchen, up on a pantry shelf. We get pests easily, so let's not put it on the floor. We have some food at the research center I can grab tomorrow, looks like you're running out."

Then, with a salute, he descended down the step ladder.

"Goodnight, Jane."

"Goodnight Abe."

"I'm closing you in!" The trapdoor closed, almost silently, and just like that Jane was left with her thoughts, her trash bags, and Cooi, who had leapt almost immediately to the bed, an iron frame twin covered with a Pendleton blanket and headed with two generously stuffed pillows, with cases matching the blue and white ticking of the crisp sheets. Jane looked around the rest of the room. An armoire that would hold everything in her trash bag luggage stood in one corner, with a sink and a small toilet housed in another. One side table, stacked with hand towels and toilet paper on the shelf underneath, one chair. The walls, chair, armoire, and side table were all whitewashed. *Very 1800s Ikea*, Jane thought.

Suddenly she was incredibly tired. Peeling off her clothes and draping them over the chair, she went to the sink and turned the faucet. After a moment of chugging, water as cold as ice came forth, and Jane splashed her face. The reflection she saw in the mirror above the sink looked sad.

The same face that had been staring back at her for almost 50 years, just a little more lined, a little more worn.

"So, I guess you're starting over again, huh." She shrugged at herself. "You've done it before. You're good at it. It'll be fine."

She dug into the trash bag that she (correctly) suspected held her charger, and plugged the phone in. Watching it slowly power up, she unlocked it, and went to her messages.

The sadness about the loss of Paul, the Boyfriend of So Many Chances, surfaced as she felt herself disappointed by not seeing his name among her messages, bobbing up like a cork in the sea of grief created by Kimmy's death.

His lack of empathy and inability to comfort her after Richard's phone call had been the final straw that broke the back of a relationship strained by emotional immaturity and excessive drinking.

It had almost been without thought, as if she'd been waiting for a signal, and after she'd packed her two bags for the trip, she simply went and got trash bags, and continued packing–taking photos off the wall, mementos from drawers, her favorite towels and blankets, and books and albums off shelves.

Jane had grown up in Tornado Alley, and had run from at least three serious storms in her lifetime; it felt almost like that, as she made split-second decisions about what was absolutely necessary to take with her, knowing she would lose everything else.

Paul had expressed surprise and a desperate, drunken defensiveness, as he watched her drag it all to her car. While listening to him Jane had replayed in her mind all the childish antics and low points of the relationship preceding this one. It was as if the scales had tipped, and these sad occurrences had finally outweighed the emotional highs of the passion they shared. Her only response to him, before she rolled up the window and drove away, had been a three-word, first person restatement of a phrase Kimmy had said over and over, after listening to her recount the times something like this had happened:

"I deserve better."

Now, looking at her phone, with the perspective of time and space, she opened a message to him, and began typing.

"I made it, I'm here. The rent has been paid for next month–don't worry about sending me your half, we'll call it a penalty for breaking my part of the lease. I want to change what I said, when I left. "I deserve better," sounds like I'm saying "better than you". I'm not. What I want to say instead is...I need different. I need different circumstances, I need to be different. I called you emotionally immature, but I'm realizing I am too. And my emotional immaturity and yours are not only incompatible, I think they're each exacerbating the other. I love you and I wish you well...but I have to stop chasing and begging. Or at least stop doing what feels like it. I have to stop feeling like the only good I'll get will come from chasing and begging. I should have let you go when you tried to, so I'm doing that now. Goodbye."

After taking a deep breath and hitting "send", she typed a reply to the text from Whitney, her best friend, that she copied and pasted into the other concerned queries from friends and neighbors.

Made it safe–it's a lot to process, but I'm fine. Or I will be. Left Paul, staying with family for now...I'll update soon.

Jane crawled into bed in just her underwear, sliding her feet under Cooi, already curled into his customary half-moon at the foot of the bed.

She repeated it again now, out loud but whispered, and this time it was more of a prayer, a reassurance, and it lacked the force of when she had thought it before.

"I need different."

The gentle rumbling of the voices below was comforting at first.

Jane was reminded of being a kid, and feeling safe going to sleep with the sound of her grandfather laughing at Carol Burnett in the next room. She would leave her door open even though he always suggested she'd sleep better with it shut. Now the muffled conversation had the same effect, until one phrase, inexplicably clearer than the rest, made her eyes snap open.

"...but she needs to stay here. It's the safest way."

It didn't last though. Too tired to try to understand, Jane fell asleep to the feel of Cooi warming her feet, and the sound of the wind whipping the snow against the tiny window.

2

Just as she'd fallen asleep to their voices, Jane woke to the murmurings of Abe and Richard below her in the kitchen, rattling pans. The scent of bacon, eggs, and coffee wafted up, and she stretched.

Cooi stood, shaking his head, whining his I-need-to-pee announcement. Jane stood too, pulling on Kimmy's sweatpants and her sweatshirt from the chair, and moving over to the toilet in the corner.

"Me first, boy." Cooi, ever clever, was scratching at the trapdoor, cognizant of its use to get him down below, to fresh snow waiting to be christened. Jane padded over, and examined the trapdoor for a moment.

Again, she realized how extraordinary the craftsmanship was. Like the fireplace wall and mantel, chair, and armoire...everything neat, expertly hinged together, made of pine or whitewashed in that simple Scandinavian way. Lifting the interior latch sprung the door into place to be lowered, ensuring that no one could simply fall through by stepping on it. The fact that the steps were wide enough for a mid-sized dog like Cooi to semi-comfortably walk down, with help, was another marvel. Woodworking perfection. She held Cooi back until the steps were firmly in place on the ground, and hefted him by his collar to allow herself to go down first, backwards, guiding him in order to keep him from falling. She greeted Abe and Richard, and went to the door–shivering a little at the sight of the claw marks–and let Cooi out.

As he relieved himself, she stepped back slightly, to look closer at the marks on the door.

Primal response or not, the feeling that crept along her spine was not anything she could ignore.

They were deep. An inch into the wood—which was thick—and starting almost at the top of the door, at least six-and-a-half-feet high, was her guess.

How could this be a dog? She told herself that wolves were large, not animals to be taken lightly,

Cooi ran back around her legs, and she shut the door.

"Coffee?" Richard held up a pot of French press, and she nodded. "Bacon and scrambled eggs? Toast?" She smiled and nodded again and he chuckled. "Have a seat!"

Enameled plates and mugs, a Mason jar of silverware. Jane took a seat, picking up one of the hand towels laid out as napkins. Richard poured coffee; Abe shoveled food onto plates. They moved like clockwork, the ease of routine making their movements look like a dance. For a melancholy moment, Jane wondered how her aunt had fit into the breakfast choreography.

Jane could see out the window over the sink the blanket of snow mirroring what she'd seen out front, and from her window upstairs. But this view had a breathtaking addition of pine forest, undulating up and away along the ridge behind them.

"It's beautiful here," she said, quietly.

Richard grunted agreement through a mouth of food. "It really is. We're on the very verge of pristine forest."

"I wish I could take a run; it's been days." Jane was wistful, and knew on top of everything else, the lack of cardio accentuated her heavy heart.

"We have a trail, you could snowshoe it if you want." Abe's enthusiastic retort deflated with a stare from Richard, and Jane found herself wondering why the silence was so awkward.

"I mean, I don't want to impose…" she trailed off, still not quite sure why Abe's suggestion had caused such a reaction. "I don't have any winter gear, anyway." Suddenly profoundly and surprisingly disappointed, she found herself fighting back tears, staring into her eggs and bacon.

It was obvious that her despondency had an effect on the atmosphere. Richard's stare moved to her, and took on a fatherly comfort, instead of the "what-is-your-problem" vibe it had held when he was looking at Abe.

"You're not imposing, don't be silly." He reached out and touched her arm.

"It would be good for you to get outside." He tossed a glance back at Abe, who spoke as if on cue. "I'll go with you, just to be sure that you don't get overwhelmed by the path." He inclined his head towards the back of the cabin. "Richard can go through...Kimmy's things... and get you some winter gear."

Suddenly Jane wondered if that was the issue. Her aunt was also an avid runner, and the trail he spoke of was likely one she'd run regularly. And the thought of putting on Kimmy's clothes was just as heartbreaking as it was comforting. The sweatpants Richard had given her the night before were enough of a grim reminder...what would covering herself in her aunt's clothes feel like? For her, and for Richard?

"Really, Richard...I don't want to stir up unwel–"

He touched her arm again. Looking directly into her eyes, his words were soft, and so direct that the honesty was palpable. "I would actually really like for you to get some use out of Kim's things, sweetheart. I'm being completely truthful with you. I think it would be good for all of us." Jane nodded, and finished her breakfast, swallowing eggs over the salty lump in her throat.

Taking her dishes to the sink, she noticed a bristle brush and bar of solid soap for washing dishes, just like the one Kimmy had sent to Jane when she discovered them. *So much better for the environment...* Jane felt as if she could actually hear Kimmy's voice. The dish drainer to the side looked like a replica of the one in the house where Kimmy, Jane, and Jane's grandfather–Kimmy's dad–had lived together for years, and suddenly Jane understood where her aunt fit into the breakfast routine. She grabbed the bristle brush, scrubbed across the bar of soap before wetting it, and washed each plate the way Kimmy had taught her, rinsing and placing each item into the drainer.

Silently, Abe grabbed a dish towel and began to dry, and Jane saw him wipe his reddening eyes.

Each time it abated, the loss of Kimmy flooded back in some other way. Jane was starting to understand that for these men who had lived with Kimmy day in and day out, as she once had, her absence in these menial moments, the ones where she'd completed tasks with a whistle and her melodious laugh– where the times when missing her could be almost overwhelming.

Just as the last pan was rinsed, and Jane dried her hands, Richard stuck his head out of the hallway and beckoned her back.

The neat construction of the cabin belied its size; Jane was reminded as she walked down the surprisingly long hall, of the circus funhouses that held rooms that seemed to never end.

They passed two, three doors, before entering a small bedroom.

A pile of clothing and shoes lay on the bed. Richard gestured to them.

"Wear a base layer, then another layer over that, a neck gaiter, these leg gaiters, a hat, and gloves. Kimmy's shoes are in the mudroom– wear the turquoise ones, they're waterproof." He motioned with his head. "When you're dressed, come outside and I'll show you how to put on snowshoes."

"If I'm wearing waterproof shoes, are snowshoes really necessary?"

"Yes! It's deep right now. You'll go better with them. The trail is somewhat protected, but there's a lot of accumulation out there."

He left.

Jane sat on the bed with her aunt's clothes, touching them as if they were holy relics. Picking up a wool hoodie with thumbholes–a staple of Kimmy's wardrobe–she lifted it to her nose and inhaled. Of course it was clean, but the scent of the same fabric softener that Kimmy had used for years was a memory trigger for a thousand feelings.

For a moment, Jane considered not going. She didn't understand running in snow, Richard's seemingly negative reaction still bothered her, and she wasn't entirely sure that Abe was as thrilled to be going for a cold-weather run as Richard seemed to think he would be.

But it was a way to feel close to Kimmy.

There were pictures on the mirror, Richard and her aunt, smiling at the camera, side-by-side at a gorgeous mountain view, kissing at a party, and

there were a few medals hanging on the corners of the frame; racing medals. Not participation trophies, but first-in-group placings, the most recent one a year before.

She always–always–thought of Kimmy when she ran. It was Kimmy who had encouraged her to run as a girl, first as a way to build cardio endurance for other activities, then to deal with the racing thoughts and attention problems adolescence had brought (years before scientific research recommended it, simply because Kimmy herself had discovered that it helped her). Then, in later years, just as a consistent, accessible way to stay moving and healthy as an adult.

"Running isn't reliant on anything but your ability to move. And a pair of shoes. You don't need money for a gym membership or expensive equipment. It gets you out of your head...and you and I both need that..."

Both she and Kimmy had led somewhat itinerant lifestyles–Jane mainly working as a freelance writer and Kimmy as a researcher, both subject to move across the country on a moment's notice–so Kimmy's advice on fitting things into non-traditional schedules and minimal suitcases was valuable.

They were not similar in the level of financial success they had achieved as "vagabonds," as they called themselves. Kimmy had a doctorate in animal behavior, and consistent offers. Jane had dropped out of a community college veterinary technician program three decades before, and had huge resume gaps that she didn't want to fill with the bartending, dog-walking, and grocery store jobs she often had to take to make ends meet.

Like recordings, Jane could hear the conversations with Kimmy, when the depression and anxiety about money would be in high gear. It was almost always a variation on the same theme—and they were like actors improvising new lines that still carried the same message.

"No serious clients will take me because I don't have a degree... and I can't get one at this point—I probably couldn't have at ANY point...I don't have the ability to focus like that..."

"You're selling yourself and potential clients short. All they'll see are your sample pieces—you're the smartest writer I know, Jane. The only real obstacle is your lack of belief in yourself."

A tense exchange could follow, usually containing an anecdote about how the last client interview didn't ask about Jane's "belief in herself," but her education, and then to keep from ending on a sour note, the topic of conversation would be changed by one of them.

Even with that sore subject—and its twin, Jane's repetitive relationship problems—Kimmy was the person that Jane believed loved her best. No one else had ever seen the things in Jane she had seen, no one had encouraged her so uniquely and solidly.

Now, she was gone.

Sniffling, Jane sifted through the pile, finding a base layer top, then pants, and lined leggings to go over them. After pulling on everything she needed—down to wool socks—she slipped on the gaiters, hat, and gloves.

When she came into the kitchen again and Richard looked up from the table, she could see the pain of recognition in his eyes, seeing Kimmy's clothes, but not Kimmy. But he smiled and nodded.

"Very good. Let's get you outfitted for snow."

Going out the door on the side of the cabin led to a mudroom, lined with a variety of outdoor gear. Richard walked to several pairs of snowshoes hanging from the rafters, and took a pair of narrow pink ones down. He explained how to step into them, and gestured outside.

Abe stood, dressed in running gear, feet in snowshoes that mirrored hers.

They were facing uphill, and the vague outline of a trail was visible, although only as a dip in the snow. Abe demonstrated technique.

"This should really be a walk, not a run…your first time, you need to go *slow*," he said, accentuating this as if he knew her, "and widen your stance just a little. Lift your knees a *little* higher, but don't overcorrect."

He smiled broadly, like a kid, and Jane realized it was the first time she'd seen him do so.

"Let's go!"

Jane didn't understand at first why Abe insisted on staying behind her…until her first misstep. He didn't manhandle her, just reached out to offer a little stability. She regained her balance and took off again.

She was tired before they had gotten more than 200 feet from the house. *What is wrong with me? How am I this out of shape?*

"How far do you want to go?" Abe pranced alongside her like a gazelle, more energetic and talkative than he'd been at any point in the last twelve hours. Before she could answer, he waved ahead.

"There's a deer feeder at the side of the trail near the one-mile mark," he explained. "We'll see how you feel then, and if you want, we can turn back. It's different, walking and running in snow. It takes more out of you."

Indeed, it did.

Jane was astounded how quickly her muscles were tiring. She had seen Abe warming up, and in her desire to get started, had neglected to do so herself. Even through the layers she was wearing, the chill was biting, and she was moving stiffly, both from the unfamiliar movements and the temperature.

Her lungs were already burning as well, and she guessed that both the cold and the altitude were working against her. Her toe caught in something beneath the snow, and before she could get her other foot in front of her to stop, she was on her face, snow filling her mouth and crunching through the gap in her gaiter, going down her neck.

"GODDAMMIT," The anger she felt surprised her, although it didn't seem to faze Abe. He came up beside her and offered a hand, which she refused at first, then took after sinking into the snow when she tried to push herself up.

They took off again, Jane going even slower than before.

She had only slogged a few steps when she fell again, flat on her back, from overcorrecting in exactly the way Abe had said not to.

"FUCK!" Her scream echoed in the stillness, and even in her rage, Jane took a second gaze at the forest, the view breathtaking from her prone position. The memory of the night before and the stars that had spoken so sweetly to her soul flickered through. Tall pines frosted with pristine white snow, as far as the eye could see. Not a sound, not another house or creature in sight. It was stunning.

She rolled to her front, pushed up to her knees, looked down at her freezing hands, touched the packed snow that was falling down the front of her shirt, and sat back on her heels...jumping as the snowshoes' latches jammed her in the ass.

Jane thought in defeat, *I just wanted to run. I just wanted to do the one thing that I can always do, the one thing that makes sense and is always the same.*

But it wasn't the same.

It did still make her think of Kimmy, but this time was different because she wasn't smiling, thinking Kimmy might be running too, wherever she was, because Kimmy wasn't ever going to run again, anywhere. It would never give her the same comfort to run again.

Jane burst into tears.

She sobbed, sinking forward onto her forearms and heaving. Her face stung, her lungs burned, but more than any other part of her body, her heart ached.

Kimmy was gone. Forever. She would never see her again.

She felt Abe come up beside her and kneel, and when he reached out to her, she fell into his arms and cried until she couldn't cry any more.

He didn't say a word or move until she had stopped, wiped her face with her freezing, snow-covered mittens, and looked at him for a long minute in silence. He returned her gaze for a while, then nodded, and looked down.

"Kimmy got me into running," he said. His eyes were bloodshot, and Jane could see they were brimming with new tears, but his face was not drawn with sadness. There was happiness there. He looked back up at her and smiled, and then pointed down the trail. "She flogged me down this trail, and then a lot of others." The love on his face comforted Jane. She felt herself smiling at the simple realization that Abe and his father really knew the goodness that made Kimmy such a special person. They understood.

"I know she did the same for you."

Jane looked down the trail and then back at Abe.

"The trails she flogged me down were Oklahoma streets. So hot in the summer that the asphalt would bubble." They both laughed, and for a moment Jane's grief was assuaged by a comfort that was both odd and familiar.

"It *won't* ever be the same again," Abe said. "But that doesn't mean the difference can't be sweet too." He pointed down the trail. "This feels harder than it really is right now. Don't quit."

Jane wondered for a moment if he meant the trail or her grief, and then realized it didn't matter.

He stood, and offered his hand again. "Let's walk to the one-mile mark, get used to the shoes, *go slow,"* he leaned forward and laughed as he enunciated that instruction, "and just enjoy it. We'll run a little on the way back."

They set off again, not running, but at a good pace. This time when Jane staggered, she was going slow enough to catch herself, and she began to understand the movements and anticipate when and how to correct.

"Now, you've got it!" Abe's excitement was contagious, and Jane found herself laughing and speeding up. By the time they saw the deer stand her legs were worn out, and she was glad to turn around, although humbled that a two-mile endeavor was taking so much out of her.

"Don't discount the effect that the altitude and cold are having on you," Abe said. "And don't be discouraged. It'll get easier and more fun the more you do it."

As they came up to the cabin, Jane noticed the loft where she slept had a twin on the other side of the structure. There was also, she noticed in the daylight, an amazing amount of detailed carving on the crossed posts at the roof's ridge.

"Are those...swans?" She glanced at Abe. They stomped the snow from the shoes and Abe showed her how to take them off before they entered the mudroom.

"They are. My...grandmother's family name was Joutsen. It means swan." Abe hung his coat and then hers on hooks in the mudroom, and took the snowshoes and placed them on racks directly over a spill guard next to the door. *A place for everything, and everything in its place,* Jane thought.

"The Whooper swan was sacred to ancient Finns. They're also known for loyalty...they mate until death." There was a strange, quiet quality to Abe's voice as he related this, and Jane could tell it was more than just trivia for him. She suddenly became very curious about her "cousin".

"Have you ever married? Or...are you married now?" Kimmy had never spoken about a partner in Abe's life, although she had related a few details about him to Jane. His work with the foundation, his skill in the outdoors, his kindness. *"You'd like him,"* Jane remembered her aunt saying. *"I'd love for you to meet him. You need to come out for a visit."*

Was she trying to set us up? Jane stifled a laugh, but then did the math, quickly. If Richard was Kimmy's age, or a little younger, that would put him in his mid- to late sixties. He looked great for his age–whatever that was–and Abe seemed to be in his mid- to late thirties.

Not unimaginable for someone on the precipice of fifty–especially since she had dated much younger men before–but Jane couldn't help but think Kimmy would have been more open about an idea like that.

Unless she didn't want to scare Jane off.

"I was married once," Abe said slowly. "A very long time ago."

Kimmy's invitations to visit had been sporadic, but as she thought about it now, Jane realized they had followed a pattern of changing tactics.

Normally Kimmy would nag and nag–playfully, then seriously–until her niece came out to visit, wherever she was. But in the three-and-a-half years since moving in with Richard, Jane realized Kimmy had tried several other methods as well. Negotiating, offering to pay, framing it around interest in the job, *"We could use someone to help redesign the website and write our marketing collateral and grant proposals."*

Enticing her with talk about the natural beauty of the place…and yes, gushing about Richard and his son, who lived with them as well.

As she watched Abe pointing out the wood structure to the east of them–a traditional Finnish sauna–she couldn't imagine Kimmy insinuating more than a friendly connection. He was handsome and funny…but what Jane was feeling was familial. Richard's son, her adoptive-mother-aunt's "stepson," the brother she never had, and might have connected with.

It added to the sadness, wondering now if she would have fit in with these men and her aunt, a possible surrogate for the family Jane had lost over the years.

Abe was asking a question, about the sauna…was she interested? She could get one of Kimmy's swimsuits, a towel, and meet them inside…it was a great follow up to a cold-weather run…something about traditional methods…she simply nodded. Was it odd, to think of tromping through the snow in a bathing suit to sweat in a little lean-to with two men she barely knew? Yes.

But when had odd ever stopped her before? Hell, yes, people I just met yesterday…let's sweat together.

Abe called to Richard to find a swimsuit for her.

She moved through the motions of removing the snowshoes and outer gear, and through the cabin in a sort of trance, back to Richard and Kimmy's room. She could hear Abe, in the living room, heard him call Cooi's name. She smiled, thinking about how naturally they seemed to fold Cooi and herself into their little world.

They miss her, Jane thought. *I'm a connection to her.*

Jane undressed quickly, laying the leggings over the side of the old-fashioned bathtub that stood in the corner of the bedroom. She laughed remembering Kimmy relating Richard's desire to put up a screen around the toilet, after she moved in. *I asked him, "Why?!"* Kimmy had giggled. *Do you think a flimsy room divider is going to shield me from the sound of your shits?*

Jane grabbed the towel hanging on the wall behind the bathtub before donning the swimsuit laid out for her on the bed, and then wrapped it around her body, and started for the kitchen.

In the hall, she could hear Abe's voice speaking to Richard. "Just come out for a few minutes. You know it will make you feel better." There was a tender, paternal quality to his voice. For a moment, she felt a pang of specialized sympathy for Abe, taking on the role of parent as Richard dealt with the death of a partner.

"I'll get undressed after Jane comes out," Richard said, quietly, and as Jane entered the kitchen, his head turned, and her heart warmed when she saw his smile.

"I guess we're taking a sauna," he stood and made his way to the bedroom. "Abe is right–it's probably overdue."

Abe pointed towards the hall and made for it as well. "Let me grab my towel and rinse off, and we'll go out. I started the fire before we went on our run–it should be at the right temperature by now."

She stood in the tiny kitchen, under Cooi's concerned gaze, before the two men reappeared, towels around their waists, not a scrap of self-consciousness between the two of them.

Abe seemed excited. "There are slides by the back door, in a basket."

As Jane followed them out, she took a pair of slip-ons from the basket. The path was shoveled, but narrow, and the crisp air made Jane suck in her breath sharply.

Abe pulled the wooden door open and stood to the side. Richard went in first, and as she followed, she could see that the opposite wall was glass…they were looking out into the beauty of the woods. No painting could have been more gorgeous. Two benches lined the north and south walls, with shorter benches in front of each–Jane guessed that six adults could sit on each side, if they were *extremely* comfortable with each other–and a pile of stones sat near the entrance, with buckets of water next to them, one containing what looked like birch branches with a ladle balanced on the rim.

It was hot as hell.

A thermometer on the back of the door read 195 degrees Fahrenheit, as Abe stepped in and closed it. He went to sit beside Richard, across from her, and with a big sigh, closed his eyes and leaned back against the wall, his relaxation almost instant. Richard took a moment to loosen up, but Jane could see him visibly relax as well.

Jane closed her eyes as well, letting the heat curl around her. Sweat began to form almost immediately, everywhere at once.

"Have you ever been in a sauna, a traditional one?" Abe asked. Jane shook her head.

"We'll give it a few more minutes, and then we'll go out and cool down," Abe said. "If we're here for five minutes, we stay out there for five minutes. Then we come back for another round, if you feel up to it."

Jane looked out the glass wall. "Go out and cool down?"

Abe nodded. Several heat-filled minutes passed, and then he motioned towards the door. Jane stood and followed him out.

Initially a relief from the heat–which had just started to feel oppressive–the cold bit into Jane after a few seconds, just a mild discomfort. Abe stepped off the path, and fell backwards into one of the drifts to the side of the sauna, piled high with shoveled snow. Getting to his feet, he laughed.

"You don't have to cool off that way," He grinned. "You can simply stand in the–"

Jane turned and fell into a drift next to his, *ooofing* in alarm when her fall felt a little too close to the ground. The shockwave of cold made her gasp, and she jumped to her feet.

"Oh my GOD..." She jumped up and down, laughing. Abe watched her for a moment, smiling, and in that space and time Jane felt a sincere reverberation of joy from him. *This man must really love saunas*, she thought. *He looks like someone who has just converted a soul.*

"Give it another moment or two," Abe picked up a handful of snow and rubbed it over his arms and then his legs. Jane mimicked him, gasping again. He laughed, and reached out to stop her when she moved towards the sauna door.

"You have to cool down for about as long as you heat up," he said, his voice taking the same paternal tone she had heard him use with his father. She indicated the sauna. "Is Richard coming out?

"We're used to taking longer saunas," he explained. "He'll stay about half an hour, then cool down."

Jane repeated the process once more, again laughing and feeling the childlike joy. Towel flying up around strange men? Who cares. Feeling like a hot dog cooking? No worries.

Because it abated her grief like nothing else had.

Finally, she felt she'd had enough, and scurried to the outdoor shower. After a quick, but thorough rinse, she scuttled inside, briskly rubbing herself as dry as possible with her soggy towel, and headed up to her loft bedroom to change.

Later, downstairs in front of the fire, Jane realized she felt clean for the first time in days. Sad, yes, but it was lessened by the physical invigoration the run and the sauna had given her. She could see a visible difference in Richard as well, and as Abe made tea for everyone and brought it to the living room, Jane had a newfound respect for her "cousin"; he was doing a good job keeping his father going.

As they all sipped their tea, Abe cleared his throat.

"Jane, would you like to speak tonight?"

For a moment, Jane's mind was blank. Then, gradually, the somber reality came creeping back in. Kimmy's wake was that evening.

"Oh, I don't know..."

"Of course, you don't have to do anything you don't want to do," Abe said, softly, and Richard nodded. "But...if you could...I think it would be...nice." He shook his head and shrugged his shoulders, acknowledging how lame the final word was for the situation, but Jane nodded her understanding.

"Okay, I will." *It doesn't have to be long,* she told herself. *It's the least I can do, after all Kimmy did for me.*

"If it's too painful, don't do it," Richard said. He looked at Abe with something like admonishment.

"No, no...I want to." Jane really did want to, she realized.

Abe nodded and stood. "I'm going to call the bar and–"

"The...bar?" Jane repeated, unsure she'd heard correctly.

"Well, yes..." Abe looked to Richard for help, and then back to Jane. "We..."

"Kimmy wasn't big on churches," she said softly, in understanding. Abe nodded and wiped his eyes.

Jane laughed, "But she did love bars." The men laughed as well.

"The man who owns Rue's is a close friend," Richard said, hoarsely. "We were there often."

Jane found herself hesitant to ask her next question. "Where...is Kimmy going to be buried?"

"Kimmy was cremated. I'm going in an hour to pick up her ashes."

Jane heard the shock in her own voice. "Cremated?" *It isn't your business*, she quickly told herself, as she saw the confusion on her hosts' faces.

"I'm sorry–that's not my decision, I just...I just pictured a gravesite, a ceremony..." she waved, as if to diffuse her thoughts into the air. "Please, don't listen to me, I don't mean any offense."

"No," Richard reached towards her, shaking his head. "I understand, it's not something people really think about a lot, and

I know a wake at a bar might seem a little..." he shrugged, "... lowbrow." He looked at Abe before shifting his gaze back to Jane and looking intently into her eyes.

"But you have to know, Abe and I–and this community, as well as the larger circle of Kimmy's colleagues–we all loved her very much. We respected her, and we intend to show our respect tonight, in our own way."

Jane nodded, embarrassed that her reaction had made such an explanation seem necessary.

"I know you loved her. And she loved you all, and this town, very much as well."

Cooi stood and stretched, heading for the door. Jane stood and let him out, the cool air softening the blush in her cheeks.

"Could I go with you to pick up Kimmy's ashes?"

The question seemed to have an odd effect on the men.

"Er...are you sure?" Richard glanced at Abe again, and Jane thought for what was surely the thousandth time, that it often seemed as if Richard, in his grief, had regressed from the role of father and routinely looked to his son for guidance.

"It might be more comfortable for you to stay here," Abe said, his voice quiet, but firm. "And one of us can stay with you."

There was an odd undercurrent to the conversation. *There's something going on they're not telling me,* Jane thought. Was it her reaction to the news that Kimmy had been cremated? Had she offended them?

"If I offended you, by my–"

"No, no..." Richard touched her arm, gently. "That's not it at all, Jane. We just want you to be–" his voice froze and he shook his head before starting over, with the mannerism of someone who had forgotten their line in a play. "It's just that we want you to be comfortable while you're here."

He was going to say something else, Jane thought. And for an unknown reason, she intuitively knew what it was.

He was going to say, We want you to be safe.

"Okay." Jane nodded, deciding to stop pushing. For the moment.

Abe left and Richard stayed, the weight of the errand seeming to be too much for him. Jane realized it might be better this way, the two of them relieved of the trip, left waiting for the return, given the gift of another hour or so without the physical reminder that Kimmy was not alive anymore.

Richard asked for help looking through pictures, and Jane obliged. There would be a slideshow at the bar, he explained, and so the two of them set about going through albums and a few boxes of photos that Richard brought from the bedroom.

The minutes flew by with both of them by turns exclaiming over a photo, sharing a memory—most of Richard's came from the album, made in the last few years he and Kimmy had lived together—and the boxes were Jane's domain.

She organized her moments with him, Jane thought, with a pang. The portion of her life where I had her is the chaos, contained in shoeboxes.

Pictures of her mother, her grandfather…her own children, Lucas, Anne Marie, and Robin…the sight of them as fat toddlers, and then graduates with Kimmy's arms around them, cast a pallor over the walk down memory lane. The sudden longing for them was too much, and Jane put their pictures back in the box.

Richard could see the sadness was compounding, and it was obvious his was getting to be too much as well.

"I think we have enough," he said softly, just as the sound of Abe pulling up next to the cabin signaled the return of Kimmy's ashes.

He looked at his watch and sighed. "We'll leave in about an hour."

Jane nodded, and walked stiffly to the little ladder to her loft to get changed for her aunt's wake, the reprieve of the sauna-induced comfort gone, once again feeling like she was in a bad dream.

3

Rue's was the epitome of the small-town bar caricature seen in movies; an outdated jukebox in the corner, television above the bar, pool table in the center, a small, raised stage in the corner, linoleum floors, and Naugahyde covered barstool cushions and booth seats, all cracked and faded.

As Abe, Richard, and Jane filed in, the small crowd that was gathered around the perimeter of the bar became still.

The man who broke from the group and came to them extended his hand to Richard first, but his eyes were locked on Jane. He clapped Abe on the shoulder and then reached over to touch Jane on hers.

"I'm Will," he said, his voice surprisingly soft for such a big man. "You must be Jane."

Jane smiled and nodded.

He was a tall man, taller even than Richard and Abe, with shaggy blond hair and big, kind brown eyes. They filled with tears as he cleared his throat and then said, "We all loved Kimmy. All of us. She…was special."

And there it was. The agonizing crush of grief had mercifully abated into a dull, but manageable throb, until this reminder of the huge loss Kimmy's death was. How much everyone who met her loved her.

A tiny, childlike, selfish impulse in Jane wanted to wail, wanted to shout to these people who were mere friends, or just acquaintances, wanted to ask them–*Can you imagine how I feel? She was just a blip in your life–she was everything to us.*

But instead, she nodded silently, whispered a *thank you* and moved along with Richard and Abe towards a curtained doorway, following Will.

As they moved through the crowd, though, she saw it in each face…the same sadness Will's eyes held. Not a polite pity, but genuine sorrow. Jane suddenly realized what she was experiencing was different from other funerals—she did not ever remember seeing this kind of pain on faces, aside from the immediate family.

Kimmy's role in her life as her surrogate mother was a special one, and Jane had always felt the depth of her love and her specialness in the way she fulfilled it. And that personal loss hurt. It had hurt from the moment Richard said the words, "Kimmy's gone," in that terrible phone call, and it had not really stopped.

But this she was feeling now…was deeper. This loss she felt when she thought about Kimmy simply as a person, and knew—from what she understood about her aunt and what she was seeing on people's faces now— Kimmy wasn't just a special presence in her life, she had been a singular influence in almost every life she touched.

The world was different without her.

Will drew the curtain aside and Jane stepped through, surprised at the size of the room behind it. An auditorium with descending stairs, rows of movie-theater style seats, and a stage, where a screen and podium stood.

"This is our movie theater and our town hall," Abe said, in response to her expression.

The three of them were ushered down to the front, and as Will gestured, they filed into the center seats of the first row.

Jane heard the rest of the group file into the theater behind them, quietly, and fill the remaining seats in the theater. When she turned to look back, she could see that all of them were filled, and people crowded into the aisles at the side of the theater, and at the door from the bar.

Kimmy's wake was standing room only.

When the shuffle ceased, Jane saw Richard nod to Will, who in turn nodded towards the back, looking up at what Jane assumed was the projector room.

The lights dimmed, and as a sound system sparked to life, Jane recognized the opening notes of what had been her favorite song in the summer of 1988, and in fact, for years after...*Don't Change* by INXS. The screen lit up and an image of Kimmy with her arm around a 15-year-old Jane splashed onto it, larger than life. It was taken at an INXS concert at the Oklahoma City Zoo amphitheater, and the bittersweet gratitude that rushed through Jane's heart was almost unbearable.

She had smoked pot for the first time that night, with the friends she had gone to the concert with, and the initial euphoria she felt had given way after only a few moments to a panic attack of epic proportions.

Convinced she was dying, she had left the boundaries of the outdoor venue and her confused friends behind, sobbing and looking for a pay phone.

Terrified to call her grandfather, who thought she was studying at her best friend's house–she dialed Kimmy's boyfriend, willing her aunt to be there.

She was.

"I'm ten minutes away, don't move!"

It took less than that for Kimmy to arrive, jumping out of the passenger seat of the boyfriend's car, and waving him away.

Jane could still feel the panic, the relief at seeing her, the feeling of Kimmy's arms around her and her laughter.

"Why are you crying? No, you're fine! No, he's not taking us home...we're going back in!"

Even though Jane wailed, begged...Kimmy dragged her around the arena's side, to a gap in the fence...and they went back in.

Don't Change was playing.

"You love this song–and this is perfect! Just listen, kiddo, listen to the words..."

Kimmy, dancing, laughing, screaming the lyrics.

Kimmy taking her hands and touching them to the grass...its rough, summer-burned sensation a call back to reality...

Kimmy pointing to the star-filled sky, still singing along at the top of her lungs.

The fullness of that memory, that remembered turnaround, the snapshot of how Kimmy's Kimmy-ness, as Jane always called it, infiltrated Jane's heartache and incredibly, made her laugh. From her peripheral vision she saw Richard look at her, and she turned to smile at him. He was laughing through tears too.

Photo after photo followed; Kimmy with her father, Jane's grandfather, Pappy, in his arms as a fat, joyful toddler, then as a just as joyful teen, with a mohawk…Kimmy painting six-year-old Jane's face like a tiger for Halloween. Kimmy at Jane's wedding (the only photo where she wasn't smiling), Kimmy holding Lucas, then Anne Marie and Robin in succession…Kimmy at the table playing cards with Pappy, Kimmy teaching Lucas to ride a bike.

Jane continued to cry, but also laugh as well. The sight of Kimmy and their other family members was comforting. Kimmy's smile, her shining eyes…Jane could almost hear her voice and her laugh.

Pappy, wearing a party hat, laughing, with Kimmy next to him, one party hat on her head, the other on her face like a beak.

Now Kimmy was gone, just like Pappy. Jane suddenly felt, not just the stab of Kimmy's loss, but the echo of his as well.

And then, just to cement the cataclysmic walk down the memory lane of loss…a picture of Kimmy and Renee, the beloved sister who had died way too young. Jane's mother.

Kimmy had all but replaced her mother, but Jane still remembered her. Or rather, she thought she did.

Jane had been only three years old when her mother had been killed in a car wreck, and she thought for the thousandth time since hearing about her aunt's death that it was a horribly cruel coincidence, to lose the two key women in her life the same way. Renee's image, the sound of her voice, the coarseness of her wild, curly hair, and the intensity of her gaze were things that Jane always considered her own memories. But now as she looked at these photos, she acknowledged for the first time they were likely planted and supported by a grieving Kimmy. After all, Jane remembered nothing else of her early life, before age five, and so the mental snapshots of Renee were likely kept alive by the same set of pictures always shown to Jane by her mother's sister. By the same anecdotes, the same stories. The sister who was now gone. In the same way. The same horrifying kind of death.

So much loss. Too much.

Suddenly Jane felt angry.

The song ended and another one started. MC Hammer's *Can't Touch This*.

The anger disappeared like smoke and Jane laughed out loud. One of Kimmy's favorites.

These images were of Kimmy's pursuits. Everything she excelled at. Kimmy in a lab coat, administering an IV to a sedated wolf. Kimmy at the finish line of a handful of 5Ks, Kimmy in snowshoes, Kimmy paddleboarding.

Jane laughed again, simultaneously with Richard and Abe.

It helped the grief, the tiniest bit, to have people to share it, and the funny memories with.

The song wound down with a video clip of Kimmy, riding a bicycle backwards, around a pool. Jane's breath caught at the moving image–seeing Kimmy in motion–and she leaned forward. It cut to another video; Kimmy at the same house (Jane recognized it as the house she had rented in Boise, Idaho, the last time Jane had visited her), jumping from the roof into the pool.

The room erupted in laughter and a few scatterings of applause that soon filled the whole theater.

Another song queued up...The Rollings Stones.

This was Kimmy with Richard. Kimmy with Abe. Kimmy sitting at the very bar they had passed to come into this theater. Kimmy at parties with her arms around people Jane had never seen, Kimmy lecturing in front of a hall of students, Kimmy and Richard standing beside a lake, both emanating pure love, their expressions so happy it felt like being slapped in the face, to know that the beautiful woman

Richard was looking at this way was gone. Jane turned to look at him, sympathy momentarily assuaging her own bereft state.

Richard was silently sobbing, tears running down his face.

Kimmy with half a dozen of the people Jane had seen in the bar–sobs could be heard now, in the audience–Kimmy with three half-grown wolf pups.

Kimmy with sixty-something lines in her face, but still radiant. Still the same smile, the same dancing eyes.

Richard leaned forward, putting his head into his hands, unable to look anymore.

The sound coming through his hands was heart-rending…a child's wail. Without even a thought, Jane reached out to touch his shoulder. He put his hand over hers and sat up again.

When the song ended, Will took the stage again, and gestured to the back of the auditorium.

"We have a microphone set up, at the back. If you'd like to say a farewell to Kimmy, or have thoughts for the family, please feel free. I'll just…I'll just say…" His voice faltered. "Richard, Abe, Jane…I'm so sorry for your loss. I'm sorry for all of us."

The first to the mic at the rear was a gruff looking older man in biker leathers, who couldn't even get a word out before dissolving into tears. He was quickly replaced by another gentleman, who hoarsely offered

condolences to the family and said that just the loss of Kimmy's laughter alone would leave a hole in all of their lives.

It felt brutal. Desolate.

Jane's appreciation for this community's love of her aunt was quickly overshadowed by the difficulty of hearing how much of a positive fixture Kimmy was in each of their lives. Not only because it compounded her own heartbrokenness, to be reminded of what a good person–what a uniquely good person–Kimmy was, but also because, she realized with a twinge of shame…it hurt to realize that she had been depriving herself of her aunt's generous and singular love by staying away these last years.

And she was jealous of these people for getting to receive Kimmy's love when she wasn't able to, even though it was her own fault.

At last, thankfully, there was a silence that indicated everyone was finished speaking. Beside Jane, Abe took a deep breath and stood. He went to the mic on the stage, and cleared his throat.

"Um, there were…so many reasons to love Kimmy. She was the funniest person I've ever met–seriously, just, comedian-level funny–and also had the biggest heart. But the main reason I am grateful she came into our lives, was that I've never seen Richard happier." His voice broke.

"Thank you, Kimmy."

He returned to his seat. Richard started to get up, then stopped. Then, after a sigh, he stood and went to the back.

For several long moments, he simply stood. Finally, he spoke.

"I knew when I met her, that my life would never be the same." He took a moment to compose himself.

"And now, it's changed again. If there isn't…an afterlife where I'll see her again, then truly…the best part of my life is over." That was all. He returned to his seat. Jane could see that he was shaking.

She knew they would expect her to speak. There was so much to say, but also…what could be said that hadn't been, already? Jane considered shaking her head and declining the chance, but her legs moved almost on their own and she felt as if she were being propelled by something other than herself as she went up on the stage.

Without thought, words came.

"My grandfather didn't shy away from talking about death. He used to say, "One day you'll die. But the thing that never dies is the judgment on how you have spent your life." I didn't know, as a kid, what that meant but…" Jane looked out at all of them, nodding animatedly at her words, as if they recognized them, "I know when I look at Kimmy's life what it means. She spent her life well."

She turned and headed towards the stairs, surprised at her own brevity. *Maybe the Ulfsons are rubbing off on me.*

Abe smiled sadly at her as she passed, patting her arm as she sat.

Richard seemed to be lost in time, staring ahead, no indication that he was hearing or seeing anything around him.

Will took the stage again and thanked everyone for coming, and mentioned that the food and drink was already set up in the bar. Mercifully, there was no traditional passing of the family to offer condolences, and so Jane stood with Abe and Richard to make her way out of the theater.

There was a spread on the bar and a long table that had been set up beside it. An ice chest with beers and bottled water sat on the floor, and guests filed in, nodding to the family and picking up plates and bottles.

Jane stood by the door with Abe and Richard at her side. None of them seemed to know what to do next. A woman came and offered to make plates...they all shook their heads in unison, as if they had practiced it.

I don't know any of them, Jane thought, sadness and an odd sort of panic overtaking her. Immediately there was a longing for her children–none of them could make it in the short window of time, and just as quickly as the wish for them appeared, guilt for not being more responsive to Richard's phone calls replaced it.

Had she known sooner, they would have too, and perhaps could have gotten off of work, made plans to travel. They had all said as much, when she had called them, their grief eclipsed by their disappointment with her. It was a natural and easier feeling to process, she knew, although it didn't make it less painful.

"Excuse me for a moment..." Jane brushed past Richard and Abe.

Heading for the front door, she murmured something about getting air, and that was initially her intent...but as her feet hit the gravel they kept moving, almost of their own accord.

They had only traveled a mile or so to get to the bar, and it wasn't dark yet...she realized that her feet were taking her back to the cabin.

It's rude, she told herself. *I don't care;* she retorted. *My mother– essentially the person who was one of my mothers–has died. I've been polite, I've received condolences...I'm tired. I want to be alone.*

The crunch of the gravel under her feet against the relative silence felt like a relief. Almost meditative. *Yes...I just need some alone time. This is fine. It's understandable.*

But she still paused for just a moment, realizing that Abe and Richard might be hurt by her vanishing act. Jane sighed. Would she ever get a break from disappointing people? She pulled her phone from her pocket, as she started walking again, deciding to mitigate her bad manners with a phone call.

It took a moment for Richard to answer. The second curve in the road had taken her out of sight of the bar and towards the trees that bordered the road their house was down. She'd made good time, the road was clear, and Kimmy's shoes were only a little tight.

"Hey...where are you?" He sounded a little worried.

"I'm sorry, it was just...it was just getting to be a bit much. I was just going to get some air, but I kind of started walking and just didn't look back. I hope I'm not being too rude, please tell Will and everyone else it was lovely...I'm going back to the cabin to lie down. It was just a little overwhelming."

"Jane, wait–she left, she's walking to the cabin–" Jane could hear Abe talking to Richard as he attempted to talk to her and explain at the same time, "Listen, Jane, we'll come get you, we're leaving now..."

"Please don't leave on my account, that wasn't my intention. I'm fine to walk..." Jane stopped, staring ahead of her. "Oh my God..."

"What is it? What's happening?" Richard's voice sounded immediately concerned. "Abe, Howard, catch her–"

She lowered her hand slowly, not taking her eyes off of the road in front of her.

A large black wolf had slowly ambled from the brush to the side of the ditch that ran alongside the road, and stopped directly in front of her.

She heard Kimmy's voice in her head.

Don't run, don't look away.

His eyes were deep and dark. Yellow, but shadowy, and his tongue lolled out in an easy wolf grin. He stood for a moment, staring at her, and then the grin slowly faded into a snarl.

Jesus, God...

Jane took a step back. But she hadn't moved more than a few inches when a rustling behind her tore her eyes away from the wolf in front of her and saw yet another wolf–a timber wolf, white and gray–coming up from the opposite side, positioning himself behind her in the road.

Shit.

Kimmy's voice came again. *Don't run, don't look away, make aggressive noises.*

Jane's chest felt like her heart was going to beat out of it. She began to step back and wheel so that both wolves would be in front of her, but the white and gray one kept moving, and she could tell he was trying to get behind her.

Her mouth went cotton dry. No sound would come for a moment, until she willed herself to yell, a weak, *"Hey!"*

The black wolf barely flinched at the noise, then snarled again and moved forward.

"Go!" Jane stomped toward the white and gray wolf...who didn't break eye contact or show any response to her noise, just kept inching behind her.

This is how I'll die. The thought wasn't as terrifying as it was preparatory.

Jane had a vision of her children, screaming in grief.

Her keyring was in the pocket of Kimmy's coat that she was wearing, and there was a small canister of mace on it, and a pocket knife. Scrabbling for them now, she flicked open the knife and turned the nozzle of the mace, but even as she made the movements, she knew they would be useless for stopping two wolves this size.

Oh, God, please, please...

For the briefest of moments, she wondered if she was dreaming it, if it was a hallucination–*wolves* on the road? Two of them? About to attack a person? It didn't make sense.

But now both of them were closing in–they were narrowing in on her. She held the mace up threateningly and yelled again, only gaining a slight pause from the black wolf, who looked for all the world as if he glanced at his companion in question. *Were they hungry? Where did they come from? Why were they so aggressive?* It didn't matter, it wouldn't matter if they made it to her. Jane was trying to look behind her as she slowly backed away, but she knew they were backing her into the ditch.

It occurred to her that they were purposefully doing that, to trip her.

Wolves are smart…again, Kimmy the Researcher and Life-Long Lupine Advocate's voice.

This is how I'll die. Jane's body felt as if it were becoming lighter–is this how it felt before death? A flash, a memory–of a car crash that bloodied her nose as a teenager and how there was a blank before the realization she'd been hit, and the pain. Would it be that quick, to be mauled by a wolf? Would she languish in pain for hours?

She felt her heel slip and knew she could not back up further.

"Get BACK!" Her voice shrilled at the end. Panic.

This time neither wolf even flinched. The white and gray's teeth bared in a smile that held a low rumbling growl she could barely hear.

Her mace held two shots, no more. She had no idea how effective it would be against a wolf–especially two of the biggest wolves she had ever seen–but she could not go backwards another inch, and she could not, under any circumstances, run.

She tried to glance behind her, knowing she could not let the wolves out of her sight, trying to see how close the nearest tree was, but she knew there was little to no chance of being able to swing herself up before they caught her legs.

But that was likely her only chance. She visualized what she felt was the likely outcome–one of them grabbing her legs before she could haul herself up–and then added the image of being able to kick them away and pull herself completely up. *You're going to regret skimping on arm day, bitch,* she sighed inwardly.

Jane took a deep breath. Suddenly the black wolf settled back onto his haunches and Jane knew he would spring forward next. She pressed the top of the mace, and then pressed it again when it caught and refused to go down, finally releasing a stream that she had to wave back and forth a little in order to hit the wolf's eyes.

She saw when the stream hit its mark and felt a burst of hope that it would handicap him. The wolf shook his head and yelped in pain and in the split second that her attention was turned from the white and gray wolf, he leapt at her. Jane turned back to him, putting her arms forward and aiming them underneath his neck, pushing against the brunt of his weight–heavier even than she had imagined–as he knocked her to her back in the ditch, so hard that the air left her lungs as she hit the ground.

Her arms had kept his teeth from her neck but he thrashed his head side-to-side, attempting to get between her hands at her face and neck. She could hear herself screaming in between gasps to regain her breath, pinned by his huge body, his back feet scratching her legs, his teeth tearing the fabric of her down coat where she was using her forearms to ward off his jaws.

A shot rang out, and the black wolf, still standing on the road up to her left, shaking his head, fell to the ground.

*Help me…*Jane screamed it over and over to the rumble that was approaching and the shouts she could vaguely hear. She could see nothing but the wolf's eyes, gray as the ring around his neck, and his teeth, snapping and flying as he lunged again and again at her face and neck, her arms stopping him just short of tearing her throat.

She could smell his breath. And his weight felt as if it was slowly crushing the life out of her, his thrashing driving her into the ground.

Another snarl erupted and another black wolf–*another one? How many are there?!*--came leaping from the embankment and hit the white and gray wolf in the shoulder, knocking him aside. Sheer terror engulfed her, and she screamed, flailing, waiting for the sensation of organs being ripped from her body.

But this black wolf lunged again, and as the white and gray turned to address him, the black wolf jumped, pushing him completely off of Jane and snapping at his throat. Jane kicked herself away, scrabbling backwards as the wolves rolled, a mass of howling, growling, snarling, and biting fur.

"Jane!!" Before she could see that it was Abe, or recognize his voice, he had her by the sleeve, pulling her up and towards him, and in a second, she was over his shoulder, and he was carrying her. Another shot, and Jane jumped. Abe swung her down in front of the open truck door, and immediately swept her feet out from under her and lifted her into the seat. Richard was getting back into the driver's side. He passed a rifle to Abe, who jumped in, Jane in the middle, and shut the door.

"Howard!" Richard called out, and to Jane's horror, the second black wolf leapt, like an antelope, into the bed of the truck. She screamed, instinctively, and Abe put his arm around her, turning her towards the front and away from the rear window.

"No, no, it's okay, it's okay!!" Richard put the truck in gear and they sped away.

"Hold on, just...hold on." Abe patted her shoulder. He was shaking, Jane could feel it. Or was that her? He held her, tightly, for most of the short minutes that the drive took, his breath short.

"Jane, are you hurt? Badly hurt?" Abe turned her face to look at him. He pulled at the mangled ski jacket, shaking his head. "I'll call Doc Buchwald and tell him to meet us at the cabin."

"It's them, you know that now, you see it, don't you?" Richard's voice was angry–or indignant? Oddly high-pitched, seething with a quality Jane had not heard in it before. She stared at him, thinking that he seemed so changed it was almost like seeing another man entirely.

"Not now, let's get her home and look around and see if there are more." Abe had pulled out his phone. "Doc–we have her, we're going to the cabin, please come quickly. Be careful...it looks like...." He trailed off and Jane could hear the man on the other end say something. "Yes, I think so." He hung up and put the phone back in his pocket.

Slowly Jane turned so that she was looking out the rear window again.

The black wolf who had leapt to fight her white and gray attacker was sitting in the far end of the truck bed, facing out. The jostling caused him to put out a paw now and then, but for the most part he sat still, watching, his large head moving back and forth, eyeing the road behind them.

A pet? The hybrid that left the marks on the door? Jane let out a breath. The odd feeling from the night before. Although not strong enough to penetrate the shock and disbelief of what had just happened.

The truck pulled into the driveway, and Richard and Abe both looked around before they got out, Abe motioning to her to give him her hands. She tried to say that she was fine, but no sound came out, and as she let him ease her to the ground it felt as if her limbs were not working in concert with her mind.

Her mind was still a mile behind them, on the ground, screaming and fighting for her life.

"I got you," Abe swung her up into his arms again and Jane let him. They were on the porch, they were in the cabin, Richard bending down to grab a savagely snarling Cooi and call over his shoulder, "Howard, you're going to have to change to come in–Cooi doesn't like you like this. And you need to come in–we don't know if there are more. Help is on the way–we need you inside."

As Abe gently sat her on the chair directly in front of the fireplace, Jane turned her head, and beyond Richard and Cooi, she could see the black wolf standing just off of the threshold, his head cocked as he gazed into the cabin, looking directly at her.

"Cooi…" Jane's voice was a weak rasp. Abe was kneeling in front of her and she turned to look at him as he gently pulled at her sleeves, freeing her from the decimated coat.

"Jane, I need to look at you, I need to see how bad it is."

How bad? For the first time, Jane looked, really looked at the front of her coat and her arms.

There was blood. There was also mud, pine needles and grass, but there was unmistakable blood as well, and Jane felt her body going light again.

"Easy, easy...okay," Abe spoke in a calm voice, but Jane recognized fear in it. The door closed and Richard was beside them as well.

"Is she hurt? Jane, are you hurt?" Richard knelt, Cooi at his side, whimpering and nuzzling Jane's leg. For the first time, she felt pain and looked down. Long, muddy tears exposed some skin beneath her jeans and there were red streaks where the wolf's claws had lacerated her leg.

Jane looked at her arms too, and saw them much the same; dark blood coagulated on her left wrist, on what looked like a bite, and there were gashes on her right arm, and scratches–the ski jacket had cushioned some, but not all of the attack.

"She fought him well," Jane jumped at the sound of the man's voice, pushing Abe and Richard out of the way as she forced her way to her feet.

Standing in front of the door was a man.

Dark hair, dark eyes, dark eyebrows, and sharp cheekbones. Muscular, but whip thin. All darkness and angles.

Completely naked.

Blood stained his mouth, chin, neck, and hands. He had mud and pine needles all over his sides, hands, and feet.

Jane stood, looking into his eyes, and immediately recognized that they were the same eyes that had stared back at her, from the wolf in the truck bed.

"Hello, Jane," the man said. "You can call me Howard."

Jane's consciousness had taken all that it could stand, and so it fled, leaving her to crumple to the floor.

4

As Jane slowly came back to herself, she realized a few things all at once. She was on the bed in Richard and Kimmy's room, staring up at the slowly oscillating ceiling fan blades. Cooi was beside her, his bristled back against her hand. And she was wearing a cotton hospital gown.

Slowly, she sat up, surprised to see a man sitting on a stool next to her. He seemed young, maybe in his twenties, and he held up a hand and smiled.

"Hi, Jane. Sorry we're meeting this way. My name is Cordial Buchwald…I'm the town's doctor."

An odd name for such a young man, Jane thought. She looked down at the gown. He pointed, reaching down into his bag.

"Yes, I had some help getting you in here, but I changed you and dressed your wounds alone. Sorry, but the clothes didn't make it. Had to be cut off so I could assess how much damage you suffered." He had retrieved a roll of gauze, and he began to wind it around her left wrist. "The good news is, you're in pretty good shape, all things considered. Only the one puncture wound here, the rest are gashes and scrapes, although the one on your stomach is fairly deep. I've given you a tetanus shot and prescribed a course of antibiotics, so these should heal up well." He taped the bandage and smiled.

"If you develop any fever, if the wounds start to look–" he almost tipped over on his stool as Jane quickly threw her legs over the side of the bed and leapt to her feet, grabbing the coverlet off of the foot of the bed to wrap around her and shield her ass from exposure through the open back of the doctor's cotton gown. Cooi also sprang up, his nails clicking on the floor beside her as she threw open the door and strode out of the bedroom.

Richard, Abe, Howard (wearing sweatpants and a flannel shirt, hair slightly wet), and another man sat at the kitchen table, talking quietly. Three more men stood in the living room, one looking out the window, one standing in front of the fireplace looking at a map, another talking quietly on a cell.

All of them turned to look at her.

"What…is going on?" She asked.

Abe stood, gesturing to the three men in the living room. "We're good here–if someone's in the fire tower and we have a perimeter, that's it for tonight." The men all nodded and left; Jane could see through the door that it was dusk.

Cordial Buchwald, Boy Doctor, carefully edged around Jane, his bag in hand, nodding to Abe as he quickly left as well.

Richard looked from Abe to Howard, but Howard's black eyes were fixed on Jane. She stared back.

"You," she said.

"Yes," he responded quietly. "Me."

"You were attacked by two stray wolves," Abe began. "We killed–"

"No," Jane said quietly. "I want to know what's really going on."

"Tell her what's really going on, Abraham," Howard continued to look at Jane, addressing Abe, who slammed a large hand on the table, the first expression of non-calm Jane had ever seen from him.

"Goddamit, Howard, I will do this my way. *Eng boudoux michte–*"

"*Nai,*" Howard replied, calmly, in the same unintelligible language. For a moment Jane thought she was passing out again, or having a stroke, until she realized that they were indeed speaking in a foreign tongue.

Swedish? Norse? French?

"She deserves to know the truth. She won't run, she'll understand. You're underestimating her."

He had an accented lilt to his voice like Richard, only more pronounced. Thicker. He continued to stare at Jane, and she felt like he was somehow familiar.

'Do I know you? Have we met?"

He smiled, an animal's grin. "Yes, and no."

"You...were the wolf. How...how is that possible." Jane could scarcely believe she was saying it out loud, could hardly comprehend how she could think such a thing, much less *know* it.

Howard looked to Abe, and so Jane did too. He seemed tired, and frightened. He ran a hand over his short-cropped hair, and looked at Jane with his sad, kind eyes full of...love. She could see it; she could feel it. It was love, mixed with fear.

'Let's all sit down, and I will tell you."

They all moved quietly to distinct seats around the fireplace, as if their places were assigned. Cooi passed by Jane to drop at Richard's feet, to both her slight dismay and amusement.

It became so quiet the grandfather clock's ticking sounded like drumbeats.

For long seconds, Jane looked at each of them in turn. Howard, cool and calm. Richard, oddly still, but smiling weirdly when he would meet her eyes. Abe, looking at his hands until he finally cleared his throat and raised his gaze to meet Jane's.

"What if I told you we were shapeshifters?"

Jane looked at each man. "What...all three of you?"

Abe nodded. "Yes. And the three men who were just here, the doctor, and most of the individuals you met today at Kimmy's wake. As well as the wolves who attacked you."

She half laughed, knowing instinctively, on a deep level that he was telling the truth, but unable to simply accept it without question.

"Like, werewolves?" The word produced an expression of distaste on the faces of all three.

"We call ourselves *lugaru*."

The word stirred something in her. "Wait...like, like the Cajun stories? Like the *rougarou*?"

Abe tilted his head. "Kind of."

"My grandfather–" she noted that the men all glanced at each other when she said this– "my grandfather used to tell me ghost stories when I was little. Cajun stories about the *rougarou*, a man who turned into a beast." Jane smiled; the bizarreness of her current situation lifted momentarily by the memory of her grandfather. "It's funny, when I got a book of Cajun fairy tales, all of the *rougarou* stories were meant to frighten children, but–"

"But, your grandfather," Abe said softly, with a touch of fondness himself, "Told them differently, didn't he? The *rougarou* was the hero."

The familiarity with which he said this gave Jane an eerie feeling, and she was suddenly, inexplicably hostile. Emotions swirled, until her mouth was able to work again and form the question that came as a statement.

"You knew him."

"Yes, I did."

"How?"

This stopped the interchange momentarily, and all three men exchanged glances.

"Stop looking at each other and tell me what the fuck is going on!" Jane had lost all sense of decorum, all gratitude, all patience, all at once.

Abe swallowed. "I knew him because I'm your father, Jane."

Long seconds passed, and Jane burst into laughter. She laughed for several minutes, and then finally stood.

"This is ridiculous, I'm leaving…"

Howard stood, holding up his hands in a universal symbol of passivity when she bristled.

"Please, Jane, will you hear him out? He's hesitated to tell you any of this because he's afraid you'll run. And he doesn't want that. Not only because he wants to get to know you, but because you're in danger. You can see that, right? From this afternoon? They attacked you for a reason, and we want to be sure you're safe. We also want you to understand what's going on, but…Abe should be the one to tell you."

"Why, because he's my father?" Jane laughed again, then felt the anger return. "How can you expect me to believe this? First, that you're werewolves and then that a man who looks like he's twenty years younger than me is the father I haven't seen for 47 years? So, Richard is my paternal grandfather, then? Are you serious?

"Actually," Richard's voice was quiet. "I'm your brother, Jane. Abe is my father, not my son."

His statement stopped Jane's protest for the same reason Howard's calm admission he was the wolf did; she knew it was true. A primal nudging told her it was.

She had noticed small instances of paternalism in Abe, towards Richard, and now, she realized…towards her as well. Suddenly she thought of all the times Kimmy had mentioned Abe, what a good man he was…how much Jane would like him…how she would love for them to meet…

"Did Kimmy…believe all this?" A sudden incredulousness took her over. Was Kimmy brainwashed? Was this some crazy cult? Did that explain her feeling of belonging that first night, after drinking the tea–had she been drugged? The sense of having met them before, of feeling at home…the wild stories…did *they* loose the wolves on her to save her? To set up this story? Jane's head swam with every story she had ever read about how cults inculcate a sense of home in their victims…

"Jane, please…" Abe stood. "Please, just let me explain. Let me–" he turned to the hearth and held up a finger, signaling her to stay put. He crossed to a wooden box on a shelf, and pulled it down. "I want to show you something."

He put it on the small table in between all of them, and opened it. Inside were documents and photos, and he took out two small frames. He looked at them for a moment before slowly walking to Jane and handing them to her.

She took them, hands shaking, and stared at him for a few long moments before taking a breath and looking down.

In one photo, Abe sat with his arm around…

Renee. Jane's mother.

Renee was not smiling, but Abe was. In his arms, he held a baby, small, grinning a toothless grin, a shock of golden-brown hair standing up on top of her head. Jane felt tears stinging her eyes and felt her breath catch in her throat.

It was her.

Her grandfather had baby pictures of her, and she recognized not only herself, but the pink romper she was wearing.

Pictures can be faked, she told herself. *But this one isn't, and you know it,* she responded.

Jane looked at the other photo, and more tears welled. A younger version of Richard sat at a Formica table, with baby Jane balanced on it in front of him. He was beaming. She shook her head.

"I don't understand…how, how do you both still look the same? Why do you look younger than Richard?"

"When we…change, it preserves us." Abe was clearly emotional, seeing her reaction to the pictures. His voice was thick.

"Changing provides us with health and anti-aging benefits," Howard said quietly.

Jane met his gaze. "That sounds like a commercial for acai berries." She shook her head. "So, the more you change, the younger you stay?"

"That's a simplified version of what happens, yes."

"How…how old are you?" Jane turned to Abe. He cleared his throat.

"I don't know for sure what year I was born, but it was in the 1700s."

Jane sank back into the chair, still holding the pictures. She looked up at the shelves again and gestured to another photo.

"It's you, isn't it? In front of the cabin?" She glanced at Richard, "He's the baby in the photo, isn't he?"

Abe nodded.

"Rikaarti Ulfsson, 1915." She shook her head. "That means Richard–Rikaarti– is 111 years old."

"Around that," Richard's voice was soft.

"Where is your mother? Is she still alive?"

"No, no…there aren't female *lugaru…*" Richard seemed to fumble, and looked at Abe.

"Oh my god, this is unreal!" Jane shook her head. "You are all men, you have human women bear your children, and then you live forever?" She shrugged. "Sounds wonderful."

"No, not forever," Howard's voice had a patient quality to it. "Our lives can be extended if we change often, but we can be killed. Not easily, but we can be killed. If we don't change, after a while, we begin to age."

They were all quiet for a moment, as Jane digested this. The kitchen sink was dripping, in concert with the clock, and Cooi's soft snoring. Jane cleared her throat.

"That's why Richard looks older than Abe—he doesn't change, as much?"

"Yes, until recently, that was the case." Abe glanced at Richard, who was looking down at his hands.

"Was it…because of Kimmy? Did you not change as much because of her?" Jane looked down at the photo of the younger Richard, holding her. His wide, toothy grin made her heart contract.

"Yes, that was why."

"She didn't know."

"Oh, no, she did know. I just…" Richard's voice cracked. "I just wanted us to live as normal a life as possible. I wanted to be with her, like her, for as long as possible."

This revelation brought a new swirl of questions to Jane's mind. "She knew. She knew what you were?"

"She knew what she was, as well." Howard's enigmatic, cryptic words brought a look of consternation from Abe, and Jane could tell their guest was pushing Abe, goading him to reveal more.

"What does that mean?" Jane looked at Abe, then looked at her father. God, so many things to absorb, so much to ask. "What does he mean, she knew what *she* was?"

Howard stood. "I'll put on a pot of coffee…it's going to be a long night."

5

Jane refused the coffee at first, but then relented, knowing the caffeine would help her brain to begin to sort the anger, confusion, wonder, and sadness that was overfilling it.

"Your aunt, like you, was what we call a 'tamer.' Women who are able to…" Abe sighed and ran a hand over his hair. "Howard can explain this part better."

"Tamers are women whose presence can act as a comforting agent to a *lugaru*, put simply," Howard said. "It can help them resist the urge to change, if that's what they want." He sat with his legs crossed at the knee, quietly blowing on his cup of coffee as if they were discussing their favorite movies. Jane laughed.

"I'm sorry…I'm still stuck on the werewolf part–"

Again, the very visible cringe from Richard and Abe.

"What is it you don't like about that word? Is it incorrect?"

"I don't think it's necessarily incorrect," Howard sipped his coffee. "We consider it pejorative." He shrugged. "Centuries of its use in tales that…well, don't tell the whole story." A polite smile.

"But the stories were based in fact? You've existed that long and surely they were describing…" Jane gestured "…you."

"Well, yes and no." Howard leaned forward and set his cup down. "They described events from one side. Our side tells a fuller story. It has all the facts."

"What are the facts? What is this…condition? Has it always existed? Does it have a cause?"

Howard became very still and cleared his throat.

"As far as we know, we have always existed alongside humans. It's hard to know for sure, but the oldest among us, at least, the oldest among us after we began writing our history, remembers a father who looked...different...from modern humans. There were others like him who walked among us, here and there, in the times before modern history. We believe that interbreeding with them resulted in a genetic predisposition to be *lugaru*. Now, if a man who is *lugaru* has a son, there is no guarantee that the son will be *lugaru*, or a daughter will be a tamer--"

"Wait," Jane leaned forward. "This gene is what creates tamers as well? And what do you mean by "others?" That's pretty broad. Do you mean, like, aliens or something?"

"Some think they were aliens, some call them gods. They looked like what humans would call vampires, with pointed ears, fangs, but they weren't. Jane, you understand that–"

"Vampires?!" Jane interrupted. "Oh my God." She shook her head, looking down at her hands, twisting the blanket that she had around her shoulders.

Everyone was silent for a moment. Howard leaned forward a little, an encouraging expression on his face.

"You know, you're taking this very well—"

"NO, I'M NOT!" Jane's voice was almost a scream, causing Cooi, Abe and Richard to jump. She could feel her heart racing.

All of it—werewolves, tamers, vampires, a father who looked like he was thirty—swirled around her brain, the unreality of all of it too overwhelming.

And no Kimmy.

"This is crazy," she whispered, looking at each face around the table. "You're all crazy!"

"Jane," Richard seemed the most concerned, his eyes big. "We could call the men back here, the doctor, Will—would you believe them?"

"No!" Jane laughed, almost hysterically. "This, this could be some kind of weird cult, you, you could be brainwashing people into believing this. Kimmy---" the suggestion died on her tongue. It had sprung into her answer-seeking mind to say that they had deceived Kimmy, but in all of the wild revelations, all of the unbelievable things, the one thing she knew was true was that Richard loved Kimmy with all his heart. She could see it, feel it. And as she looked at him now, face etched with pain and desperation, eyes haunted with sadness, that was what she knew she could believe. This man loved Kimmy, would have died to protect her, and if that was real, then the rest of it, somehow, crazily, was too.

Howard's expression was serious. "Jane, you understand that everything I tell you has to remain secret, yes?" He leaned forward; intense eyes boring into hers. "This is a sacred trust, telling you these things. Only certain ones of us can obtain permission to share, and only with those who understand how tragic the consequences could be for our kind if human society at large knew about us."

Jane nodded. Now, along with absorbing the reality of this new culture, she began to see why secrecy was so necessary. But also, how difficult it must be to hide differences this big in a world that rushed to dissect and destroy "otherness."

"And yes," Howard continued, "a genetic mutation in those who carry DNA from those forebears causes both *lugaru* and tamers. And the…others."

Jane blinked. "What others? What else is there? Are you going to tell me that Sasquatch is real now?"

Howard ignored the jab. "By others I mean that there are those among us who…can see. They have the sight." He gesticulated a little when he saw Jane's blank look. "I guess you would call it magic."

Jane laughed, a laugh that trailed off. "Wow. This just gets better and better. Are you guys magic? Is that both men and women?"

"It's those who are in between."

There was a long silence as Jane looked from man to man quizzically. "What is that supposed to mean? Who is in betw–" She realized it before Howard could answer, and he saw her understanding, and affirmed it with a nod.

"Yes. Those who are in between what we usually closely define as men and women."

"Are you trying to delicately say "non-binary" and "trans", Howard?"

He nodded. Jane felt an odd pull at her chest...the thought of Robin. Instead of focusing on it she leaned into indignation.

"So only people assigned male at birth get to be werewolves, only cis-women are tamers, and only non-binary or trans folk can practice magic. Perfect. Makes absolute sense."

"I can leave some reading material for you, if you'd like to learn all we know about our origins, and how DNA has been discovered to play a role." Howard completely missed (or ignored) her caustic sarcasm, and the excitement and the reverence with which he spoke prodded a realization in Jane.

"You're an historian, aren't you?"

Howard shrugged. "An historian, a scientist, a bodyguard...I am what my people need me to be."

Jane looked to Abe and Richard. There was so much to absorb, so much to ask, about this insane unveiling. Not just about how the world contained a society of shapeshifters and women called tamers, and queer magicians, descended from aliens or gods, that looked like vampires (but weren't), but also about this new family she never knew she had.

And about the attack she had just suffered. Even though her adrenaline was high, the wounds were beginning to ache, and make her move slower. She touched her stomach gently.

"Why did those wolves attack me?"

"We aren't exactly...a united society." Howard was an intense man. Even though his movements and expressions revealed little, there was an energy to his speaking that punctuated it with feeling.

"There are *lugaru* who believe tamers make us more balanced, and there are those who feel their existence is a threat to who we are." He leaned toward her slightly to enunciate his next words.

"Among those who believe them to be a threat are extremists who...have been known to kill tamers."

In all of the flurry in her foggy mind, Jane felt an epiphany come out of the confusion.

"You all knew this was possible. Is this..." she stood, slowly, "what happened to Kimmy?"

Their stricken faces were answer enough.

Jane felt a sudden sob wrench her body. She clasped her mouth, shock and then anger shaking her.

"*How could you not stop them?*" her voice was a shriek, and even though the looks on Abe's and Richard's faces grieved her, she said it again. "*How could you...not protect her?*"

She collapsed in tears, head in her hands. Howard came to her side and gently guided her back to her chair. He replenished her drink, and even though Jane welcomed the gestures and felt somewhat calmed, something irritated her, and she suspected it was because his actions seemed so...automatic. As if he knew what would happen next.

He had done this before.

Even though she knew her words had hurt them, she could see it in their faces, Jane would not apologize. "There's so much I want to ask...why did you leave me?" She looked pointedly at Abe, still wiping tears away, her voice still catching with sobs.

"If this is all so dangerous, if tamers are at such risk...why did you leave me? Why did you leave my mother?"

Abe wiped his own eyes. "I thought..." he held his head in his hands for long moments, composing himself. "I thought it was best at the time. I actually assumed I was protecting you by leaving you with Agricole. And..." he composed himself again. "Your grandfather thought so too. In fact, he insisted, and I made a promise to him that I would go, and not contact you."

Jane stared at Abe. The more she sat with the knowledge that he was her father—as ludicrous as it sounded and seemed—the more her emotions battled for first place in her mind. Anger, relief—he was alive, he was a good man—and hurt, at his abandonment. Disbelief, that her beloved grandfather would orchestrate something so hurtful.

"He wouldn't do that to me." Even as she said it, she knew it wasn't true. It sounded exactly like something Pappy would do. Threaten someone with violence if they were endangering her. And if he knew about all this–

"How did he know what you were? Did you tell him?"

The looks from Richard and Abe made her dissolve into laughter, an inappropriate response she often had to stressful situations.

"You want me to believe that he was..." she fell silent.

Howard was the one who finally spoke, softly.

"Your grandfather was a *rugaru*. A lone wolf, you might say. Even though he was technically a *neoto*, a leopard–"

"A *leopard*?" Jane's laughter turned to a snort. "Is this just going to get more ridiculous as it goes on? Wh–why a *leopard*? How many different types of were-animals–sorry, I don't know what else to call them, are there?"

"*Lugaru* is our word for what we are," Abe's voice was uncharacteristically soft, and Jane could see that in spite of all that was happening, all of her anger, he really did want her to understand.

"Our type of turnskin–that's our word for what all of us are--changes into wolves. Other men who are descendants from other places, other cultures...they turn into different animals."

"Some men whose ancestors come from a particular part of Africa turn into leopards. We call them *neoto*, because it sounds like what they call themselves. Most turnskin types have their own language, like we do–it's a byproduct of having a society within society. But we call any turnskin of any type who does not live within the rules of the group a *rugaru*, like we call wolves who live on their own in our culture. Does that make sense?"

Jane shook her head, as she began to piece together memories and the present. "Like I said before, he always told me Cajun stories about the *rougarou*. And when I was an adult, after he died, after we took his ashes to Louisiana, I saw a book of folk tales, and bought it, thinking it would remind me of him, that it would be a good way to keep some of the tales he told alive, when, or if, I ever have grandchildren." She shrugged.

"But they weren't the same stories. In fact, I was confused, because all of the *rougarou* stories in the book were...cautionary tales. Horror stories. And in Pappy's version..."

"The *rugaru* is the hero," Abe said quietly, exactly as he had said it before.

Jane rubbed her eyes, willing the tears away. Her Pappy. The man who had always seemed bigger than life. Who had raised Renee and Kimmy alone, and then Jane. Pappy, who Jane's boyfriends had always declared to be the scariest individual alive. The man who had carried a picture of her, at age 5, in his wallet, until the day he died. He had been her hero. And all that time...he had been a *rugaru*. One of the monsters he was telling stories about. Now she realized...he had been sharing his most personal truth with her, in the only way he could.

Agricole. No one ever called her Pappy Agricole...no one knew that was his name. More proof that this unbelievable tale was true. She hadn't known his real name herself until she found an old photo album as a nosy teenager, that had the name *Agricole Roubideaux* scrawled next to the image of him with his parents.

The photo had always seemed odd. His birth certificate, when she found that, said he was born in 1926, and he looked like a ten-year-old, at least, in the photo.

"1936" had been written on the back...next to something else, that had been scribbled out. And the birth certificate seemed too new. He had lied to her at first, saying that his had been destroyed in the hurricane that hit New Orleans in 1947, but then when she began to question her own birth certificate–which said she was born in Oklahoma, not Louisiana–that was when he told her that he moved them and changed their last name after her mother's death. Jane had already figured out that her mother was a drug addict, and when she had asked if the move and name change was to get a fresh start, Pappy had simply said, "Yes." And then looked at her sadly and said, "I can't talk about it yet, *tête dure*, but I will someday."

And "someday" had just never come.

With a sigh, Jane held up her hands in a hopeless gesture.

"When you get married, when you father children…how do you explain this?"

All of the men looked at each other.

"It's different for each tribe," Abe said. "It's also one of the reasons we are so careful about having children–it's a huge responsibility and every male child born must be prepared for the first change, which usually happens in puberty. The ones who change without a father around usually become *rugaru*, like your grandfather, and learn to deal with it, but it's a lonely life."

A pang of love for Pappy shot through Jane. She had loved him before, and held respect for the struggles his life had held, but to know that he carried this secret in addition to all that, made the bittersweet feeling in her heart grow even more.

"But, Pappy had a father. Unless…" She knew from their expressions that what she'd always suspected about the man who raised her grandfather was true. "That wasn't his real father."

"Probably not." Howard shook his head. "Our ancestry records aren't complete, but they are quite meticulous, and with Kimmy's help, we were able to connect some missing pieces from your family tree. Your grandfather's mother was the daughter of another *rugaru*, a man called

Panther Dan; a discovery we made with Kimmy's help, by testing her DNA."

"The man who raised him, Andrew Spears, wasn't a biological match for your family. There was another *lugaru*'s DNA, but it doesn't match any in our database."

"What does that mean?"

"There are tribes who don't want to be profiled–we don't have DNA samples for every branch of *lugaru*. Not even close."

A sudden knock at the door caused Jane to jump, and Cooi yipped as it swung open, swiftly.

Jane recognized Will, the owner of Rue's, the bar. He was breathing heavily, as if he'd been running. The sound of commotion outside caused all of them to get to their feet.

"Alistair just radioed—he's seen something in the woods; we think it may be more of them." He glanced at Jane, nodding almost imperceptibly.

Abe pointed at Jane. "Get in that back room again." He touched his son on the shoulder and Richard nodded.

"Jane, come on." Jane let herself be led, moving slowly, her body shaking in either panic or a continued shock reaction to the attack in the woods. Suddenly, she could again feel and smell the gray wolf's breath on her face and hear the ripping of her coat under its teeth.

Men's voices were shouting, and Howard and Abe retrieved rifles from— from where? Jane hadn't even seen them—and disappeared out the door. Cooi stood staring at the door, with its deep claw marks, whining and then barking.

"Cooi! Come!" Jane's voice shook, like her knees. He followed them into the bedroom and Richard shut the door, reaching up onto a chest and retrieving a handgun, which he handed to Jane.

"Can you use one of these?" She nodded, sitting on the bed, then standing again.

What do you do in a shootout? She thought, almost laughing at the ridiculousness of it. Cooi growled his low, purring growl, and she shushed him. Richard reached under the mattress and retrieved another gun, a revolver. *Jesus, how many guns do they have?* She wondered, and then immediately hoped that it was a lot.

"Do you think it's them?" Jane wanted to sound calmer than she did. She straightened as she saw that Richard was pulling off his sweatshirt, after laying the revolver beside her.

"If it is, we stand a better chance if I change, and you shoot," he said, taking his eyes off the door for a moment and looking at her.

He smiled a sad smile. "As bad as this all is, I'm glad that you know now." He turned his attention to the door again, stepping out of his shoes.

She took a moment, in the terror, to look at her new-found brother. He was about to change to protect her, something he had stopped doing in order to try and age along with Kimmy. Jane felt a love well up, along with an instinct.

"Those claw marks on the door. They were from you, weren't they?"

His shoulders slumped. Richard cleared his throat, but then just nodded, instead of speaking.

"Does changing—help with the pain?"

"Nothing helps with the pain," he said, quietly. "But it lets you forget for a little while."

The outside door slammed, and Abe's voice called out.

"False alarm, we're okay. Come out."

Richard sagged with relief, then picked up his sweatshirt and put it back on.

In the living room, Howard and Abe were propping rifles against the fireplace. Both sank into chairs, and Richard and Jane did the same.

For long minutes they sat that way, until Jane quietly asked Abe, "I still don't understand—why would you, why would Pappy, think it was safer for me without you? What about safety in numbers?"

"Because *rugaru* avoid association with a family, they are difficult for the Brotherhood–the *lugaru* who hate tamers–to find."

Jane shook her head. "Are they seriously called the Brotherhood?"

Howard lifted his hands. "Of course they are."

She sighed, suddenly very, very tired.

A short stint of therapy (snagged during a brief period when she had insurance that covered it) after her divorce from her children's father had brought up issues that Jane had never put together with paternal abandonment. Now, the knowledge that he was healthy, and in a position to write letters and make phone calls, but chose not to, was bringing up all of the things her counselor had helped her see as outcroppings of that deep hurt that came from...him. "So much pain, from knowing that you left me," Jane's voice was soft. She was surprised at how soft it was, how shy she suddenly felt. "It crept into so many areas of my life."

"I knew you were well-loved, and taken care of..." Abe's voice was gentle as well, and even though there was no tone of excuse-making, Jane shook her head.

"That doesn't matter...you...you...why couldn't you at least still be in my life?"

"I made a promise to your grandfather," Abe leaned forward, "A vow is a serious thing in our culture–"

"Is it more serious than taking care of a child you make?" Jane stood. Abe and Richard looked at their laps.

"I can't imagine leaving my children, any one of them, just... abandoning them." Jane shook her head, and even though the horrified look on Abe's sad face pulled at her heart, she said what she was thinking anyway.

"I wish I didn't know. I wish you hadn't told me."

Abe's eyes filled with tears. "I'm sorry. I just want to say...I'm sorry. I would do it differently now." He stood and crossed the room to come to her. He hesitantly took her hand. She let him. His hands were strong and rough, and she was stunned at how comforted she felt at his touch.

"I thought it would keep you safe, and I believe it did. But I wish more than anything that I could have lived life with you. With your children."

"Jane," Howard was still sitting, but he leaned forward. "There is still much we need to tell you."

"I don't want to be here anymore."

"Please," Abe had a look of panic. "It's safer for you to be here, with us." "Even if it weren't safer," Richard's voice was soft and tearful. "We're your family, Jane. You're here now, if you can forgive us..."

"Yes, I suppose I need to forgive you as well." Jane was hurt. Growing more hurt by the minute, she realized. "Do you know how often I wished for a brother or sister? And I had one...I had a big brother all this time."

Richard looked gutted.

Silence.

Jane snapped her fingers and Cooi scrambled up from his blanket by the fire. "We're leaving."

"Jane," Howard stood now too, and walked ahead of her to a large knapsack on a bench near the entryway. "I want to show you something." He pulled out a large, rectangular felt bag that clearly held a book, along with a pair of white gloves, and inclined his head towards the kitchen.

Jane did not follow him until he carefully pulled the leather-bound tome out of its cover and laid it gently on the table. Then she slowly went to his side and gazed at it.

Cracked, stained, and bound with a brass clasp, it looked old. Howard held out the gloves to her, pulling them away when she reached, so that she would look into his eyes.

They were so black you could hardly tell where his pupils began. *If you're a pot smoker, I bet those are handy,* Jane thought, almost laughing, but the intensity of his gaze quickly caused her smile to fade.

"This is a very old, very important book," he said quietly. "But it has things in it that will help you understand our story. And yours." He held the gloves up by his ear and wagged them. "And it has to stay with me. If you want to read it and want your questions answered– all of them–you have to stay here." Howard inclined his head back towards the living room, in Abe and Richard's direction.

"You may not believe it right now, but they love you, Jane. Your father has always kept track of you–that's how Richard met Kimmy, Abe was making one of his pilgrimages to check on you. During that time, she saw him and tracked him back here." He glanced at the men, and then back to Jane.

"What she learned made her understand his decision. And also made her think long and hard about revealing all of this to you. There were many, many discussions about it. Everyone wanted to tell you, but wanted to be careful, and our society has rules. She tried to get you to come here–that was the only real safe way. None of us do this perfectly, but we care about you."

Jane shook her head, as the stab of the phrase "she tried to get you to come here" was all the more painful because it made her acknowledge she had been dodging her aunt's pleas to visit for almost four years. Howard reached over and touched her arm.

"You'll understand too, if you keep asking questions, and listen to the answers. But…" he handed her the gloves. "Let's take a break from that part for a while. Some of the best stories jump from point to point occasionally in the narrative," he smiled a wide wolf's smile and Jane shivered and smiled back, simultaneously. "We can look back and get some history lessons before we return to your father and brother, and how they absented themselves from your life for so long. You have a lot to take in, and many questions…let's handle what I can answer for now."

Howard called over his shoulder, "Abe, Richard…why don't the two of you get some rest. You've had a long day. I can take the first watch in here and sit with Jane for a bit while she reads."

Jane noticed both men hesitated, looking at each other, but tiredly began to amble towards the back of the cabin. Both looked at her as they passed, and nodded, with Abe stopping and gently touching the corner of the table, his eyes worried.

"Abe, she's curious, a book nerd and history buff. She's not going anywhere for a while, and she'll be sleepy once our chat is done. You'll see her tomorrow."

Jane allowed her father a slight nod in affirmation, and his shoulders slumped with relief before he disappeared towards his room.

Left alone with Howard, Jane slipped her hands into the gloves and sat down in front of the book.

Taking a long breath, she gently lifted the cover.

Yellowed parchment, dark ink...her skin prickled with the realization this was probably the oldest book she had ever touched. During her infamous stint at community college, while working in the library, she had scored a chance to see a sixteenth-century Mexican catechism book in the Zapotec language behind the scenes, before it went on exhibition.

She could feel the years in the air around that book, a time-imbued energy. She felt it in this one too, as well as...something else.

Her eyes traveled over the page, and then met Howard's.

"I can't read this; it's not in English," she said softly, raising an eyebrow.

"I know," he retorted, raising one of his as well. "I have an English paperback translation in my bag. I wanted you to touch the original, though." He pointed his chin towards the book. "Even if you don't understand every word, I wanted you to see what you were actually reading. It's important."

Jane reverently touched a gloved fingertip to the parchment, turning a few pages. There were scant illustrations in the first several pages, more towards the middle, and then fewer towards the end. The book looked to be written in three parts; three different hands, three different languages.

"This is Latin," Jane indicated the last third of the book, "And this is French..." the middle... "...but I don't recognize this," she motioned a finger along the first page. "Is it...your language? *Lugaru* have their own language, don't they?"

"The first part is Old Norse," his voice was soft, and Jane wondered if she was imagining that he sounded emotional. "You are familiar with sagas, of course...this first part is a saga. The beginning of *lugaru* history, and also that of tamers." Jane squinted. "Is that the language *lugaru* speak...Old Norse?"

"Our language is a mix of Old Norse, Old Frankish, Latin, and a few other things."

She looked up at him. "How did you know this would get me to stay?"

Howard's inscrutable black eyes glistened, and he swallowed before answering, in the same soft voice Jane was beginning to understand indicated deep feeling.

"I have known various women in your lineage for many, many years." Howard said, and Jane could feel the wistfulness in his voice. "The best of you always have a few predictable traits."

The best of you.

"I have so many things I want to ask you."

"That's why you need to stay with us. I have so many things I want to answer."

Jane laughed. "Very smart. It makes me believe you *have* known generations of my forebears, and they must have been at least somewhat like me, for you to lay a trap this compelling."

"It's not a trap, Jane," Howard's dark eyes were like obsidian, but their depth was oddly comforting. "You are drawn to knowledge and understanding because it's part of who you are. Our culture is part of who you are. You will feel more complete with knowing it, and it will benefit from your presence. This is just…" he shrugged, "…destiny."

She laughed again, but inexplicably, just as quickly as she had started to chuckle, the laughter turned to tears, and then she was sobbing into her hands, with Howard touching her shoulder in comfort…after very quickly sliding the book away from any danger of dropping tears.

"I don't—this is too much. It's all too much," she sobbed.

Howard made gentle shushing noises, letting her cry for a little more before pulling a chair to sit beside her.

When she was able, she pulled off the cotton gloves, wiped her eyes, and shook her head. There was that prickly sensation again, the usual preceptor of an anxiety attack, a feeling of unreality.

"Jane," Howard's voice was as gentle as she had heard it be. "I meant it when I said you're taking this very well. You've lost the woman who was essentially your mother, you've been attacked and injured, you've had information that would boggle the mind on a good day dropped on you— along with a father and brother. Old psychological wounds opened up." He patted her shoulder. "I wasn't patronizing you—I am impressed. But I have to remember that you're human, and we've dropped a lot on you. You're entitled to a breakdown. And maybe this will also help you understand even more why there are rules about what we reveal, and reasons why people, especially people who love you, are hesitant to do so. It's overwhelming. It can cause breakdowns, it can rupture families."

Jane nodded, calmed by the acknowledgement. She laughed as she took a napkin he pulled from the holder on the table and offered it to her.

"It sounds as if you're the man they call when new recruits are brought in. Are you the Tamer Whisperer?"

Something like a grimace of pain flitted across Howard's chiseled face, then he smiled.

"Only the tamers who come from your family."

Jane couldn't describe later, what she felt exactly, when Howard said this, but it was all that was needed to convince her. Why, she couldn't say. But it ushered in a feeling of finality, a confirmation, a sense of both awe and comfort, and a deep knowing that this, for whatever reason, was exactly where she was meant to be.

And where else do you have to go, anyway? She asked herself. *What else do you have going on?*

She nodded her head and looked down at the book, touching it gently once more before looking back up to Howard.

"I don't know if I can handle anymore tonight. But I will read it.."

He smiled, handing her the small paperback he had taken from his bag, and taking the cotton gloves from her when she handed them back. When she took hold of the paperback, he did not immediately relinquish his grip, causing her to look up at him. He held her gaze for what began to feel like an uncomfortably long time before saying, quietly...

"Time is a sphere."

Jane stood completely still for a moment, wondering what she was supposed to say in response.

A hesitant, "Okay," was what she finally managed.

Howard pointed, in warning.

"Go upstairs, pull the stairs after you, I'm taking the first watch here. We can talk more in the morning."

He went to the door where Cooi was pawing the doorknob and let him out, then stood and waited for him to come back in. Jane whistled and Cooi came to her, obediently scrambling up the stairs with her help. Before she ascended herself, she turned to look at Howard, who was positioning himself on the loveseat. He looked up and smiled. Jane smiled back.

"How long are you staying?"

He blinked at her. "Until it's finished."

Once up in her loft, after sliding carefully into the sheets, adjusting herself so that her wounds were as comfortably positioned as possible, taking a few deep breaths and switching off the lamp, Jane realized that even though she was incredibly tired, she could not fall asleep.

Her mind raced. A father. A brother. Werewolves–no, sorry, *lugaru*. Ancestors who look like vampires, but weren't. An inborn power that made her a calming agent to werewolves. Her aunt not killed by a random car accident, but possibly murdered.

God, she thought, staring at the bright square reflected on the ceiling through the tiny window, from the moon shining on the snow outside. *It's all so fucking ridiculous.*

Sleep would not come. It came for Cooi, softly snoring at her feet, yipping now and again as he dreamed, but not her.

Finally she turned carefully, wincing as the bandage on her stomach rubbed the wound beneath, switched on the lamp again, and picked up the book.

Okay, she thought, *maybe a little light reading will do the trick.*

The Tamer's Saga

"It may well be fate that I lose my children, my friends, and this patch of ground in addition to my life today. But if the gods are truly gods, they will not begrudge me the chance to make them earn their will."

Unn the Deep-Minded on the day of the Sunset War

Írland, in the year of the Christian Lord, 875

The tales of Unn, also called the Deep-Minded, that appear in other sagas written and read by mere men speak of her wisdom, her strength of will, and the skill with which she commanded the men who served her.

This is the chronicle of another of her gifts, and how it came to be understood.

Unn was born in the Romsdalen valley, in the shadow of the Trollveggen. Her father was Ketil Flatnose, who took his family with him when he journeyed to the Suðreyjar, the isles off the coast of Lothlend to quell the rebellion of the renegade chieftains there, in service of King Harald Fairhair.

Once the chieftains were subdued, Ketil revealed that he did not intend to administer this land in the name of the king, but in his own.

"How should Fairhair rule this far from the reach of his arm and mind? Each man should rule what he conquers himself, and a king is only a man strong enough to hold what he conquers."

It was bold, everyone agreed. But no one challenged him, and so Ketil ruled in the style of a king. All of his children were loved, but little Unn was close to his heart, and he was to hers--she marked everything he said.

To make a pact with Olaf the White, King of Dyflin, Ketil gave Unn in marriage to him. It was a sign of the strongest truce, since everyone knew Unn was his favorite.

Ketil did not perceive that Olaf was a cruel man from his dealings with him, only that he was a cunning warrior, and a strong leader. Men are often blind to each other's faults. Unn's mother told her as she left the shores of the Suðreyjar on her wedding day; You must do the best you can. Raise your children to be kind. Don't forget that you were loved for the first part of your life...many don't have even that.

In her later life, Unn would only occasionally refer to the man she spent years married to as "the children's father," and that was only when it was necessary to speak of him. She never mentioned his name, never spoke willingly of the time spent in his court before his death.

There were four children born to Unn. Two sons; Thorstein, called the Red, and Bjorn, who was the youngest of all her offspring, a daughter, Yngvild, who was called Yngvild the Fair, and a child who was neither girl nor boy called The Eye.

Thorstein was the oldest, and was fostered with Ketil, his grandfather, growing into a strong warrior and ruling half the kingdoms in the Suðreyjar. When Thorstein was betrayed and killed, Ketil knew his daughter, Unn would suffer. So he sent Olaf, Thorstein's young son, to live with her. Unn insisted that Thorstein's wife Helga, the baby's mother, come as well, saying, "I will not strike another mother to heal my own heart."

King Olaf the White of Dyflin was a shrewd ruler, and was fair to his own people, but his family did not receive any kindness from him. His wife, above all, bore the brunt of his ill nature.

His court was a place of debauchery and wildness before Unn came to Dublin, but in the years after her arrival, there was a gradual, but unmistakable change.

Olaf had always drawn the strongest and fiercest warriors to him--this was why he was feared, and why his campaigns were so successful. The wantonness he not only allowed but encouraged brought forth all the men who were the boldest fighters, and also those who were the cruelest. It was well known that Olaf did not only defeat enemies...he obliterated them. It was always stated when battles began that there would be no quarter, and no one would be left alive. And no one was. No one was left to give account of how Olaf's men fought, or what happened. Once in a great while a survivor, or a witness--usually a villager caught unawares--would rave hysterically about the bloodlust that took Olaf's army, and the rumor began that some of them actually shapeshifted and became beasts.

This account has been put down for eyes that will understand, for those who know without it being said that these men--said to become animals when their blood ran hot--were your fathers. They were perhaps not the first, but their coming together--drawn to the court of Olaf the White by a thirst for violence-and their recognition of each other as a kind was when your known history began.

When Unn came, something changed.

Her entrance to the court was at first not of much consequence. The men raged through the longhouse as always. Taking the women they wanted, fighting amongst themselves, and even occasionally changing into the beasts they were at heart to fight each other, or a hapless merchant or other traveler who happened to wrong one of them, or provoke them in some way.

Olaf laughed at these times, and reminded everyone in the fortress walls that the penalty for speaking about what they saw was death. And a slow death, at that.

Unn said nothing, only watched. She had spent her childhood in the shadow of the Troll Wall in Norway, and knew that magical things were sprinkled into the everyday world. Men who became beasts did not frighten her.

In fact, as the first months passed, there was a subtle change that eventually became more and more obvious.

These beast men not only did not shake her peace, they became calmer in her presence.

At first it was only for a few moments. A group sitting at table while Unn wove by the fire with her women would lower their voices to listen to her singing. If one of them went to grab one of the girls, Unn might catch their eye, or simply shake her head without even looking at them, and they would back away. Eventually, the shift grew in both size and effect. Men who would have turned their skins in broad daylight to rip the throat of a baker trying to protect his daughter now bathed, and paid respects and bride prices.

Warriors who tore through men like bread on the battlefield sat and laughed in the longhouse, telling stories and drinking only moderate amounts of mead.

They began to sleep in beds.

Their rage was still in place on the battlefield, so Olaf had not lost any of his might when it came to waging war, but he did not like the change in his home.

He had always been a harsh man. Unn often had eyes red from crying, and had her body been visible, bruises would have told the story of life behind her bedroom door. She said nothing of this, and simply made sure to follow her mother's injunction; she was always strong with her children, but made sure they received kindness and laughter from her, as well. Olaf was not gentle with his sons or daughters, but his hands seldom touched them. Never in affection, but also rarely in anger.

One day, however, young Olaf Thorsteinson broke a drinking horn of his grandfather's, as he examined it in the great room of the longhouse.

He had been holding it up near the fire, and it slipped from his hands, falling to the hearthstone and then into the fire itself.

Olaf the White happened to be nearby, with a good number of his beast men on hand as well, speaking of battle season, and his anger caused him to cross the room in a fury. He grabbed the boy by his neck and threw him, almost the length of the room. Unn and Helga had been seated at a table near the fire, and Unn leapt up and jumped at Olaf.

Olaf struck Unn to the ground, with his fist, and made as if to do so again.

Before he could reach her, four wolves fell on him and tore him to pieces.

There were men in the longhouse who were not shapeshifters; one found his way out the door, to find others of his kind, and the rest--who rose in protest over what was happening--perished the same way Olaf did.

The man who ran for help found it, in the form of the soldiers who were mere men like him. But the alarm had also sounded for the brothers of the beasts who had gone against the leader who thought he was their master.

In all there were fifty turnskins, and with the help of fifty soldiers who were mere men, but berserkers loyal to Unn, they slaughtered almost two hundred of Olaf's warriors. Men of renown.

Unn, and her children and daughter-in-law fought beside the men. In the aftermath, as they all looked at each other, beginning to understand fully what they had done, Unn said, "My mother told me to raise my children with kindness. But my father told me to protect them."

In the heat of the battle, some of the men loyal to Olaf had loosed the fortress's horses before they were killed, sending them into the night. It was meant to strand them, and as the bodies were burned on pyres and the blood washed from the longhouse floor, Unn sat and thought.

Her name, "The Deep-Minded" was well earned. Even at his most hateful, Olaf himself had consulted her on almost every matter, and generally followed her suggestions, and earls under his rule had frequently asked for her advice as well. People listened when she spoke.

"This was a clever act," Unn said. "Olaf's man who did this knew that word would spread that so many warriors, as well as Olaf himself are dead, and we are left few, alone here, and vulnerable. With no horses to escape."

The bloodbath that had freed the world of Olaf and made Unn the sole ruler in the fortress that was her home, occurred after a heavy snowfall that was not typical for Dyflin. The loose horses were irretrievable for the moment, because the majority of the people were natives of the region, not used to conditions like this. Unn called together those who were Norse, and gave them instructions.

"Quickly fashion yourselves some snowshoes. Go to the woods and begin to build two knorrs. Make sure you're in the deepest part of the forest, where no one will see you."

They began in earnest, and worked in shifts. By the time the snow melted, the boat was finished.

Word did indeed spread about Olaf, and when the roads cleared, a message arrived, addressed to Unn. It caused a cloud to cover her face, and for the space of a day, she was quiet and withdrawn, speaking only to Helga, her daughter-in-law, and her children and grandson.

The next day, she called the fifty shapeshifters to her, and addressed them, in the presence of her family. On the longest table in the great room were fifty small bags.

Each shapeshifter had been given a bronze arm ring–twisted metal strands with wolves' heads on the ends–by Olaf to wear, not as a sign of simple loyalty, as was the custom with other rulers and their men, but as a reminder to them that he believed he owned them; Olaf laughed and called them 'dog collars' every time he put one on a warrior. Each of the shapeshifters had been given reprieve by Olaf for a crime committed, and the price was their servitude. They used their skills to kill for him in battle, and he believed he owned them the way other men owned hunting dogs.

Unn went to each man and took his band, ringing them on her forearm and then placing them on the table once every single one had been removed. When this was done, she spoke.

"You are not simply men," she said in her melodious voice. "But you are not animals, either, and you will be slaves no longer."

"My children's father thought to harness your strength, and kept you here as weapons, bound to him through your condition, thinking that you had no choice but to accept a life where you were offered a way to give vent to your passions."

She smiled. "But you're not a slave to those anymore, either."

"Earl Einar is on his way here, and he means to take me as his wife by force." Unn paused to let this sink in. "My children and I have decided that we will resist him, and I will die here before I become the wife of another man without honor, but I cannot expect you to give your lives for us."

She gestured to the table with the arm bands and the bags.

"You're free men. I release you from your bonds, and I offer you each a bag of silver to start a new life." Unn looked at each face lovingly. "You do not have to die here. You can go out into the world, and now you know that you can live in it peacefully."

There was silence for several moments. At last, the man called Hord, who had become a confidant of Unn's, stepped forward. He took up one of the small bags, hefted it, and then tossed it back onto the table.

Then he picked up the band she had removed from his arm, and put it back on again.

One by one, the remaining men all did the same.

"It may be that we could leave you here and go out to live in the world as other men do," Hord said, "But I doubt it. I believe that you are the source of our tamed spirits, and if we leave you, we will be as we were before." He looked to his companions and then back to Unn.

"None of us want that. And we would never leave you to die, or become a slave again. You have freed us through friendship, we will keep you free through it, as well."

Unn nodded with a smile, and tears.

Hord sighed, and crossed his arms. "And now, Unn the Deep-Minded, will you tell us your plan?"

She did indeed have a plan, and when the men had heard the whole of it, they laughed the howling laughs of wolves, throwing their heads back and baring their teeth. When they left the longhouse to share the plan with the mere men who stood outside, waiting--the fifty soldiers who had stood with them during the rebellion against Olaf--the laughter rippled out from there, as well, and Unn's daughter-in-law and her children looked at each other and laughed too, believing that there might be a chance now that it could work.

When Earl Einar rounded the bend in the road that led to the Dyflin fortress, he and his men were traveling at an easy trot. His scouts had reported that it was true, all of the horses were gone from Olaf's refuge, and he was most assuredly dead, along with the majority of his soldiers. They said at most, there were a hundred warriors guarding the woman and her children, and the common population of the fortress would most certainly surrender to them, after knowing Olaf's cruelty.

Battles to decide the fate of the lands Olaf had ruled as King of Dyflin were already being planned, but there was no sign of resistance from the king's fortress.

Rumors said that the handful of men left were the fearless, raging warriors the Norse called berserkers, that defeated numbers three times greater--but Einar had fierce fighters as well. He imagined that whatever petty dispute had caused the infighting could be smoothed with gold...and he was bringing plenty of it.

It was said that the man Hord had taken to living in the longhouse, along with King Olaf's personal bodyguard, the fiercest berserkers. It was also speculated that it had been his lust for the queen that birthed this madness. Einar was counting on the gold and the chance that a battle to keep Dyflin unified would be more trouble than a simple captain might want. He believed this would persuade Hord to give up Unn and the fortress without a siege or fight...but was certain that his mounted retinue could quell a few dozen mercenaries if that was not enough.

There was also the hope that his message to Unn had accomplished its goal, and that she would find the prospect of being his lawful wife *preferable to being kept hostage by a common soldier, if that was, in fact, what was happening.*

As Einar and his retinue cleared the turn, the horses started.

He smelled the smoke before he saw it.

Huge pillows of it were rising from the fortress, and also from their left, and as they urged the horses forward, they saw that the hay houses were aglow with fire. Turning the next bend that brought them into view of the fortress, they saw that smoke was also beginning to rise from every structure inside. They saw this because the gate in the wall was standing open.

No siege would be necessary; they rode right in.

The horses balked and reared upon entering the fortress, and men began to exclaim and mirror the animals' distress when they saw what was causing it; to each side of the road, dead and bloody animals were piled high.

Einar glanced quickly around him, and realized that what seemed to be true was; not a goat, pig, or chicken remained alive. Every stock animal had been slaughtered, sloppily so as to be useless for eating, and then piled high.

Anger began to burn in his chest, along with the smoke from the fires.

He dug his heels into his distressed horse, and rode faster.

The road took them through the shops and shanties that made up the fortress's village; not a soul was present. No families, no men, or women; no one.

They came into view of the longhouse that Olaf the White had built for himself and his family. He had brought Norse carpenters to fashion the timbers which lined the roof--thatched, but bordered with beams of wood--and they had painstakingly carved his sign, the two-headed dragon, into each one, and it was a structure that had been spoken of widely.

It was now burning, orange and scarlet flames licking the monster's heads, reaching to the darkening sky.

The door was wide open.

Einar urged his horse forward, glancing to each side and looking for warriors, but seeing none.

As he drew up in front of the longhouse and leapt from his mount's back, he strode angrily to the stone steps, drawing his sword in preparation to face Hord.

When he reached the steps and stood in front of the door, however, the only person he saw was Unn.

She stood in the middle of the floor, in front of the stone hearth, wearing men's breeches and a long vest, arms behind her back. Her face was calm, and her amber eyes glowed with the reflection of flames--the rafters had been lit inside, and she stood in a burning house looking calmer than he had ever seen any woman.

He blinked and then took a step forward.

"You?" He asked incredulously, "Did...this?" He gestured to the longhouse, and behind him to the horrific piles of animal carcasses. He rose to the second stone step.

"This is how you thank me for taking you as a wife and saving you from dishonor? Burning your home and belongings was better than sharing them with me? Killing every living thing you own to keep it from my hand?" His voice was full of rage, but also surprise that bordered on awe.

Unn stayed quiet, arms solidly behind her back, legs slightly bent. She was still, watching his feet bring him closer. He was now on the third step. His men had been given no order, and so they stayed where they were, astride their horses, trying to calm the animals, gaping at the fire.

"Do you think I'll just turn around now? Do you think you did yourself any favors by angering me?" Now Einar was giving full voice to his rage, which had completely replaced his amazement. "I was going to let your children live!"

Unn still said nothing, but raised her eyebrows quizzically, and inclined her head as if she could not hear him. This small gesture shocked him still for a moment, but when she locked her gaze with his, and cocked an eyebrow...malice propelled him forward, and he stepped fully into her house.

When his foot crossed the threshold, Unn pulled the bow from behind her back, fitted the arrow she held in the other hand to it, and put it through his heart.

The wolf men flew from where they had been hidden, just to each side of the open wooden doors, and fell upon the men outside as they poured out of the longhouse. Unn's warriors who were not turnskins came out of their hiding places--among the dead animals by the front of the fortress--and attacked from the back.

The children and Helga, in the forest, sitting in one of the wooden boats resting on logs, heard the clamor and cries of the battle, and hugged each other, surrounded by belongings and food for the journey that lay ahead...if there was to be a journey.

It seemed that the noise went on forever, when in truth it only took minutes, and then the ensuing quiet was slowly replaced by the sound of horses approaching.

The outlines of riders were not clear at first, and the children and Helga, wife of Thorstein gripped each other's hands.

When it became clear that the leader was a woman, with long, curly, golden-brown hair, they breathed a sigh of relief, and Bjorn and Olaf were the first to leap from the boat to run to Unn.

She dismounted, and tossed her mount's reins to Hord, so that he could begin to harness some of the animals to the knorrs. They would pull them to the bay that would spill them into the Western Sea, and propel them back to Lothlend.

"Let's go home, my loves," she said, embracing each and every one of them and baring her teeth in a wolf's smile.

"Let's go home."

6

When Jane's eyes opened, it took a moment to realize both where she was, and what from the past night was a dream, what was revelation, and what was reality.

She sat up, and Cooi did as well, giving her the look he always did when he was trying to figure out if she was truly getting out of bed. She nodded to him and he leapt to the floor.

Jane went about peeing, rinsing her face, dressing–carefully, because her wounds were actually more painful now–doing the things to make herself presentable before going down the hatch into the cabin's main floor, where her father, brother, and Howard were waiting. As she did these tasks, she also did the mental equivalent; calming her anxiety from the attack, formulating what her next questions were going to be, and simply trying to digest everything that had happened the day before.

It seemed impossible, but she felt as if she was beginning to adjust to the understanding that this was all real.

She carefully picked up the book she had fallen asleep reading.

Abe, Richard, and Howard were all awake, quietly sipping coffee, and waiting for her and Cooi to descend.

Richard let Cooi out. Abe and Howard stood.

Jane went to the dish drainer, got a cup, and poured coffee.

She sighed when she sat down, and pointed at the book she had laid on the table.

Howard picked it up and opened it up to where Jane had marked her stopping place with a scrap of paper.

He nodded, then put it back down and looked from Jane to Abe and back again.

"Who do you want to start with?"

"You."

Abe nodded and stood. "I'll make some breakfast until it's my turn."

"Wait–" Jane held up a hand to stop him. "Before you do that, I want to ask both of you something…" she took a deep breath. "Are my children in danger?"

Abe seemed to hesitate, but Howard responded immediately. "Of course they are. We all are. It's a matter of degrees."

Her father jumped in. "We have eyes on them, Jane. Our people are watching."

"The way they watched Kimmy?"

Both men seemed humbled by this. She shook her head.

"No…I want them here."

They looked at each other, and then at her. "Of course," Abe said, "We–"

"If I am what you say I am, if you are my father, and if all of… this…" she gestured at the book, at the door, all around her, "…is true, then I must have them here. I need to be sure they're safe."

Howard nodded. "We'll get them here. But we'll have to work together and you'll have to be sure, yourself, Jane. You'll have to convince them."

"Is this just something that's…normal? Living with this kind of danger from this–" she rolled her eyes and gestured. "Brotherhood?"

"It's…ramped up in recent months. And this…" Howard let out a sigh. "Is possibly the result of a change in order, a switch in leadership."

"A zealot?"

Howard replied calmly. "A true believer. We can only speculate right now, though; we don't know. The Brotherhood doesn't exactly have a PR agent, and since information in our society has to spread carefully, that often means slowly, you understand."

Jane shivered. "How does this happen? If you know tamers are in danger, why isn't there some sort of–"

"System in place to protect them? There is. It broke down in ways we didn't expect. Now we have to revert to an earlier system, one we haven't used for decades."

Abe quietly added, "One that was instituted when your mother died."

"Why then? Was...was she...murdered too?" Before Abe nodded, she knew. As she sat at the table now, Jane felt as if interest was being compounded to the grief that had dwelt in her from childhood. The mother she could barely remember, but whose loss had devastated her as a child. The grandfather who raised her. The father who abandoned her. The aunt who had acted in place of her dead sister by mothering Jane, and grandmothering her children. And now, the knowledge that at least two of these deaths were orchestrated, not cruel acts of fate, but events that had been carried out by...beings who hated them, without even knowing them.

"I can't believe this. It's too much." She looked at both of them, but her gaze landed back on Abe.

"That's why, isn't it? That's why my grandfather sent you away. He didn't believe you could protect me, and he blamed you."

He nodded. "Yes. He believed attention and danger would be less, if I went away. He didn't know that I was sending surveillance, to help protect you. He knew we had a system for watching over tamers, but he didn't like it. He believed he could do better alone.."

"When did the program for protecting tamers end? And why?"

"The year you got divorced, it formally ended. Too expensive for all of the others in our extended tribe–our clan–but we kept it on you and your children." Abe shrugged.

"Your clan is the most...humble," Howard said, emphasizing the last word with raised eyebrows, "But your father–" Jane still could not get used to the word. "He insisted we keep men on you and your children, and Kimmy. No matter the cost. And the rest of the tribe agreed."

"That's how Kimmy found us, in fact." Abe smiled sadly. "She noticed that she was being followed, and tracked her tracker. Here."

Others. Jane found herself stuck on that word.

"There are more than just our family in your tribe? Other tamers?"

Richard was rubbing his eyes as he stood. "I'll make breakfast and some more coffee." His voice was hoarse.

"Yes," Howard said softly.

"My mother's death...it was a car accident. Like Kimmy's." Jane was remembering all of the times she asked her grandfather and Kimmy about her mother and her death, and how they were too grief-stricken to speak about it.

Howard exhaled, sounding as if he was choosing words carefully. "They are easy to orchestrate, and often don't provoke questions. Easy to cover up."

Abe chimed in. "Your grandfather was explicit; no one was to contact Kimmy or you, or tell you what you were."

"Your mother's killing set off a political and actual war among us," Howard explained. "Between the factions I described to you. One so big and messy that it threatened to expose us to the human world. All sides knew that it would end with our obliteration so a truce was reached."

Jane shook her head. "What do you mean, a truce? This Brotherhood is a recognized entity?"

Howard leaned forward.

"We have tribes, clans, and regional territories. Think of our people as being organized by family, by region, and by...belief system."

"*Lugaru* who adhere to older, more traditional ways–" he gestured to Abe, and Richard, in the kitchen, "--support finding and guarding Tamers. Other, more radical individuals...either don't believe they're necessary and don't find it profitable to find them, or, on the far end of the spectrum...think they are a curse on our culture."

Jane exhaled, blowing a long breath through pursed lips. "Great. Those are the Brotherhood folks, right?"

"Yes. Think of our people like…the hearing-impaired community. Some identify as Deaf, and look upon interventions like cochlear implants as insinuations that something is wrong with them. This suggests a need to be fixed, and therefore they eschew them, and embrace who they are, and how they were made."

Howard's description was too concise, too well-explained to be objective.

"That's what you believe, isn't it?"

He smiled. But held up a finger. "However, I believe Tamers exist for a reason. I do not want their influence, and don't use it anymore–although I have in the past–but I would never…" he leaned forward to look into her eyes and clearly enunciated it again, "…never…advocate for exterminating them. I am the first and most faithful friend to your kind."

My kind. Jane felt as if she were in a dream.

"But the Brotherhood does…advocate for extermination."

"Only old school extremists. Not the current leader. To believe tamers unnecessary is not the same as seeing them as anathema."

Jane leaned back, shaking her head and reaching for the coffee Richard sat on the table.

"Are tamers really this big of a deal? Is the effect you feel that huge?"

The three of them looked at each other.

"I mean…what does it feel like? Do you know someone is a tamer right away?"

"It feels like–" Richard seemed to be struggling to articulate his response. "--it feels like, the sensation when you recognize something. It's also almost like a scent, but not really."

Jane looked at the other two men, who added nothing.

"Wow. Okay, not super helpful."

"I would describe it like a lulling," Howard said. "You have to understand that we feel a compulsion sometimes, to change. When we are angry, when we're frustrated." He looked at Richard sympathetically. "When we are grieving."

Abe interjected. "It can feel like a relief to change, but we have to be cautious, and only change in certain conditions. The need to wait can feel bad, and make it into almost a compulsion."

"When a tamer is present, that compulsion is lessened. Sometimes dramatically, if the effect she produces is powerful. Alcohol and drugs can accomplish the same thing, unfortunately. Many *lugaru* abuse them, for that reason."

"When I say, 'lulling'," Howard interrupted. "This is what I'm talking about. It's good to have something to help a *lugaru* not change, if it's going to draw attention. If he wants to age more normally. If it suits his desires. But it's also good to be able to feel, and be in control. To manage the impulse yourself. And to not be swayed away from changing, if it's what you want–or need–to do."

Jane pointed her coffee cup at Howard.

"If you don't believe the effect is good for you, then why are you the "first and most faithful friend" to us?"

Howard was a study in economy of movement, Jane thought. The more she watched all three of the men she had gotten to know so quickly over the last couple of days, the more she realized that they all had movements that made them seem similar. She wondered if it was their…*lugaru*-ness…that she was seeing, or if it was the power of suggestion, now that she knew they were wolf men.

But even of the three of them, Howard was different.

They all responded a little quicker than humans to sound and smell, and seemed to be on some level of alert all the time, even when in relaxed postures. But Howard had an air to him that felt old. Not aged, but ancient. Again, Jane wondered if she was intuiting it, or just thinking that after learning his true age. But she was fairly certain that she could see–she could *feel*–a depth to him and his movements that cast him as a living relic. His energy reminded her of what she felt looking at the book he uncovered for her.

He didn't fiddle with things when he sat down. He didn't glance around much. He made direct eye contact, watched you, unblinking, while you talked. He moved from one place to another with purpose. In fact, most of what Jane saw him do, he only did with purpose.

He was, she slowly realized, the most wolf-like of the three of them.

"I never said the effect you exude isn't good for us," Howard's reply was clipped, and close, while also being articulate, a vocal mirror of his physical movements. "And it's not a simple subject, and I'm not a typical example of someone who believes what I do." *Ah*, Jane thought, *An underdog. Or underwolf.* "The effect you produce allows a *lugaru* to resist the urge to change, if he wants to." He shrugged. "I don't resist the urge. I change often. I can be happy with who and what I am and still respect there are beings who... seem to have evolved to serve as a calming presence, or a balance to our existence."

"*Lugaru* are not always blessed with self-control," Howard continued. "And early in our history, before we understood ourselves, or had a society of our own, some of us could be wild, abandoned to our passions." He said this with such succinct clarity that Jane knew at once he was including himself in that group. She thought of the saga, and how Unn's influence had led the *lugaru* to a focused existence, one with the choice to funnel those passions into good, where before, her husband had exploited them, and encouraged the worst in their natures.

"More than anything I believe tamers and *lugaru* all benefit from greater understanding."

Understanding is love's other name. One of Jane's favorite quotes came to mind, a reminder of the secret longing she had carried all her life...to be understood.

Howard squinted, and once again spoke as if he read her mind. "Isn't that what we all want, deep down? To be understood?"

Jane responded, "Understanding biology isn't the same as understanding an individual's personality." Something about her response elicited a laugh from Howard, and when it finally died down, his obsidian eyes were glistening with what looked like tears.

"Well said."

Jane looked at Abe and Richard. "How does what you believe differ from that?"

Richard took a breath, stirred the eggs he was cooking, and shrugged. "Our ancestors who share our beliefs thought our condition was a curse." He indicated Abe with a motion. "Our dad..." Jane still couldn't get used to hearing this man who looked thirty years old called her "dad." "...won't call it that, but it's close to what he believes. Me? I guess I look at it as...maybe a health condition? Something to be managed. And I saw Kimmy as..." his voice caught, and he steadied himself against the stove before shaking his head and turning and walking to the bedroom.

Abe stood and went to the stove, taking over the breakfast prep. He cleared his throat.

"*Lugaru* who mate with Tamers are believed to get an even more dramatic ability to resist turning and start aging on par with their partner. But, the drawback of that is the grief they feel at separation seems to be...overwhelming."

Jane looked at the closed bedroom door. "What happens now? Does he still age naturally?" She had lowered her voice to a whisper, and despite her frustration and anger at the situation, found herself feeling a sisterly concern.

"If he can resist the urge to change, he may." Howard also spoke softly. "But it's hard to do, when you are grieving." Something in his voice let Jane know he knew this from experience.

Abe added a quiet comment.

"The Brotherhood, and those who consider tamers a threat also point out that when *lugaru* live without changing, and have shortened life spans, it dwindles our numbers, which were small to begin with. Right now there's a dropping birthrate crisis, and we've considered the possibility that this has set off some extremists."

Jane sighed, and rubbed her throbbing wrist. She glanced at Howard.

"You said you were the oldest known *lugaru*," she said. "You must have lost more people over the years than I'll ever even know."

"I've only lost people whom I love a few times, because those few times taught me not to love humans too much." It sounded so matter of fact that Jane laughed. And once again, she saw the scrutiny of the deep black eyes.

"Let's get back to my kids," Jane put her hands flat on the table, and thanked Abe as he sat her plate in front of her. "How do we get them here?"

"Just call them," Abe said, and in the quiet intensity of his voice, Jane heard grandfatherly concern.

"But I don't have the—"

"The money is not your concern," Howard said, once again intercepting her thoughts. "People are guarding them right now without them knowing, and if you will just tell them that those who approach them are to be trusted, they'll get them here by tonight."

Jane exhaled slowly, looking at her plate.

"They have lives. They have jobs and friends they love. I can get them here, I just—"

Abe reached out and placed his hand on hers, and repeated himself with even more quiet insistence.

"Just call them."

7

It was not, in fact, as easy as "just call them."

While Jane knew her determination to raise her children to think for themselves was one of her best decisions, she wondered sometimes if she should not have done such a good and complete job of it. She pleaded and haggled with each of her three offspring to come to Kimmy's graveside service.

It was a contrivance she and Howard developed to get them on a plane from Ft. Worth, where they all lived. Richard said later he actually wanted to scatter Kimmy's ashes on the property behind the cabin, which made it a stretch of the truth rather than an outright lie. This didn't make Jane feel any better about deceiving her children for the first time ever.

Jane loved her children so deeply it sometimes felt abnormal. She didn't have many friends who were also moms of adults, or "semi-adults" as she called them– with whom to compare feelings and stories. Kimmy was childless, also overly protective and in love with Jane's kids, and so had not been a good source of objectivity.

The highs associated with being their mother were high; they told her details about their lives that those few mom friends she had seemed surprised about, and they all shared a sense of humor that had seen them through really dark times.

But the lows were low. Anne Marie, the second oldest, in particular seemed always frustrated with Jane about something, and the last conversation they had before Jane called to tell her the news about Kimmy had been an emotional one.

Or at least, emotional on Jane's side of things.

"I think I need to take a break from talking to you," Anne Marie had said, after Jane tearfully expressed the depth of her depressed state over relationship problems with Paul. "I mean, no offense, Mom, but sometimes I feel more like your therapist than your daughter."

Jane simply said, "Okay." And that was that.

Until she had to call and relay the news of Kimmy's death.

The twin desires of wanting to be a good mother to her children and also desperately wanting their love, which she felt would only come from them understanding her, seemed often to be at odds in Jane's relationships with the kids. Her idealism told her it was possible to do both, but a nagging little voice inside told her that every conflict with Anne Marie had risen out of Jane oversharing some part of her life and showing her daughter just how far she was from perfect.

Anne Marie, at this stage of her life, Jane believed, simply needed a mom. A mom who was strong, supportive, and didn't cry over electric bills they couldn't pay, or emotionally unstable men who couldn't be good partners.

Jane knew that wasn't her. But she had resolved after the last conversation to try even harder to be.

Lucas, the oldest, was easy. He was simple, straightforward, both in his appreciation and his criticism and the good and bad with him was that you always knew where you stood. It was both blessing and curse.

And Robin, well...Robin was Robin. Different.

Both closer to and farther away from Jane than the other two, in ways tangible and otherwise. Some of the differences could be chalked up to this child's "otherness"--as a non-binary person with autism–and some of them were difficult to categorize. Just like Robin.

Jane loved that the siblings were all close, and told herself many times that even if they weren't impressed with her as a mom, the most important thing was that they had each other.

In the end, it had taken tears to convince them to travel to Oregon. Crying was something Jane would not have chosen to do, but it was dramatic enough to be effective, and the very real tears were easy enough to produce.

Each of them worked jobs with very little time off, and needed every dime they made, much like Jane, so when she added, "I'll send you money to cover the lost wages, in addition to the plane tickets," each of them also knew something else was afoot, without further explanation. It was a harsh reminder of how much of a role financial struggle played in all of their lives, and even though it wasn't her money, Jane relished the feeling of being able to, for once, say those words.

Then, after they were convinced, and on their way, Jane was free to worry about the next piece; how they would react to the news that had blown apart her sense of reality.

She had called them from the burner phone Howard provided her, telling them each to save the number, that her phone had been damaged. (Not a lie, Abe had destroyed it). Howard's explanation that the Brotherhood might have found a way to tap hers had spiked her anxiety even more.

"Can't you tell for sure? Can't you track *them*?"

"We have our version of the FBI, but they aren't *the* FBI." he said. "There is only so much we can do with the resources we have, and we need to be as cautious as possible, while also planning for this to take a while to resolve."

Abe had explained that in addition to funding that was available to *lugaru* worldwide, each tribe found ways to fund their own members.

"*Lugaru* need help constantly–medical, legal–I'm sure you can understand that there are a million reasons why we have to stay as far off of the humans' radar as possible. There's a limited amount to go around. We have to put our people in high places, to have allies, in addition to relocating others, and securing housing. And…" here he became somber, "The financial situations of each tribe vary wildly. The Brotherhood is one of the richest, due to familial wealth that had been passed down for generations."

Jane sighed. "And of course, with my luck…just the same as the outside world, I don't have the good fortune to be a part of one of the wealthier tribes." She looked at her father sympathetically, understanding too well the pressure of trying to keep a family group afloat with limited resources. Now she could see more clearly why the practice of constant surveillance had been difficult to maintain... and also appreciate that it had been carried on for so long, despite the financial constraints.

"I know you said the threat seemed to have disappeared...what made it come back? Why do you think they killed Kimmy?" Jane spoke in a lowered tone, helping Abe wash the dishes. Richard was in the bedroom, bogged down by grief, and she did not want to aggravate it.

"There may have been a death in the ranks that led to a radical taking power. That's the only thing I can think of. There has been no announcement, so it's that, or...rogue activity." Abe dried his hands and motioned to the living room with his head.

He continued speaking softly. "There are people looking into it."

"What people?"

"Investigators. From our...culture."

"Not actual policemen?"

"They are policemen. Not human, but ours."

Jane fought the urge to get angry. "No offense, but shouldn't we have...real cops helping us? Not that I'm a super fan of the police, but this–" "Remember," She could tell Abe was actively trying to speak calmly and patiently. "We are a very old society. We have laws, we have people who handle these sorts of grievances—"

"These sorts of grievances?" She looked towards the bedroom, trying to control her voice. "My mother was murdered, my aunt possibly as well, and now my children and I are in danger... that's beyond a grievance. And the fact that it's repeating through generations seems...well, forgive me if I'm not impressed with *your* police."

"Don't you think I would do everything in my power to protect you and your children?" Abe was as impassioned as she had seen him since meeting him, his pale complexion flushed. He took a deep breath.

"They are investigating. They will also send reinforcements to help us guard you and the kids until this is resolved, and after, as well."

Jane blinked. "What do you mean, after, as well?"

Abe looked confused. "I mean...after this is over."

They sat looking at each other as Abe slowly realized she had never agreed to stay after the threat was neutralized. Jane could hear the tick of the clock in the living room, and Cooi's short barks and the stamp of Howard's feet on the stoop. The two of them came in.

"Things are ready whenever you are."

Abe saw Jane's question and said, "We need to move you to a place large enough for you and your children."

"You have a place that large?"

"We do. We use it mostly for recreation and when there's a need to be...inconspicuous."

"Oh. It's a...*lugaru* place, not yours."

"My tribe's place is mine." Abe didn't say this with an air of any affectation, just a simple statement.

Jane suddenly realized she may have underestimated her father's position. The way he gave orders, the deference shown by the men who came to help.

"Are you the...leader of this...tribe?"

He smiled a tiny smile, and looked at Howard, and then back at her. "Is it that hard to tell?"

"I'll pack my things."

She wanted to go with Richard and Howard to pick up the children from the airport–Eugene–and ride back with them on the long drive, but Howard had effectively argued against it.

"You can be better protected here, and I don't think you would offer that much help protecting them, we can do it better without you," he said, over and over, each time she raised a point.

Two other men–Jane recognized them from Kimmy's wake–had come to pick them up in a 15-passenger van, and the four of them would take turns driving and watching so that they could return more quickly. An ambitious plan, but one they seemed rather confident about carrying out.

A group of men had been posted outside, a few came in now and again for food or coffee. Abe and Jane packed things and brought them out to be loaded into yet another van. As they were introduced to Jane by Abe, she could feel, literally feel, their wariness or awe, or a combination of both.

"This is Canute..."

"This is Robert..."

"This is Peter..."

"Do you remember Dr. Buchwald?"

"Do you remember Will?"

At one point when they were alone, Jane reached over and touched Abe's sleeve.

In a hushed voice she said, "I don't know if I'm going crazy, or if you guys have gotten into my head or what...but I can feel them."

"Of course you can. You simply haven't been around many *lugaru* before to feel the effect."

"'Many'?" Jane laughed. "You mean, 'none'!"

Abe didn't respond outwardly, but she saw the statement in his eyes before she remembered one of the biggest shockers of her new reality.

"Oh...Pappy. But I never..."

"You certainly felt the calm you brought him. But it existed in his love for you."

Grief that was old, but new, folded around Jane. Multiplying the horrendous hole in her heart Kimmy's death had opened–or was it the other way around? She had spent years after her grandfather's death picking up the phone to call him...and feeling as if he had died again every time she remembered that she couldn't.

"How...do you ever get used to seeing people you love die?" It was almost a rhetorical question, but she wanted to hear an actual answer as well.

Abe said nothing for a while. He shuffled the bags to the door, and signaled for one of the men to come get it.

"I don't think you do. No matter how long you live. At least I never have."

To dispel the sadness, she asked another question. "Their calm also feels, sometimes a little like...I don't know, reverence. Is that delusional of me? Is that normal? Is it because...Kimmy...was so loved, or is that what the effect feels like?"

Abe smiled. "I don't know, I've never been a tamer. And yes, it might be because of love for Kimmy–she was highly respected here–but remember, Jane–I know you're reading her saga–you're also a descendant of Unn. That would be like..."

He shrugged. "I don't even know what to compare it to. I would say it would be like...being related to...a president? No, that's not even close, there's not an equivalent of what she was, in the human world. She was how we realized what we were, how we codified our existence. And how those of us who are proud of what we are came to be that way. That's the true shame in what those who feel hate for tamers think...they don't realize she championed our changing. She encouraged us to be proud of what we are."

Jane touched her backpack, where the paperback she had read long into the night was lodged. Howard had asked her about it already, and required her to show him it was secure before he had agreed not to take it back, and to let her be the one to transport it to the lodge.

"It's written to look like a novel, to ward off suspicion in case it falls into the wrong hands, but..." He shook his head. "You must keep it safe."

They trundled into the van, Cooi bounding onto the middle seat beside Jane. She brushed off the snow he tracked onto her jeans, laughing as he shook, and put her arm around him as the driver, Will, put the van into gear and they took off.

Again, the wariness. The tightness in her chest. Looking around, halfway expecting to see wolves tearing towards the vehicle at every turn, Jane only relaxed slightly when Abe took her hand.

"We're safe. They've combed the forest; no one is around for miles. It's a straight shot to the lodge, and believe me, no one can sneak up on us there."

It took almost half an hour for them to reach it, a multi-level building higher up the mountains with a steep A-frame roof with black shingles, walls and trim painted a flat, dark charcoal gray. Snow decorated its edges, and the dark glass of the windows was lit from within, giving it the feel of a slightly goth gingerbread house.

It was surrounded by forest, like the cabin, but with a larger clearing cut around it.

A guard shack sat at the head of the drive, what looked to be guest quarters and a sauna were to the back and west.

As the SUV crunched up the long, snow-covered drive and pulled to the front of the door, Abe pointed out trees at the perimeter with barely visible stands in them like those hunters would use. Had he not shown her, Jane probably would not have seen them.

"This place is engineered for safety," he said, matter-of-factly, "This is where we'll stay until this is figured out."

Figured out. Jane exhaled and wondered for a moment what that even meant. How does something like this get figured out? What are our lives going to look like after this? What will the kids say? She looked at her phone. Abe saw the motion and said, "They won't be here until late, remember?"

"They should have landed; I'm just wondering how it's going. What they're saying? What's happening?"

"Nothing out of the ordinary. Richard is introducing himself. He's spoken to all of them on the phone, so they'll recognize his voice and they'll chitchat on the drive."

Jane laughed. Chitchat. She knew her children. Even though the men had been able to convince her it was too much of a risk to take her, and that they could explain the basics of what was happening, she still knew her kids would have questions. Lucas, in particular, and they would not be easy or polite ones.

Will helped them carry in the bags; Jane's suitcases and the ones Abe had packed for himself and Richard. She had noticed that Howard carried one large backpack everywhere with him, and she had also observed another interesting fact; while his clothing was simple, it was always stylish. As were his shoes and socks. They also never looked as if they came from the bottom of a backpack. In fact, he was one of the most well put together men she'd seen, since she arrived.

Did werewolf historians carry steamers with them, when they went on escapades to rescue tamers? Were Pinterest boards of current fashions part of their research?

After stepping out of her boots, Jane went up the slick plank stairs just off of the foyer, sticking her head into each of the doorways of the five small, but tidy, bedrooms before choosing one and putting her bag on the quilt-covered, iron frame bed. She sat beside it and took off her coat. After looking around the room for a moment, she took the book out of her bag. The cover was black, the title–*The Tamer's Saga*–embossed silver. She ran her fingers over it, relishing the feel. Jane was remembering Howard's words; *It's fashioned to look like a novel, in case it's discovered, but we must keep it safe.* She flipped to the back, where there were appendices and illustrations. So much to learn.

The next few hours were almost silent, with Jane trying to read more, but finding it difficult wondering about the kids, and listening to the rustling below as her father busied himself in the kitchen, putting together dinner.

Her father. Still such a foreign concept.

The sun set. Jane went downstairs.

A fire burned in the living room fireplace, a welcome change from the chill of upstairs. She went through to the kitchen.

Cooi sat, his big ears standing tall, watching every move Abe made. Jane noticed the same thing she had perceived about Howard and Richard; they anticipated Cooi's needs many times, seemed amused by him, but weren't overly affectionate the way "dog people" generally were.

"Kimmy always had a dog, you know," she said. "It kind of surprised me that she didn't get another one when she moved up here." Kimmy's last dog had died before her move.

"We don't really keep pets," Abe said, matter-of-factly. He looked up from his dinner prep and smiled when he saw her expression. "It's just a *lugaru* thing. Call it a...belief system...or an aversion, whatever."

"But Pappy always had dogs," Jane mused. "In fact, he told us that, constantly. 'Always have a gun and a dog'.

"*Rugaru* are different." Abe said simply.

Cooi whined quietly, and Abe tossed him a piece of chopped chicken, which he delicately ate. Jane chuckled. Cooi's mannerisms had always been elegant, causing Jane's kids to joke that his soul was that of a millionaire's Afghan Hound, trapped in the body of a poor woman's coydog.

"He seems to really like all of you. I guess that surprises me, given what you are. He doesn't usually like other animals–I can't imagine him liking a wolf– and he doesn't really like a lot of people."

"Well," Abe said, matter-of-factly. "We aren't exactly one or the other, you know."

"Can you communicate with him?" It felt like a childish question and Jane wasn't surprised when Abe laughed a little.

"No, we can't communicate with other animals, exactly, although I guess it's kind of like that." He scraped the chicken he was chopping into a casserole dish. "We have a sense for each other, kind of like feeling vibes, and we have it for animals, especially dogs." He indicated Cooi with his head. "He's protective of you–remember, when he first met me, he wasn't keen. But he respects confidence. Whether it's from other animals or people."

"Why don't you have pets?"

Jane knew as she asked it, she might not like the answer. She watched Abe's face and could tell he was choosing his words carefully. She laughed.

"Don't worry about offending me. If you tell me that it's cruel to have pets, that they hate it, I would understand."

"No, no, I wouldn't say it's that, exactly."

Abe looked at Cooi, who cocked his head, and cut his eyes to the casserole dish. "As I said, we can't communicate with them directly. It's a sense. Some humans have it, to a degree. An understanding of animals. Ours is just a little deeper. This guy here," he pointed at Cooi with a grin.

"His general feeling is that he's fine. He's fine with you, he'd be fine out in the wild. His only frustration is that his ability in our world is limited."

No matter how unscientific the source, the idea that Cooi didn't see her as a jailer made Jane relax with relief. She went to him and rubbed the top of his bristly head.

"Maybe he senses that you're family." She said it much more quietly than she intended.

"He senses that we love you, and that you're safe." Abe responded, simply, putting the dish in the oven.

It was the opening she needed.

"We have to talk."

Abe nodded and went to the living room and sat down. Jane sat across from him, He leaned forward, elbows on knees. Again, she noticed the precise movements, similar to Richard and Howard, but Abe was different. He always seemed to be moving, finding things that needed doing, the first to jump up to handle something that required physical exertion. Jane marveled that the man sitting in front of her was not only old enough to be her father, even though he barely looked 40, but had been alive since before the Revolutionary War. She scanned his face, remembering she had thought he looked familiar, and realizing as she looked into his eyes, they were the same golden-green as her children's. And hers.

A long silence ensued until Jane finally formed the words that she had been rolling around in her mind for days.

"I can't believe I'm able to see you, to speak to you. I've spent my whole life wondering what I would say to you if I had the chance, and it's changed over the years."

"I've had times when I thought everything wrong in my life was your fault. My years of feeling like I lived or died by whatever man I thought I loved at the time returned my feelings...I blamed you for that, for a while."

"And I realize that we all have our challenges to work out. I've seen women who grew up with loving fathers go through worse than me."

Abe swallowed. Jane noted that it looked as if he were carefully listening, not just waiting for a chance to respond.

"You're right to blame me," he said. "I should have been there, and I wanted to be. I let my...misguided sense of honor keep me from parenting you. And...I thought you would be better off with Agricole. He was a good father...I didn't know if I could be, especially to a little girl." He lifted his hands in what seemed like a helpless gesture. "I wasn't the greatest father to Richard, either, in his younger years–I sent him to my mother's family in Finland, after his mother died. I was overwhelmed and...didn't know what else to do. It sounds like an excuse, but I really did think he would be better off with them, not me...I felt that way a little about you, too."

"I've watched, from a distance, as you struggled. Job to job, man to man, place to place. After your grandfather passed and Kimmy found us, and realized the truth of what she was...what you are... we discussed traveling to you, revealing the truth, getting you to come here, to us. I would daydream about you coming here, living with us–"

Jane stood up suddenly, hot tears blinding her out of nowhere.

"I hate you for leaving me," it didn't even sound like her voice. It came from somewhere deep in her chest.

"I needed you. Not just then, I needed you five months ago. I've needed a father hundreds of times in my life. Not a grandfather who was called in to pinch hit. I've leaned into being a vagabond because I have no other choice but to enjoy what life has made me. But I could have had the one thing I wanted most if you had only done your job, and been my father."

She sank back down, clueless as to why she had needed to stand to deliver that speech, her heart racing as if she were running.

Tears were streaking Abe's cheeks. "I went to Texas five months ago. I was standing on your porch, and I didn't ring the doorbell."

Jane's mouth dropped open in surprise. "Why didn't you?"

"I was afraid."

"You were afraid?" Jane laughed, the memory of that month still like a feverish dream. "Do you know what was happening inside my apartment? That month, possibly that very night? I was thinking about killing myself."

She had never told anyone.

Paul had walked out one balmy night. The man whose infectious laugh had made her heart sing. The boyfriend who had told her over and over, tears in his eyes, that he had never felt the way he had with her.

That feeling, that came from his love, had felt in the beginning like it was the cure for a thousand ills. It felt like Fortune, which had seemed to be so against her for so much of her life, had finally come around.

She knew in her heart that he loved her, the way she had always wanted someone to. She could see it in his face that it was true when he said it.

She had also known, in the same place in her soul, that there was no predicting when his next dramatic, drunken exit would be. He had done it once before, and called days later, hungover and in tears, regretting the emotional decision. A misunderstanding about dinner plans had caused him to explode, and then snowballed into something neither of them expected.

She had let him come back. And then, one night not long after, he had left again.

She had called Kimmy, who, of course, implored her to come up to Oregon. Jane had declined, and she distinctly remembered leaving the fact that she believed something had died in her out of the conversation.

"I came so close," she was explaining to Abe. "It wasn't only that Paul felt like the only man in the world that I'd loved like that, that loved me back, it was the feeling that if something that I felt was so sure, so real, so right...if it could go away that quickly... what else wasn't real? If your father can just go away, if your kids can just stop talking to you...if the man you think is your soul mate can get so frustrated he walks out...what can you really count on?" The fire crackled, and Jane looked into it for a moment before going on.

"I couldn't even understand why it hurt me so badly when he left. How it could take me so low? How I could be that codependent, that I didn't feel life was worth living anymore without the person who supposedly loved me so much. But then I realized, it was because it was an echo."

Abe looked confused. Jane cleared her throat and went on.

"I don't really remember when my mother died. But you do, right?"

Abe nodded, looking down at his hands.

"How did I react?"

He started to speak, then had to stop and rub his eyes before going on.

"You...you asked for her every day. You cried yourself to sleep every night."

"I also don't really remember you leaving. Pappy never talked about you, but Kimmy told me, when I asked."

Jane felt her anger dissipate and empathy for Abe move into its place, as she saw the look on his face.

"She said that it was heartbreaking. For days, I went to the window, looking for your car. That I cried for you at night, and not even Pappy could comfort me—the man who always could before. It took weeks for me to go to sleep without sobbing, and when I finally did, Pappy told Kimmy never to mention you again."

"Kimmy said one day I looked out the window and and just said, "Daddy left," and then I never mentioned you again, either."

Jane wiped away tears. "That night, after Paul left, I realized it was an echo I was feeling. That this must have been how it felt, to three-year-old me, to realize I'd been left." She shrugged. "I'm only guessing, because I don't remember anything about those years. It's all blocked out."

"Maybe it's codependence to be so completely broken when one person leaves you, if you have others in your life who do too, but that doesn't make sense to a toddler. And I guess the toddler in me was still there, looking for someone who loved me more than anyone else in the world, and I thought I had found him. I was devastated when he left, it felt...it felt apocalyptic. And I let him come back. In fact, the second time, I called and begged him to..." She had not told anyone the last part, and as she said it out loud, embarrassment flooded her. To be so weak, so needy, so starved for love.

"Jane," Abe took a deep breath and looked into her eyes. "I'll do anything I can, after this is over, to make this up to you. To show you...to be the father I should have been all these years." He shrugged. "And honestly, I know I don't have the right to say anything, since I haven't been there, but Paul–" he cleared his throat and Jane almost laughed at the fatherly disgust his tone took. "He didn't strike me as the most dependable guy. I know I was just spying from a distance, but–"

"No," now Jane did laugh. "You're right. I mean, I know he really loved me, he just wasn't...able to love me in a way that wasn't only passionate, and it was dependent on me being strong. I could never be weak, never be securely loved unless I was on top of everything, 24/7. Maybe I didn't end it all because deep down I knew that. Or... maybe it was something else. I don't know."

"I do."

She blinked at Abe, and he took a breath before continuing.

"Jane...I'm sorry. Kimmy told me what you said, how devastated you were, how it scared her--that's the reason I got on a flight and came to your door. I should have knocked, I should have told you who I was, and why I left, and I should have told you I wanted to make up for it, and take you home with me, and let you recover from the break-up, recover from all these menial jobs, live with me, and let me help you heal from what I did." He looked out the window, as if watching the scene unfold from his memory out in the front yard.

"I can imagine that it's hard for you to tell me this. Both that you begged him to come back and that you felt like dying. You're strong, and you rely a lot on projecting that, so that others know you're strong." He rubbed his eyes.

"I believe you didn't go through with it because of an internal optimism, a feeling that told you what you're looking for is out there. It's possible, and it's what you deserve."

"You're self-sufficient, you're strong, as you said, you've had to be. But you don't have to be that here, with me. With us."

He shrugged. "Why did you want Paul back, when he left like that? Why do you give men so many chances? Why do you love so doggedly?" Cooi lifted his head at the last word, and Abe laughed softly and patted his head. "Are you devastated when a man whose love is "good enough" or the best you've had so far, in a string of half-assed relationships leaves, because you don't think you deserve to be treated better? Is it because you don't believe there's more good coming? I could understand that. Sometimes you want to cling to every bit of good you get, and it's hard to believe and trust that there's more, or some that's better suited for you, out there."

Jane was stung, and on the verge of being offended, but then she remembered the three words that had clearly rung in her mind, like a bell, when just a few short weeks later, after getting the news about Kimmy. Paul had acted so petulant about her going to Oregon, so selfishly unaware of the depth of her grief. The three words that finally provoked her to pack her bags and leave for good.

I deserve better. She restated it now in her mind, the way she did to Paul. *I need different.*

"Why didn't you knock on the door that night?"

Abe sniffed and answered quickly. "Fear. Fear of you rejecting me, of it being the wrong thing and causing you to spiral even more. And fear of you being angry at Kimmy and losing the only family you have besides your kids. Fear of you not believing me."

Jane digested his answer for a moment, and found that her old rational reasoning was slowly returning. He was just human. Or, partly human, after all.

"I had no idea that that relationship devastated you to that level. I'm sorry."

"Well, it's over now. And I realize now I shouldn't have let him back in. I feel stronger now. In fact, I've just made peace with the idea that I may not be cut out for relationships."

It felt odd to say it out loud. But it was true–for the first time in her memory, she actually felt whole. When she had been single for stretches of time before there had still been the daydream of, what, a partner? A knight in shining armor? Now there was none of that, not even a wistful whisper of it.

And it felt good. A little hollow, but good.

Abe seemed uncomfortable with this revelation. "Don't say that–you just need some time to clear out your head. And maybe some time to think about your standards in men, and expect more."

Jane didn't know if she was actually hearing judgement or imagining it, but it irritated her anyway.

"I wonder if I would have had better standards for men if I had a frame of reference for what stable love was."

She could tell that he was becoming frustrated, and it set off an alarm bell— the old fear of being too much. Did she push too far? She hadn't even felt, until that moment, the fear of pushing him away, in the confusion of realizing who he was, and now she did.

Abe took a deep breath, almost as if he heard her thoughts.

"You can be as mad as you want, for as long as you want," he said, simply. "But can I just ask that you let me in, just a little? I want you to feel your feelings, I want you to be honest, not pretend…but I also want you to have the benefits of a father, now that this is in the open. And honestly..." he sighed. "We have kind of a time crunch here. I need to be your father in this situation we're in right now most of all, and you need one. You need me."

Jane realized she was coming to admire his matter-of-fact way, his direct but heartfelt communication style, and most of all, the way he was not giving up.

The way his golden-green eyes betrayed deep feeling.

Abe made a helpless looking gesture, and rubbed a hand over his reddish-brown hair. "Many tamers also have a strong tendency to be nurturers, not just to *lugaru*, but in general. Sometimes those urges to nurture are misapplied to human men...and not appreciated. Sometimes they're misapplied to *lugaru* too, and I just want to say... just because you have a gift, doesn't mean you have to share it with everyone. I guess I'd rather you have no man, than one that's just going to disappoint you."

Jane blinked. It was so well stated, so simple, so straightforward, and so...fatherly that she burst into laughter.

Abe looked worried, then hesitantly smiled.

Jane rubbed her knees. "I want that too. And I want my kids to have a family. We don't have anyone but us now." The statement hung in the air momentarily, and then a howl from outside took their attention away from the fraught conversation.

"They're here."

Jane jumped up and ran to the door, excited to see her children, but also worried about what was to come. What had Howard told them? How were they going to react?

Headlights were coming down the road that led to the lodge. Snow was falling, illuminated by the floodlights that shone down from the guardhouses on the side of the road and from the roof of the house, and Jane rubbed her arms and stomped her stockinged feet to chase the chill from the open door.

She could hear the arguing before the vehicles even stopped, and felt a smile jump to her lips.

Howard, Richard, and two other *lugaru* hopped out. Howard's face was drawn tight with an expression of irritation that made Jane laugh.

The men grabbed the luggage and gestured for the kids to hurry inside, and Jane's heart leapt as she saw each of them disembark from the vans, disheveled and carrying their stuff, all three of them directing loud questions at Howard and bickering with each other.

"Mom!" Robin threw their arms open, but the gesture was more of a "What the fuck?" than "So good to see you." Jane ran to Robin anyway, grabbing her youngest child in a bear hug.

Anne Marie came up next, and Jane hugged her as well.

"Can we move inside, please?" Howard and Abe both said it within seconds of each other.

Jane touched Lucas on the cheek, and hurried all of the children into the house.

Coats were shuffled off, and everyone gathered in the living room where they warmed their hands by the fire and looked from Jane to Abe and back again for a few moments.

"So," Lucas, the oldest and the one who always took charge, shrugged. "Are you going to tell us what the fuck is going on?" They gestured at Abe. "This is our grandfather?" Anne Marie looked incredulously at her mother. "Doesn't that warrant a phone call, Mom?"

"They thought it best to keep some things to in-person discussions," Jane explained. Despite the seriousness of the moment, she couldn't keep the smile from coming to her lips or the tears to her eyes as she looked from child to child, savoring the moment of being together in one place.

"It's so good to see..." a sob choked her and she sank to a chair.

Immediately all three of them were surrounding her, Lucas slipping an arm around her, Robin sinking in front, and Anne Marie awkwardly taking her hand.

"I'm so sorry, Mom, about Kimmy." Anne Marie kissed the top of her head. "We all are. We're just...confused about what's happening here. Howard–it's Howard, right?" Howard nodded, still looking exasperated.

"Howard told us that there's something to do with Kimmy's death that might be putting you–and possibly us–in danger. He said that's why they came to get us, why the service is out here, why everything has to be so hush-hush. What is going on?"

"He said," Robin pronounced, in their characteristically slow cadence, "That you were going to all explain this, and that we were not being kidnapped and inducted into a cult, or about to be murdered for our organs."

Jane laughed and wiped her eyes.

"No, it's not a cult. But it is a long story."

"And dinner is ready," Abe added. "I know it was a long drive; you must be hungry." He waved the two *lugaru* who had helped drive to the kitchen. "Laszlo, Rafe, take this out to the bunkhouse for the men." Laszlo carried one of the casseroles out the door and finally, just Richard, Abe, Howard, Jane, and the children remained.

The kids went to the long wooden table in the dining room.

As they sat down to eat, Jane stood at the head of the table and cleared her throat.

While they chewed and drank, she started the tale.

She went through all of it, even though Howard had explained most of it to them, so that they could hear it from her. The chase after Kimmy's service, the men explaining *lugaru* to her, the revelation that Abe was her father.

All three of them slowly stopped eating, one after another, and listened with disbelief.

She went on, explaining how the changing *lugaru* went through slowed their aging, hence Richard, Howard, and Abe's relatively youthful appearances. She shared the revelation that their beloved Pappy, her grandfather, was a *rugaru* and told the theories about her own mother's death. She described how each of them had been under protection, as had she, for most of their lives, until the recent past, and that was why it was necessary they stay here, for now, until it could all be settled.

"Wait…" Anne Marie looked around. "You're not saying we have to stay here–you just said that it was for the service!" she stood, looking panicked. "Are these guys, like…imprisoning us here? Mom, you don't believe all of this, do you? It's crazy, they're crazy!"

"We have lives, Mom," Lucas shook his head. "I told Emily I was going to be gone the weekend, at the most…" his voice trailed off. "Wait, she's not in danger, is she?"

Anne Marie stood as well, shrilly echoing Lucas's concern about his girlfriend with a similar query about Wade, her latest paramour, causing a nervous energy to swirl around the room.

"No, listen–listen!" Jane held up her hands. "The three of you are the primary concern–don't worry about Wade and Emily, they'll be watched." She shot Howard a look and he nodded. "And yes, I don't just believe it, Anne Marie, it's the truth. I was chased and attacked and Howard saved my life. In wolf form."

The kids were looking at each other, silently telegraphing disbelief…except for Robin.

Robin sat quietly, looking at the table for quite a while before raising their eyes to Jane's.

Jane saw something haunted in their expression. "Robin? What are you thinking?"

The others looked to Robin, who sat almost motionless. Robin slowly turned to Howard, who was looking intently at Robin already.

"Robin knows it's true." Howard said, in his low, melodious voice. "Don't you, Robin?"

Robin nodded almost imperceptibly and looked up at Jane. "Yes, I know it's true."

Lucas laughed. "You're out of your mind. You're all out of your minds, and you're not keeping me locked up here. You're not keeping any of us here. Robin, Anne Marie, get up."

He pushed back his chair and was walking to the foyer when Abe stood up.

"Lucas," he said softly, "What if we showed you that we're telling the truth?"

This halted Lucas in his tracks, and also seemed to leave him speechless, but only for a moment.

"I don't care," he almost spat.

"And I certainly don't care about anything you have to say. Not only are you insane, but if you really are our grandfather–which, I'm sorry, can't be possible–where were you when my mom needed you? When our dad was terrorizing us? When we left him and were shit poor for years? Pappy was the one who helped us. You left an old man to do your job, and I don't respect that. I don't want to hear anything you have to say. Give me a car to drive back to the airport or I'm calling the police." He moved to go around him, and Jane could see that his words hurt Abe. As much as she had been angry with him as well, she felt a pang of pity for him.

"What about me, Lucas?" All of their heads swiveled to Howard, who was standing up and making his way towards Lucas. It didn't seem like a challenge, but Jane found herself moving towards Lucas protectively, and Lucas himself turned, stepped around her, and straightened himself to his full 6' 3" height, shrugging with a half-grin.

"What about you, Howard?" There was also a not-quite-a-challenge tone in his voice, as well as something that seemed like an off-hand ready excitement. Something old and primitive, but also unique to men in their twenties.

Howard turned his back to Lucas and went to the fire. He kicked off his shoes and peeled off his socks, and suddenly Jane knew what was about to happen. She backed towards the table and put a hand out to take Lucas's sleeve as Howard pulled his sweater over his head. Abe moved between them, as did Richard, who motioned to Jane with his head.

"Come over here." She tugged at Lucas and waved the other kids behind the table.

An eerie sense of expectation had filled the room and the kids looked to each other and Jane uneasily.

"What's happening?"

"He's taking off his clothes? What the fuck–"

"Mom, seriously, what is going on?"

Howard was facing the fireplace as he pulled off his pants.

Lucas chuckled. "Jesus."

Then, a stomach-churning squelching sound.

Jane felt lightheaded as she watched Howard's body fold into itself. Anne Marie screamed and tried to run around Jane to the door, but Jane instinctively grabbed her and Richard held up a hand to all of them.

"Don't move! Be quiet"

They all stood, transfixed, as what had been the man Howard continued to fold and squelch and black fur burst out of his skin as his body dropped, hard, to the floor, flopped like an enormous fish for just a moment, and then suddenly a black wolf was scrabbling to its feet, shaking as if it had just climbed out of a bath.

A collective intake of breath and a shudder of primal fear.

Jane felt the hair on her arms stand up and looked at Richard and her father. Both men were laser focused on Howard, or the wolf that one minute ago had been Howard. But they both stood protectively to the sides of Jane and the children.

Cooi yipped sharply and came behind the table with them.

"Listen very carefully to me," Abe said, softly. "No sudden moves, no loud noises."

The wolf snorted, and shook his head. His nails clicked against the flagstone floor as he stepped gingerly towards them, dark eyes gleaming.

Jane was feeling something she had never felt before.

He was beautiful, an enormous wolf with shaggy black fur. The same wolf who rescued her from the others, and she could see, as clear as day…Howard in its intelligent eyes. He looked directly at her.

"Howard is very old," Richard said softly, "And he's much more in control of himself in this form than most of us are, for that reason, but you still have to be careful. Please don't move. Don't say anything."

A low rumbling growl emanated from the animal's throat and Jane's blood ran cold.

"Do you believe us now?" Abe turned to look at them and Jane could hear the wolf growling even louder.

"Yes," Lucas whispered. "Just tell him to turn back."

The wolf blinked at Lucas, and without a word from anyone else, turned back to the fire.

Again, the sickening sound, but this time the wolf yelped, rolled onto his back, and seemed to fold inside out while at the same time rolling forward and morphing into Howard, kneeling face down before the fire.

He stood up with a groan, shaking his head, and leaning forward to put his hands on his knees for a moment before picking up his jeans and pulling them on, followed by the rest of his clothes.

Except for the sound of the kids' rapid breathing, it was silent for several moments while Howard sat on the couch and pulled on his socks. "Well," Lucas finally said, softly, after clearing his throat. "Now that you've traumatized us and we have no choice but to believe you, I guess you have our attention."

8

It was the same introduction they had given Jane, but with multiple interruptions, interjections, jokes, and argumentative assertions. At some point, they tried to eat, but the talking and questioning made it difficult.

She offered no help, no additional editorializing to her brother and father's presentation, as they struggled to explain their history and the present situation to her very verbal and challenging children.

Abe in particular was interesting to watch. It was obvious he had an affection for them, "knew" them from years spent observing them…but it was a limited knowledge, hampered by an inability to engage with them personally.

"How do you like being a grandfather?" She wanted to ask. *"Not as heartwarming and sweet as you'd dreamed it would be, is it?"*

After an hour of this rowdy congress, Jane stood, deciding to call it.

"Listen, it's late. Let's go to bed; there are plenty of rooms upstairs, go, get cleaned up and settled down, and we'll go over this some more in the morning." Again, the sweet rush of seeing all of them, together in one place, even under the dire circumstances, and although Anne Marie and Lucas were looking at her as if they wanted to shake her.

Everyone dispersed, even Abe, after giving instructions to a man who came to the door to inform him of the guard change, outside.

Jane padded over to the fire and sat down, digesting all that had happened.

It seemed like only a few minutes had passed, but she glanced up at the clock when she heard someone coming down the stairs, and was surprised to see that it was midnight.

Anne Marie came to stand in front of the fire, rubbing her hands. "I can't sleep."

Jane nodded. Anne Marie sniffed and rubbed her nose, sitting down in a chair across from Jane. "Paul isn't here?"

"We broke up. I left him. I'm staying up here for the time being."

Anne Marie blinked. "Wow. Um, I'm sorry?" She seemed to wait for a response and Jane just shrugged.

"It's fine."

Anne Marie sighed. "I really am sorry about Kimmy, Mom."

"Well, I'm sorry for you kids too. She was basically your grandmother."

"I know, but I think you get to be in the smallest circle in this situation. She was everything to you."

"You guys are everything to me." It sounded sappy, but Jane felt compelled to say it. "What do you mean, 'the smallest circle'?"

"It's something I learned in therapy. There are concentric circles of grievers, when someone dies."

"The person closest to them should be in the smallest circle, when you're in a group. When you are in a group of people who weren't as close to the deceased, then you're in the smallest circle."

Jane smiled. "You're really wise for your age, you know that?"

Anne Marie smiled too, but just barely. She looked away from the fire to Jane.

"How dangerous is all this, really? And was it necessary to let strangers come and get us, and tell us all this?" The vaguest hint of anger in her voice.

Jane shrugged, trying to think of how to phrase it carefully. "They insisted. They just want to keep us all safe."

"I feel like a prisoner."

"You're not a prisoner. And you're handling all this really well." Anne Marie usually responded well to positive encouragement. "You are, truly. It's a lot to digest–I'm still having a hard time." Jane looked over her oldest daughter's face, round like a cherub's, with big, thickly lashed eyes and brown hair pulled into a messy topknot.

"I want to tell you something." Jane was struggling not to think about the possibility that something would happen to her, or to any of them, but again felt compelled, this time to make sure that Anne Marie knew how she felt. Anne Marie's brow furrowed.

"I know it was hard, after we left your dad. I know you had to be responsible, and I know that being strapped for money all the time and living in all those shitty apartments wasn't fun."

"But I believe it made you strong. When I hear you talk about things like the "smallest circle," and I see how you live your life, I'm just, I'm just proud of you. I know it wasn't easy when you guys were growing up,

living with your father, or after we left, but…I believe those things made you who you are."

Anne Marie looked at her mother for a long time, then looked back to the fire.

"Well," she said softly, "Being poor never made me anything but stressed and tired. And being Dad's child only made me sad and afraid."

"I'd like to just be able to be weak, sometimes."

Jane felt as if she'd been punched in the stomach, hearing this echo of her own sentiment that she had expressed during her earlier conversation with Abe, turned around on her. *You want to be the person they can be honest with, she told herself. This is honest.*

All those times when she's lashed out, or given you the silent treatment, she's being weak with you. Just like you want someone to let you be with them. Let her be weak with you.

"I'm sorry," Jane said, quietly.

Anne Marie shrugged and stood. "It is what it is." She gave Jane a funny look.

"You know, it surprises me to hear you call me strong. You always talk about Lucas being strong, and Robin being resilient."

Jane tried not to focus on the accusation she could hear under the surface of the statement and just restate the compliment, to be sure Anne Marie heard it.

"Well, I do think you're strong. And a lot of other things I think would probably surprise you." She stood too, and reached out her arms, hoping that her daughter would reciprocate. Anne Marie gave her a hug, and padded towards the stairs.

Jane sat back down and put her feet up, pulling the wool blanket that decorated the back of the chair over her, and stared into the fire, thinking about the understanding she wanted from her children, the love and admiration she craved from them.

The same things she had wanted from a father for all of those years. Apparently, what he also wanted from her, and the same thing her child wanted from her as well.

Howard's voice echoed in her mind. *Time is a sphere…*

She could suddenly see, actually almost physically see, these generational longings as timelines of need now. Emotional webs that made up their intersecting relationships. Bending and crossing around each other, providing insight to each individual about the other as time passed and their experiences built empathy.

Jane felt a little lighter, more forgiving, and more *forgiven*.

But also, still empty.

Did all parents feel like this? Did all children?

Before her mind could attempt an answer, she was asleep.

She woke to the clink of plates and cups and the smell of coffee and bacon. Jane stood, stiffly, stunned that she had slept so soundly without waking. She grunted as she stretched her aching back, happy for the sound sleep, but feeling the catches in her muscles.

A pot of coffee was on the table along with a breakfast spread. One by one, her children, along with Howard, her father, and brother filtered in and sat at the table for what at any other time might have been a vacation of family and friends.

She looked around the table, reveling in the moment at the joy the presence of her children always brought. No matter how dark things were, simply having them there, not just the assurance of their safety, but them, their irreverence, wildness, humor, their love for each other, all of it, was her favorite feeling in the world.

She wondered if this was the first time she realized that they actually made her feel safe, in addition to feeling they were safest with her.

Even if it wasn't true. Just as quickly as the feeling of deep happiness had struck her, Jane found herself feeling extremely afraid. More afraid than she had been up to this point.

The communion this new family had given her, after digesting the insanity of who they were–combined with the exhilaration of being in the presence of her children, had for just a moment, given Jane an almost unbearable delight.

Which immediately gave way to a terror at the realization that it could all potentially be destroyed.

Cooi's whining and scratching at the door snapped her back to the present.

"Aww...Cooi!" Lucas jumped up and around Abe to ruffle Cooi's ears and open the door. He watched him go out into the yard and laughed. "I'm glad he's still with us...he's my favorite of Mom's strays. Speaking of which, where's my buddy Paul?"

Jane looked down at her plate, feeling stung. The table was silent.

"Do you often take in stray dogs?" Howard asked, politely.

Jane put down her fork. "He's talking about the men I date. And no, Paul isn't here. We broke up."

Lucas snorted, "Again?"

"Hey!" Synchronized responses from both Abe and Richard. There was a silence as the kids looked at each other, then Jane, and an unusual feeling crept over her, which she finally realized was the sensation of someone defending her from her kids' insensitivity. It felt good.

"Are you always this disrespectful of your mother?" Howard asked lightly, after swallowing a mouthful of eggs. Jane started to protest, thinking it was harsh, but then stopped herself, to see the reaction his statement would bring.

"Uh, I was just joking." Lucas's voice had lowered a little, and he looked at Jane, who picked up her fork and started eating again, appetite restored.

She looked to Howard.

"They love me, but they don't have a lot of respect for me. That's probably my fault."

Howard continued eating. "Sometimes the one who was the "safe" parent doesn't inspire respect." He took a drink, as casually as if they were discussing the weather, even though Jane felt as if she'd been punched.

"Or they see you as weak for not leaving sooner."

Lucas seemed stung. "I do respect you, Mom. It was just a joke."

Jane made a small, "all is well" wave.

Anne Marie, who Jane noticed made no effort to denounce the assertion she didn't respect Jane, brought the subject back to their present situation.

"So, you're saying that this "Brotherhood" is going to kill all of us eventually? That we can't go to the police, go back to our homes, or our lives, until when? What's going to happen? I can't stay here forever."

Abe leaned forward. "It's not, forever. But…" he looked at Howard.

"We're trying to connect with their leadership. For assurances. But this is likely a faction that has gone rogue."

"When will you know?" Lucas dropped his toast, amped up again. "I mean, werewolves have cell phones, right? How is this not something that got figured out on day one?"

"First of all," Abe seemed to finally be losing his patience. "I don't like the word "werewolf." Secondly…"

"Please don't say 'It's complicated'", Anne Marie sighed, just as Abe said,

"It's complicated."

In spite of the circumstances, Jane laughed, almost choking on her orange juice.

"We have been in contact with them," Abe restated, "and are trying to negotiate a meeting, as well as get backup from other factions who do not agree with the Brotherhood. We have to be careful, though, and only use encrypted channels. I'm sure you can imagine what would happen if the world at large knew we were real." His frustration could be heard in every word.

Jane turned and caught Howard's eye, and smiled. He smiled back.

"Time is not a line," he said, so softly it was almost unintelligible. "But a sphere."

"What?" Anne Marie scoffed. "What does that mean? Is it a riddle? What does that have to do with anything?"

Howard's eyes turned away, to Robin, who Jane noticed was looking at Howard as well. An eerie feeling came over her as she remembered something.

"Wait, earlier, when you said, 'Robin knows'," Jane looked back to Howard. "What did that mean?"

He continued looking at Robin. "What does it mean, Robin?"

"Does this guy ever give a straight answer to a question?" Lucas sighed, his voice irritated.

Robin took in a breath. They looked down at the table.

"In the van, while we were driving, you said that there were... those in the DNA pool who are magical. Or...able to see things."

Quiet. The siblings and everyone else looked around at each other, but Jane noticed Anne Marie was fixed squarely on Robin, nodding assurance when Robin glanced quickly at them.

Jane felt an unsettling energy come over her, with a rush of memories.

Memories of Robin playing with an old Ouija board, gotten from a friend, thrown away by their Pappy when he discovered it. Robin asking Jane if it was possible for people to cause things to happen with their mind.

Robin, hysterical because they dreamed about the death of Fletcher, their old family dog, days before it happened. Scared because of the feeling of premonition. Begging Jane to tell them if it was real.

And Jane saying of course it wasn't.

It was coincidence.

It was chance.

It had seemed right at the time, to brush away the weight of the idea of a ten-year-old having psychic ability. "Coincidence" and "chance" seemed less scary then, even as now it seemed less terrifying to believe it was part of this.

"Those times when you were little…" Jane's question trailed off, as she realized she was not sure what she was trying to ask, only knowing she didn't want any additional dangers or difficulties for her children, but especially for this child, who had already endured so much, at the hands of other children and adults, for their in-between-ness, their difference, what Jane was only now realizing was their otherworldliness.

"Your mother has a book she is reading," Howard said quietly. "A book written by one who came before. About the experience, and what they learned." He cleared his throat, and Jane made note of how emotional he seemed. "You should read it. You remind me very much of the person who wrote it."

Jane felt her mouth drop open.

"You were there."

He nodded, eyes glistening. "Yes, I was. My original name was Hord. Unn the Deep-Minded was my friend, as was The Eye."

He indicated Robin with his head. "Even if I did not know before that this child was descended from the same lineage as The Eye, I can see it, clear as day."

He swiped at his own eyes, gesturing to Jane. "Go, get the book. There is something you must see."

Jane went upstairs, hearing Howard explain to the children about the first tamer, about the practice of keeping the biographies and diaries of tamers since, and about the *lugaru* historians, and scientists, who studied and tracked, endeavoring always to understand how it all tied together.

She grabbed the book from her backpack.

"Wait, so you're a historian; why are you here?" Again, Lucas, with his characteristic bluntness. Something that Jane was beginning to see with new eyes, as she got to know her father more.

"I mean, no offense, but Abe, Richard, you seem a little understaffed. With a name like, "The Brotherhood," I'm assuming they're big, well-funded. This…" he waved his hands around, "is a nice place, and the five or so guys you've got seem, tough, but…" he pointed at Howard. "I'm imagining a historian is important to the group as a whole." He shrugged. "Why are you risking your life for a couple of outlier *lugaru*?"

Howard's response was quick. "I'm doing it for you. You and your siblings. For Abe and Richard. And for her." With that, he looked to Jane.

A chord sounded, deep in Jane's heart. The dedication she saw in him, the love. Her eyes locked with his and the bond that had always been there was suddenly very tangible to her. As if it had been swept free of centuries of dust. The moment he had knocked the gray wolf off of her, the way his eyes–in wolf form–had looked into hers…the way he gave her the book that detailed how her forebear had been the first one to see him, understand him, and celebrate and elevate him…all of these moments suddenly became powerful with this context.

"Your forebear, the one talked about in this book," he pointed as Jane laid it reverently on the table, "Was the first we know of. I was there. I was her friend, her companion. Over the last thousand years, I've known many of her descendants, and when necessary, I've helped them survive. And I will continue to do that for as long as I live."

They all looked at the book, unmoving, until Anne Marie shook her head.

"You're…a thousand years old? Is that like…" she looked around the table, "…normal for you guys?"

Abe pointed to Howard. "Howard is what we call an Elder. Any lugaru who lives beyond 300 years–"

"300 years?" Lucas literally choked on the drink of water he was taking.

Abe sighed. "Yes, 300 years is a...well, nothing about us is typical, I realize, but 300 years is a ripe old age for us. Any *lugaru* who lives beyond that is an Elder."

The questions all exploded at once.

"Why don't all of you live that long?"

"Do you die from natural causes?"

"Do you have like, super recovery?"

"*Voi luoja...*" Abe exclaimed, shaking his head and looking at Richard, who laughed and turned to look at Jane, who was laughing as well. *Our first time laughing at our dad together,* Jane thought. Abe held up a hand.

"We will have time enough to talk about these things later, but no, all of us don't live that long. Yes, we generally die of what you would call natural causes at about 300, if we're healthy. We don't suffer from human diseases, but we have some of our own. One of them, *hememodor*, or "World Weariness", specifically affects Elders, and can be hard to disguise."

"That," he looked around the table and paused to ensure he was being heard, "Is just one of the many reasons secrecy is so important. We've been trapped and studied before, and only over centuries have we been able to obfuscate the humans' knowledge of us. And with technology being what it is now, we must be even more careful."

He took a breath.

"What the fuck does obfuscate mean?" Anne Marie whispered to Lucas.

Abe looked as if he was going to cry.

"We do recover from most injuries, things that would kill humans, but we aren't immortal, obviously. We can be mortally wounded if stabbed or shot through the heart or head, or beheaded. Or if our throats are torn out." Anne Marie grimaced at this, touching her own throat and mouthing *Jesus Christ* to Lucas, who snickered.

Howard took over, placing a hand on Abe's shoulder. "Elders have both avoided mortal wounds and disease and also have stayed in wolf form for long periods of time. That's what enhances our lifespan, time we spend in changed form."

"So why don't all of you do that? Spend more time in changed form?" Lucas wasn't letting it go, even though Abe seemed ready to focus on talking about their plan of defense.

Richard cleared his throat, signaling that he would answer.

"Some of us," emotion cracked his voice, "don't want to live a thousand years."

The reintroduction of pain from grief over Kimmy swirled around all of them, like a fog.

Abe gestured towards Howard.

"Also, you have to understand there is effort and self-control involved, in all of it. It takes a certain type of discipline to not change, when you feel the urge, and while you are in wolf form, it takes self-awareness and control to not..." he sucked in his lips, obviously remembering something unpleasant, "act in a way you would be ashamed of, as a human."

The depth of what he was saying sunk into the group, for a moment. Jane leaned forward, towards Howard.

"You've spent lots of time as a wolf, so you're able to control yourself more when you're in that state." He nodded. She looked to her father and brother. "What about the two of you? Does that mean that you can't control yourselves as well?"

"You're safe with us," Abe assured her. But then he took a deep breath. "But let's just say you're safer with Howard. And if we are engaged and any of us change," He looked around the table meaningfully, "If possible, you should keep your distance. I don't like changing, neither does Richard. We are in control of ourselves but... well, it's hard to explain."

There was silence for a moment as Jane and her children took this in.

"And Mom, you're saying that having a tamer near...moderates that urge? To change?" Lucas was getting it.

"Yes," Richard nodded, smiling at his sister. "It does. It also helps us exert more self-control while in wolf form."

Lucas pointed at Robin. "And you're saying that queer kids are magic." He laughed, raising his eyes at Robin. "We should make t-shirts that say that–we could make a fortune." Robin smiled.

Howard pointed at Robin.

"Open the book, to the back. To the Appendix, to the illustrations." Robin did so, slowly.

"Look at the fourth vision."

Robin laid the book flat, and pushed it to the center of the table.

The image was unmistakable; a line drawing of a teddy bear, Xs for eyes, inside a black heart.

Drawn by an eleventh-century seer, on a remote hill in Scotland.

That in itself was enough to shake Jane, but then Robin turned, pulled their backpack off of the back of their chair, and gently laid it on top of the book.

Pinned to the flap was a pin…black, heart-shaped, with a teddy bear line drawing in the center, Xs for eyes.

A collective intake of breath, from Jane and all of the children. The air felt as if it left the room; reality bent across generations by this one little image.

"What are these visions?" Robin's voice was unbelievably calm, as if they were discussing anything other than psychic phenomena.

"The Eye had knowledge beyond that of regular people," Howard said, "But these visions were induced by performing a ritual that our people called *seiðr*, going between worlds."

"Going between worlds?" Jane didn't want to know but was powerless not to ask. "How?

"A trance, induced by taking a combination of mushrooms, henbane, and an ancestor's ashes, as well as a contemporary female relative's blood."

"Good God," Anne Marie gasped, and Lucas chuckled.

"Could I…do something similar?" Robin asked timidly, as Jane jumped to her feet.

"Absolutely not!" she exclaimed.

"Of course," Howard responded.

She glared at him. "These aren't your kids!"

"They aren't yours, either. They are their own people, not children anymore."

"Hold on," Abe held up a hand. "Let's slow down."

"Yes, let's slow WAY the fuck down!" Jane felt hot, anger leaning her forward. "You're overstepping, dude. I don't care if you've helped my ancestors for a million years, you don't get to suggest something like that within a couple hours of meeting my kid, when you don't even—"

"Mom," Robin reached across the table and took Jane's hand. "It's okay. I'm not scared of this and you don't have to be either."

Jane looked at her child, so old for their age. She had known what Howard said about supernatural abilities applied to Robin from reading the saga about Unn, and about The Eye. She had felt the tingle of understanding about so many episodes from their life— coincidences marked up to odd chance—and had not wanted it to be true. Just like she didn't want to believe it any time during the past twenty-two years when Robin had melted down after a premonition came to pass, or slipped into a depression when a vision was heavy.

Jane squeezed Robin's hand and looked into their wide set golden brown eyes. So careworn, so innocent.

"Every single time you've *known* something, it's caused a panic attack. And you want to add henbane, whatever the fuck that is, to the mix?!"

Robin shook their head and looked at Howard. "I don't think it's going to make me afraid anymore." They shrugged. "Knowing it's real, and that there's a purpose for it—that there are others like me, that it is this way for a reason, and that it might help us…that makes it different."

Robin turned to Howard. "Because it might help us, right? That's what these visions were for; answers to problems."

Howard nodded. "That's right. It might help us."

"These," he pointed, almost reverently, to the drawing of Robin's pin, "Were a series of visions that showed the end of your kind many times, specifically your family line, and the ways it was forestalled."

"This happened after Unn? Not just to my mother and Kimmy and us, but to others?" For some reason this felt so heavy that it pulled Jane back into her seat with a thud.

"You must remember, you are descendants of the first known tamer. Throughout our history, the peace with and acceptance of tamers has ebbed and flowed. Decades, centuries have gone by without any factions bringing up this nonsense about eradicating tamers. But whenever these notions come up again, as they always do, your family is a symbolic target. It's easy enough to find you, since we keep records like we do, and yes, people die. But sometimes, they survive. Someone has always survived and kept the line going."

"The line..." Jane put her head in her hands. "I can't believe someone can look at me and feel like I'm a threat." She laughed, and suddenly a ripple of curiosity momentarily distracted her from the sadness and ridiculousness of it all. "Is it through Pappy that we're connected to Unn?" She looked at Abe. "Or my father?"

"Who," Anne Marie asked with a sigh, "in the world is this Unn?"

"Our ancestor," Jane replied, quietly, looking at Howard.

Howard smiled. "Through both of them." Lucas laughed. "Oh my God...that's some werewolf Appalachia shit!" He held up his hands in a "sorry" gesture when he saw Abe's face, however, and stifled his laughter.

"Your father is a descendent of Unn's through Olaf, her grandson. Agricole's mother, your great-grandmother, was the daughter of Panther Dan and--" This time, Anne Marie was the loud interrupter.

"I'm sorry...PANTHER DAN?" She looked at Lucas and they both burst into laughter for a few seconds. Ignoring them, Howard continued.

"Panther Dan is a legendary figure, one of the fiercest fighters and noblest of our kind," He looked meaningfully at the snorting kids and then turned his attention back to Robin and Jane.

"Your great-grandmother's mother was Amélie Roubideaux, a descendent of Yngvild the Fair, Unn's daughter. By the time the lines crossed, generations had passed." He looked very pointedly at Lucas. "That is not equal to 'Appalachian shit'."

"I have a question…" Robin's voice was so quiet it was hard to hear. "If Pappy was a…*lugaru*…why did he die? Why isn't he still alive? He died of heart failure…couldn't he have changed and healed it?"

It was quiet.

Howard sighed.

"To Richard's point, not all *lugaru* want to go on for hundreds of years. Or," he paused and looked at Jane. "Outlive all of their children. But it's a good question– heart failure is not something we usually see in *lugaru*. Its symptoms look like some of those associated with World Weariness, but it's not common in one as young as Agricole is thought to have been."

Jane rubbed her forehead, as if she could massage away both the sad memories of Pappy and the thought of her children dying.

She paged back to the first illustration in the appendix. "What is this?"

Something Jane could not understand was written next to it. "Are these runes?"

"Yes," Howard chuckled. It says, ""Cunning as a fox, let her talk her way out.""

"That could be anyone in our family," Anne Marie said, and the other kids laughed.

"Who was it?" Jane asked quietly.

"Ailis MacAuley. The 1400s, in Scotland. That's a picture of her set of dice. She used them to gamble and tell fortunes, and in one instance, it almost got her burned at the stake. I was on the brink of killing the men who were building the pyre, but she talked her way out."

"What does this say? What are these?"

Howard grew grim. "Dark and bloody lady. You can save two with these two." He pointed at the drawing, which looked like a river with two Xs positioned on it. "Countess Erzsébet Báthory. This was the river that ran behind her castle. I used these two points to enter it and exit, saving two tamers who were about to die at her hands. Two tamers who were the last we knew of in your line at that time..."

"*The* Erzsébet Báthory?" Robin's quietness was dispelled momentarily.

"Yes. Another story for another time."

"What does it say next to the drawing of Robin's sticker?" Jane knew she had to ask, although she also felt that she didn't want to know.

"A bird with a bear. This one's eyes see *Ragnarök,* and the way through."

Fear clutched at Jane's throat. A voice from another time that knew she called Robin her baby bird. A nickname that was a grim reminder of the premature birth of a baby born thin and delicate-looking, like a hatchling. A voice that knew about their gift...although this was the first time Jane had thought of it as a gift. Maybe it was. She looked at Robin and the other children, knowing that the situation was dire.

"Why are there no more drawings or runes after this one? Is it because..." Lucas's voice trailed off.

"I don't know." Howard said, in his now familiar, blunt manner. "It could be that the Brotherhood kills you all, and us, and your line ends. Or," he looked meaningfully at Robin. "It may be that someone has come along who will see the answers for the times after this."

"What does *Ragnarök* mean?" Anne Marie looked at all of them.

"It's from Norse mythology. A battle of gods, monsters, and men that represents the end of the world." Lucas, always a fan of Norse mythology, which Jane found eerily prescient now, answered quietly. "The gods die. The world is burnt, then submerged, and then two humans repopulate the Earth, like another Adam and Eve."

"But, could that be an allegory? For the Brotherhood coming here and wiping us out? Or, are they the "gods"? Do we kill them? Is this something other than what's going on now? I don't understand." Anne Marie wondered.

"Well, that's something scholars have been trying to figure out for centuries," Lucas laughed, "So I don't think *you're* going to solve it, no offense."

"You don't have to be a dick, Lucas," Anne Marie whispered.

"Please!" Jane pressed her temples, feeling a tension headache coming on. "Howard, you've looked at this thousands of times. You knew the Eye, you had to talk about this, what do you think? I know your scholars don't know, but, what do *you* think?"

They all looked at him.

"Well, I think Robin is the answer. My feeling is from this point on, if we live, Robin is the seer. *Ragnarök?* I don't know. I don't think it's this, though, but something different in the future. But something that happens at least in Robin's lifetime, if they survive."

"Whatever it is, I know I need to see." Robin's hands were flat on the table, their voice more forceful than anyone at the table had ever heard it.

Already changed, Jane thought, with both pride and sadness, but fear still clutched at her throat.

"Drugs aren't to be taken lightly," Howard said, suddenly sounding almost grandmotherly.

"No shit," Robin's mature calm faltered for a second. "But what choice do we have? You're the one who wanted me to do this!"

"Yes, I do; but you must understand the risk. I think it's likely small, because you are who you are. But it's not zero risk." He looked at Jane. "And only people who believe in positive outcome should be around. Is that you?"

She nodded. The other children did too, but Howard waved them off, as well as Abe, who had been silent, along with Richard, for the entire time.

"No, my friend!"

"It is my house," Abe said, standing, "and my grandchild."

Robin laughed, "Okay, hold on now, *Grandpa,* I just met you."

"But I didn't just meet you." His tone was grave, matching his expression. He waved at all of them. "I was not visibly part of your lives; this is true. Although I've been there the whole time; I saw all of you grow up. Multiple times a year, I lived in the towns where you were, watched what happened."

"And we intervened when we could." Richard's quiet statement provoked an angry glance from Abe and a communal outburst from the kids.

"What does THAT mean?"

"Oh my god, is this a "helping from the shadows" thing?"

"Are you SERIOUS?"

"Be quiet!" Jane slapped the table for effect. Then she turned to her father.

"I know you mean well, and that we don't fully understand why it was dangerous for you to actually be in our lives."

"Why can't you explain it?" Anne Marie's voice was incredulous. "Just explain why it was *sooooo* dangerous for you to be–"

"Because of what's happening now!" Abe's cool demeanor finally evaporated, and the heavy atmosphere lifted for Jane; it had only taken a few hours of being an active grandparent for Abe's stoicism to disappear. But a wave of sympathy for him replaced it as she watched his shoulders sag and heard his voice break.

"You have no idea how much I wanted to take your mother with me. In fact, I did." Everyone leaned forward at this, including Jane.

"The night Agricole was going to move you and Kimmy, I snuck into the house and took you. I made it 10 miles out of town and then I turned back." "He was furious, of course, that I had left. I think he would have killed me for trying it, but when I sat in his kitchen and cried..."

The shuffling and buzz settled; the emotion in his voice had stilled it.

"He told me he wasn't doing it to be cruel, but a lone wolf draws less attention. He knew I would be a liability. By keeping tabs on you, and checking in, I was being selfish–I was endangering you, even though I was careful and covered my tracks, but...he was right. And the only reason we're here now, the only reason Kimmy is dead, is because I was careless. She recognized me, and her hate for me, then her curiosity about why I hadn't aged, and then her love for Richard after she followed me here put her in the open. It all began with me."

No one argued with him; but no one said more. Jane got up, and for the first time, put her arms around him. She could feel his shoulders shake as he resisted the tears, and then tremble when he gave in.

"I don't know how much of this you all know," Richard said, quietly. "But your Pappy's name was Agricole Roubideaux. Not Cole Ruby. He killed the men who murdered Renee. Then he took Kimmy and Jane to Oklahoma, and told Kimmy that Renee's death was due to a conflict with a drug dealer, and the authorities had resettled them and changed their names for their safety. In fact, he did it all himself. And he kept everything remotely connected to *lugaru*, tamers, or Abe quiet. For the sole aim of protecting Kimmy and Jane. Something he managed for years, despite the Brotherhood being a global organization."

"Why does this Brotherhood hate tamers so much?" Anne Marie's voice sounded small. "I mean, it doesn't sound like a bad thing, to be able to help werewo–*lugaru*–control the impulse to change."

Richard answered. "There was a point when tamers were used by a particularly ruthless group to catch *lugaru* and try to exterminate them. Granted, this happened as a response to some *lugaru* acting on a belief that…consuming…tamers might be a complete cure for our condition." He glanced around when this brought a gasp. "Yes, I know. The Brotherhood was formed as a protective organization for *lugaru*, but even after that threat was over, they couldn't let it go. The fact that it happened

drove them to want to eradicate all tamers, even though the good they do far outweighs that one point in history."

"The divide between the various groups of *lugaru* grew. Conflict between those who believe Tamers were a godsend, literally, and those who feel they are the biggest threat to our kind. And…" he gestured with a slight smile. "Everyone else, in between."

"Where was that? And when?"

"France, Germany, and Romania, mostly, and a few other countries. In the sixteenth century."

Jane felt overwhelmed by the absurdity. "My mother and my aunt have both died due to something that happened over 500 years ago?"

"You have to remember," Howard said carefully. "We only exist because we protect ourselves, and we can live a long time. That was not so long ago to me. And it was not insignificant; we were more concentrated in one place then and it was almost the end of our kind.

"That's why some of us moved to America," Richard said quietly. "After a couple hundred years, when exploration began to show us in Europe that the New World was an option, we felt it was time to break away, and so we did. My grandfather, Abe's father, was one of the *lugaru* in the band of what became the organizing group of North American turnskins. It was not something entirely approved by the Old Order, our leadership in Europe. For a while…the New Worlders were very much on their own. And as has been said so many times; our kind needs each other."

"Did the Brotherhood come to America at the same time?" Lucas leaned forward and Jane could see his wheels turning.

"No," Richard said. "They waited. They saw us struggle, and build some structure, and then they came. But with the full blessing of the original, Old World Brotherhood, and their monetary support."

He, Howard, and Abe chuckled, and Lucas picked up on the joke.

"Same struggle, but now you guys have more room, and less support from your old guard, whereas the Brotherhood has the full support of theirs."

"Exactly." Jane could see the grandfatherly pride in Abe's eyes at Lucas's quickness of mind.

"We were able to blend in more here," Abe said. "So many people, from so many places. It's hard to explain what it was like then, but it's possibly what allowed us to survive as a species. The Old Order was afraid of change, that was why they abandoned us, but it was a good exchange. We're very different, as a result, in some good ways and some not. If you're interested in learning more, I would be happy to teach you. This is," he took an emotional breath. "Your heritage, after all. You're not *lugaru*, but if you have a son, he may be."

"If we make it, you mean," Lucas's tone softened his words.

"Look," Anne Marie made an exasperated gesture. "I'm sorry to ask this, but what are we doing here? What's going to happen? Are we here because we're in danger in the present? Just supposed to live out our days in this place? We have lives. We can't stay here. And we thought we were coming to a funeral. We haven't even had time to process our aunt's death, I can't imagine what Mom..." she trailed off, looking at Jane, who shook her head.

"The threat right now is immediate. Or at least, we think it is, right? After what happened to me?" Jane reminded them.

Their expressions darkened at the mention of her attack. Robin stood.

"That seals the deal. I'm doing the 'between the worlds' thing. And I think we need to do it now."

"This isn't something you have to do," Jane felt as if the situation was spiraling from any semblance of being under her control.

"Mom, it's okay." Robin smiled. "In fact, it's more than okay. We're going to figure out what to do. Viking style."

9

After much bickering and explaining, Richard, Abe, Anne Marie, and Lucas were sent to the back of the house, the farthest room from the area where the *seiðr* would take place. A drop of blood donated by Anne Marie, under extreme protest from Jane, was blended with a tiny spoon of ashes, from a many times over great-granddaughter of Unn, and a pinch of henbane, by Howard, in a mortar and pestle that Robin dubbed, "hella medieval". It had taken half an hour of arguing for Jane to convince Howard she would be both silent and supportive, two qualities he insisted had to be present for Robin to be safe.

To be sure that she could deliver on her promise, she had retired to her room to meditate. It had taken several minutes for her mind to quieten, and for her body to relax.

She knew two things; there was a force coming to track them down and kill them. And Robin was the key to figuring out how to stop it.

She knew this as clearly as knowing Abe and Richard were telling the truth about *lugaru* and tamers before they had fully explained it. She felt it as keenly as Abe's pain about leaving her as a child, and she accepted it as totally as his explanation that her grandfather knew the only way to get their lives to this point.

This point.

Three children downstairs. On the cusp of true adulthood, although in the book that held the life story of her forebears, children even younger than that lived through conflicts that held just as much danger.

Her forebears.

Jane opened her eyes and stood, looking for the book, driven by an instinct that what she needed to feel calm would be in its pages.

Lothlend, in the Year of the Christian Lord 876

The crossing had been smooth. Some of the wolf-men had been born in Norway, and others were quick learners, and those who were not either were strong, so the building of the knorrs according to the Viking fashion had gone well. They were deftly crafted, sailed sleek, and carried them across the sea without incident. Upon landing, it took some figuring to understand where they were, but once she had her bearings, Unn pointed north.

"We'll travel to the land of my brother," she said. "He can shelter us and give us supplies for our journey."

They walked for a full day, making camp in a treeless valley and setting men in shifts for watches. Earl Einar's third son, Turg, had not been in the group that set upon them, and Unn the Deep-Minded knew he might not take the news of his father and brothers' passing quietly.

"He has the land, he may not want to sail away and leave it unguarded just to chase one woman and her children," she mused, "But men are not always practical."

When the sun was directly overhead on the second day, Unn pointed to the horizon. The tops of trees were visible, and as they grew closer to the forest it became clear that it enclosed a fortress. It was raised slightly, on a hill, and a plain spread out all around it.

"This is how my father taught us," Unn explained. "You clear a space all around you, leaving the trees to shelter your home, which should always be built on high ground."

The space had done its work. Voices could be heard, coming from the trees, and everyone could see, after movement began, that there were structures built into them, housing men and women who were now raising a signal.

As the party drew closer, the fortress's gate opened, and Helgi, brother of Unn, came out.

The two embraced, as Helgi's men and Unn's tribe of travelers looked on.

"Sister," Helgi said, glancing over the group. "How is it you've gone from queen to vagabond?"

Unn related the main points quickly, then gestured to the line of people trailing behind her.

"Part of Father's lands are mine," she said simply. "I am here to claim them, and I need a place to rest until we can travel and build."

Helgi widened his eyes, whistled, and scanned the party again.

"I could house ten of you," he said at last. "Through the rest of the year."

Unn stood so still for so long that Thorstein's wife was about to reach out and touch her shoulder, but then Unn spoke.

"And what, exactly, brother," Unn said in a strange voice, "Do you propose we do with the other souls in our group?"

Helgi shrugged and waved over them with a hand. "You and the woman and the children will be safe," he said, "These men can fend for themselves easier if you are not with them, I'm sure they would tell you."

He started to say something else, but Unn turned away and spoke to the men, Thor's wife, and the children.

"Go back the way we came. We are returning to the coast."

Helgi's mouth fell open in surprise, and then he looked at his men, and then at Unn.

"Sister," he said, trotting to fall in beside her as she walked. "Surely you understand—"

She stopped abruptly, and Helgi almost ran into her.

"You should understand that these men saved me and my children from death or servitude, or worse." Her voice was quiet.

Helgi looked uncomfortable, and Unn reached out to touch his cheek, as if he was a little boy again. There was love in her eyes, those standing nearby could see, but even though she spoke softly, the words were sharp.

"You're still my brother, Helgi, but I was also looking for my mother's son."

She turned away and began walking again. Though Helgi's face was angry, he called out to her to come back, and bring the whole of her entourage with her.

Later, as they all crowded in the great hall around trestle tables, eating a quickly prepared meal, Helgi was heard to say that he supposed his love for his mother would be the death of his children, when their winter stores ran out, but a stern look from his wife quietened him, and he said no more about the visitors being unwelcome.

But after everyone fell asleep, some in the hall on the floor, some in the barns, Unn went to Hord, and took counsel with him on how to make their presence less of a burden. Both agreed that they needed rest, and plenty of food, and to wait until warmer weather to travel, but also knew that living in cramped conditions would lead to illness, and they could not depend on Helgi's stores.

Unn went to her brother the next morning with their plan.

If Helgi would agree to some lumber from the forest being felled, Unn would pay for it. They would construct a cabin for her, Thor's wife, and the children, and the men would take turns manning the treehouses that spanned Helgi's forest, living two or three at a time in them for the remainder of the winter.

Helgi said that his men would welcome the reprieve from the duty, but warned that the huts were small, and cold. Hord smiled and said that they were used to hard living, and that the huts would be shelter enough.

Unn also told her brother that she had several tame wolf dogs that traveled with them but were shy of strangers and staying some distance away, in the forest, for now. She asked her brother to make certain that his people understood that they were not to hunt these animals or agitate them in any way.

So, they passed the winter with the people of Unn's brother Helgi.

Helgi's men grudgingly spoke their gratitude to Unn's men for taking over the guard during the cold winter months. Their wives began to seek out Unn for advice. Bjorn and Olaf each grew several inches, and practiced archery and running with Helgi's sons. Yngvild the Fair smote the hearts of many young men, but fell for her uncle's right-hand man, a tall native of the Suðreyjar. Unn gave her consent for their marriage, happy that her daughter would be somewhat close to her lands, a few days' travel away.

Thorstein's widow, Helga, also had many suitors, but refused them all. When Unn gently urged her to take another husband, she responded that Thor had no equal among men, and she was content to live the rest of her life as his wife. She also said that young Olaf would never leave his best friend and uncle, Bjorn, nor his grandmother, and she would not leave him.

At first, much was made of the wolves occasionally seen lurking near Unn's cabin. People who visited out of curiosity noticed that they were not always the same wolves. More often than not a few would be in the cabin, with Unn and her children, lying on the flagstone floor in front of the fire, or on the foot of the beds.

But even more than they wondered about the wolves, Helgi's people feared The Eye.

Helgi had married a native woman, a Christian, and adopted her ways. His settlement had never had a seer, and was not sure what to make of Unn's child, neither male nor female, who interpreted their dreams, had visions, and answered to no name.

Their unease reached its height when a man shot an arrow into one of Unn's wolves that he said was too near his chicken house. The wolf was carried away to Unn's cabin and taken inside to see what could be done. Helgi and some of his people were speaking with Unn about the matter in Helgi's great hall when The Eye burst in, angrily calling for the man who injured the wolf to come forward.

Everyone looked to the man who had been seen to shoot the wolf. He was frozen in place and could only look at The Eye in terror.

The Eye had never been heard to raise their voice.

The Eye was a quiet, slight person who moved slowly and exercised great passivity in most matters, only passing along what they could discern in their visions when asked, and always reminding everyone who sought their counsel that the future was like a river, not a lake; moving and bending, and apt to change.

But on this evening, The Eye was breathing heavily and shouting that trust had been broken, and the people of Helgi were not people of their word. The Eye went to the center of the room and looked around at each person gathered there. Silence fell, and then The Eye raised a finger, pointing it at the man who had shot the wolf, without anyone saying that he was the culprit. Gasps were heard all around, and the man cried out, covering his face.

"My child," Unn stood from her place at her brother's table, her voice firm. The Eye did not turn to meet Unn's gaze. "This man has agreed to pay for his mistake and Ulf will recover from his wound." The Eye slowly lowered the finger they had raised. Panicked whispers flew around the hall and Helgi looked to his sister with concern.

"Please give these people a blessing, so that their minds will be at ease."

The Eye blinked at the man, never turning their eyes from him.

"I will not give them a blessing." The Eye paused, then shrugged. "But neither will I curse them."

With that The Eye turned and left, as abruptly as they had come.

Later, in the cabin, Unn made sure that the only people in the house were wolves and her children and daughter-in-law and grandson, and called to The Eye to come and sit by the fire.

"Child...these people are Christians. What they cannot blame the one God for, they will ascribe to malevolent powers. They don't know that you don't have the power to curse them."

Two wolves came and lay at The Eye's feet, and the black wolf sitting

by Unn's side went to The Eye as well, laying its large head in The Eye's lap. The Eye rubbed the black wolf's ears and responded without looking up.

"I do have the power, Mother. And yes, there is risk in them believing that I can be evil in my actions...but there might be some benefit in that, as well."

Since The Eye's childhood, there had been times when Unn questioned them, both about the visions that they saw and about what The Eye could understand about the world beyond this one.

Sometimes Unn asked when others were around, and sometimes Unn kept her questions for when the two of them were alone.

Unn had grown up with both Christians and those who followed the old gods. Her father had been a pagan, as had her husband. She herself questioned everything, and when The Eye began to explain the visions they saw, Unn had encouraged The Eye to see them with new eyes, not those of a Christian or pagan. Pagan seers assumed the gods were real, and the Christian priests believed that things came from the hand of the one God. But when Unn asked The Eye,

"Who are these visions coming from?", the child simply shrugged, and said, "They're just coming from my mind."

As The Eye grew older, they told Unn that from time to time in their visions, they could see the beings thought to be the Norse gods. The Light Ones, The Eye called them. The Eye didn't know if they were gods, or dreams from ancestors, showing characteristics needed to survive.

"Perhaps people who see these beings described them to others, and people choose a god from them that is the image of what they feel they need," The Eye once said, and Unn pondered this often, when asking herself the question of what she believed about the world...but she had advised The Eye not to share it with anyone else.

"Like the Christians say," Unn said, "Some have ears to hear certain things, and others do not."

Unn had seen her child called The Eye predict things that came to pass, and bless fields that prospered, despite harsh conditions, by using the words the Norse seers used. The Eye knew herbcraft and had nursed many a sick child back to health. Unn had accepted her child's abilities as gifts.

But there was one occasion that Unn had put to the back of her mind, that she thought about again now, after seeing The Eye's anger at the man who shot the wolf.

Olaf the White had once, in a drunken fit, beaten Unn badly. Thorstein had intervened and been knocked unconscious by his father. Now, in addition to being beloved by his mother, Thorstein was also the favorite of The Eye.

Almost immediately, after beating his son, Olaf the White had vomited, and instead of the usual relief that was brought by purging, when he had drunk to that extent...his discomfort had gotten worse as the night went on.

For three days, he was unable to eat, and his vision began to fade.

He became frightened, like a child, and called out for Unn and the children finally, telling them that he was sorry to be so brutal, and asked for their forgiveness before he slipped from the earth.

Each of them spoke words of forgiveness to him, with The Eye coming to his bedside last.

"Do you forgive me, child?" Olaf asked.

The tiny Eye responded with another question. "Are you truly sorry?"

There was a silence, and the fearfulness on Olaf's face changed to something else. "I am," he said.

"Then I forgive you."

Within minutes Olaf's distended belly began to shrink, and his eyesight improved. By evening he was sitting up and drinking broth, by the next morning he was fully recovered.

For a time, he was kind to his wife and children, but his normal reserve with The Eye was increased, and to even a casual observer it began to look like fear. When his usual bad temper returned, his fits of anger were more controlled, and although he still was occasionally violent, it was not like it was before.

Until the night that he once again raised a hand to a child, and Unn and her wolf men killed him.

Now, sitting by the crackling fire with The Eye, surrounded by sleeping wolves, with the other children settling down for the night, Unn turned the memory of Olaf's sickness over and over in her mind, like a stone she was examining for veins of gold.

She was almost frightened to ask The Eye what she wanted to know, but she did. This is why she was called the Deep-Minded; always she chose to know the truth.

"Can you truly curse people?"

The Eye told her that the invisible material the world was made of was like a horse they were all astride, and though it was not possible for everyone, some individuals could pick up the bridle of this horse and turn it to their will. Just as you could not make a horse fly, or speak, you could not guide the happenings of the world without limit...but much more was possible than people realized.

Unn sat up late into the night, long after everyone else was sleeping, and she was already awake, stoking the fire, when her children stirred and came to the table.

The man Hord and two others came to the cabin to breakfast and give reports, and after Unn had spooned groats into bowls and poured hot tea into cups, she said, quietly, "We need to begin preparing my land."

She outlined her plan, and asked Hord to relate it to the other men.

Working in small groups, men would travel to Unn's land–not far from her brother's, but north and back towards the coast–taking timber purchased from Helgi with them that they would use to build longhouses, smokehouses, and a palisade. Unn described where she wanted the settlement and said that she would come to them soon to be sure all was being built as she envisioned.

Hord nodded and set about organizing the men and speaking with Helgi about the timber.

Unn turned to The Eye and asked for a brew of sacred mushrooms and herbs– a tea to make hidden things plain.

She had never drunk the tea before, but explained to The Eye that she felt as if she was at a crossroads, and needed the guidance of the gods–or whatever guided humans in need of direction–to feel certain in her steps.

The Eye had a small hut to the back of Unn's cabin. It was always their preference to have a place to retreat, and now Unn followed them there, and took off all her clothes, save her shift, at The Eye's suggestion. The Eye built up the fire and brewed the tea.

After drinking it, Unn nervously asked from moment to moment what she should expect, until the normally reticent Eye grew frustrated.

"Sit still, Mother," the Eye instructed, "And just look into the fire, and wait."

It seemed like hours passed, until Unn noticed that the sound of rain falling on the roof had become particularly noticeable. Then, uncharacteristic for the season...thunder. Soft, but insistent.

Her eyes became heavy, and then, the next time she opened them—startled by the caw of a raven amidst the thunder—she was outside the hut, in an open meadow. Looking down at her hands, she could see that they were dry, untouched by the light rain.

Thunder sounded again, and Unn heard a rustling to her left. When she turned, she could see herself, sitting on a large carved wooden chair. To her sides stood Bjorn and Olaf, flanked by Yngvild, Helga, and her men.

Another clap of thunder, louder, to her right, and as Unn turned... her breath left her body.

Striding toward her, with monstrously large thunderclouds looming gray behind him, was her son, Thorstein.

Although her legs felt heavy, Unn ran to him, throwing her arms around his broad shoulders, and weeping as she felt his strong arms encircle her.

When she stood back to look at him, she gasped; arrows pierced him in five places, and a sword's gash ran down his chest from his collarbone to his belly. His blood covered her hands.

His eyes were the same as they had been as a child—full of life and merriment— but there was something else there now. An ancient knowledge, something that felt just out of her reach to understand.

He stepped a little away from her, and indicated she should turn.

When she did, her knees buckled at the sight of the woman who stood there.

A head taller than Unn, with pointed ears, silver hair, white-gray eyes...and a face half rotted away, exposing the skull beneath.

This was Hel, daughter of Loki, overseer of the underworld.

She stood aside, wordlessly gesturing towards the meadow, and Unn could see at a distance a horse, with her daughter-in-law Helga sitting on it, the baby Olaf in front of her. Thorstein, whole and hearty, walked beside her, laughing.

Unn gripped the arm of the Thorstein beside her, knowing that she was witnessing the happening that had haunted her for years, the event Helga could not discuss, would not answer her questions about; the death of her son.

Men appeared from the woods behind them—soldiers wearing the colors of Haakon Broadaxe, her father's rival—and set upon them. Thorstein turned and immediately after seeing them, quickly slung his shield off his arm and grabbed Helga's, shoving it through one of the shield's leather straps, shouting at her to put her left arm through the other strap as well, to protect her back.

Thorstein and Helga's eyes met for just a second before he slapped the horse. Unn could hear the screams of baby Olaf as Helga thundered away, and watched as Thorstein unslung his bow, and set arrow after arrow to it, dodging the arrows of his attackers and killing a man with each of his that he shot until he nocked the last one in his quiver.

Only one of the men was on horseback, and he cut to the side of Thorstein, riding hard in pursuit of Helga.

Thor glanced at the man running up to him before turning and shooting his last arrow through the back of the man on the horse, and it was that moment that gave his attackers the advantage they needed. Arrow after arrow pierced him, and still he unsheathed both his long sword and dagger, fighting with both in the style that Unn knew, just by witnessing it, that he had learned from her father. He killed two more of them before the last one cut him down with an axe.

Unn's tears flowed, but the cavern in her heart that had been created by the mystery of his death felt filled. She turned to look at him, still sad, but proud. Hel, fierce and terrible, smiled as well, and gestured to the right, where Thorstein had come from.

It was now an open hall, vast, with a long table set with a magnificent feast of roast boar, and pitchers of mead. Unn saw a vision of herself, sitting in the center. Thorstein disappeared from her side and appeared next to the Unn at the table.

"Valhöll", she whispered. Hel nodded and gestured. Unn laughed. "Me? I'm not a warrior."

Hel stepped towards her, the two sides of her face both the most beautiful and horrifying vision Unn had ever seen. She reached a white hand out to Unn, and as she touched her, Unn's vision deepened, and she could see both inward and outward, to a future that ended in a battle on a plain, wolves and men, fighting the son of the tyrant who had come to claim her. She felt herself fear for the lives of her men and children, and she felt the glory of each adversary that she felled, surprising herself with the number she killed, up until the moment she felt the death blow strike her, and then all fear and uncertainty was replaced with acceptance, and then.... understanding.

The next instant she was at the feast table of Valhöll, the axe wound in her chest oozing blood, and her appetite ravenous. The boar meat was the best she had ever tasted, and her son Thor was at her right hand, laughing and listening to her recount her exploits before she was killed.

It wasn't painful now, to remember how his laugh filled a room or how his attention felt like the sun when it was upon you, because he was at her side again. Teasing her, asking her to pass him a knife... until the doors behind them burst, and a horde of monstrous beasts fell upon them.

But then they were side by side, fighting, and Unn felt again the headiness of indulging love for battle, the feel of an axe in the hand, the sight of her giant son killing monsters, the power of standing at his back and fully engaging every ounce of strength in her, until an enemy's blade slit her throat, and she fell to her knees.

Thor was cut down as well, and she watched him fall again. But this time, the same knowledge, the same understanding, that this was part of the way it was meant to be, washed over her again. And this time, when she came to at the table once more, her peace was even greater, and the mead tasted even sweeter...even as she felt it pass through her open throat and soak her chest.

Time after time it happened; foes falling on them, a battle that was greater each time and sharpened their skills each time.

And deepened their knowledge each time. Their love of the moment. Their peace and their joy.

Unn felt as if years passed in this way. She felt pride. Calm. Purpose. Each foe that died appeared at the table afterwards as a brother and she understood that this was the path to Ragnarök, when the last of those who believed themselves to be enemies would be brought into the fold. That conflict would end all conflict, and they would all see that they had been brethren all along. They would continue to fight together each night, not to best each other only... but to feel the exhilaration of battle. Free of fear, free of purpose.

Each resurrection made her understand more and more that she was both the center of all things, and just a thread in a tapestry. Each rebirth deepened the connection with the circle that was each generation dying and giving way to the next, on and on, throughout time. They were all together, they were all distinct.

Hel in her dark power was there, and Unn watched her in battle, watched her govern, watched her look upon each addition to the table with her grave stare, watched each recipient of it bask in the glow of her acknowledgement and the enlightenment it gave.

Another guest at the table was a man pale as Hel, with the same silver hair and white-gray eyes, the same pointed ears. He watched Unn closely and smiled a knowing smile each time she looked his way. She noticed that his countenance changed now and again; one time he might be a woman, one time a wolf—but he was always recognizable to her. In the battles, he would sometimes fight at her side, using feints and false surrenders just like those her father and brothers had taught her.

Other times it was his blade that killed her.

One night when she awoke at her place, and her eyes raised to his, his hair was like dark golden mead, curly and wild, and his eyes were just a bit lighter, like summer honey, wide and large and laughing, ringed with long brown lashes. He had a long nose and a tooth to the side of his mouth was missing, only visible when he laughed, which he did now.

Unn laughed too, because she realized now, as he appeared to her as a mirror image of herself, that he was the Trickster, and that she had, time and again, called out to that part of herself that was him when she searched her mind for answers that others would not expect.

From time to time she glanced across the meadow, at the Unn in the carved chair. She was old now, and her hair was gray. The Bjorn and Olaf who stood at her sides were men, middle-aged, and there was a crowd behind them.

Unn knew without asking now that this was Sessrúmnir. These were those who had fallen not in battle, but faded away into a peaceful death. It wasn't worse, it wasn't better; it was different, but also a mirror of Valhöll.

She could tell that the crowds came to the Unn in the carved chair for guidance, for wisdom, and that they loved and honored her.

There was power in that Unn, too, but she held no axe. She did not hone her marksmanship nightly in a battle against otherworldly creatures. She did not laugh with her fellow dead over their killing of each other.

Instead of a leather jerkin and chain mail, she wore a long green dress, the same vivid hue as the field in spring; her hair grew fairer and fairer with each cycle, eventually turning as white as the wheat before the harvest.

There was a table on that side, too, a slowed image of the feast in Valhöll. The diners excused themselves each night to bed to sleep, a tiny, peaceful version of the death that the Valhöll Unn and her companions experienced.

Finally, Unn felt herself pulled away from the table, and she was in the center of the meadow again, in her shift, rain coming down around her, but not dampening her.

Out of the mist in front of her, a dark figure in a hooded cloak appeared, walking towards her.

A raven on each shoulder, and as he came close enough for his face to be visible under his hood, Unn could see that one eye in the white face was covered, and another, white-gray, stared at her intently.

He stood directly in front of her, and from his sleeves came his hands, each holding a stone. His pale eye looked first to her right, where Thorstein still sat, at the table in Valhöll, and Unn could see herself sitting beside him, her body bloody and damaged—one half of her face decayed, like that of Hel—her hair long and tangled with mud and blood, her eyes full of laughter and cunning and wildness and freedom.

She looked to the being in front of her again, and his pale eye turned to her left.

The Unn who sat in the chair was very old now. The crowd around her had grown until she could not see its end, and they all looked at Unn with love.

There were wolves all throughout the throng, and their eyes were on Unn too.

This Unn was peaceful, and there was a type of strength emanating from her as well.

But there was no Thorstein.

Unn looked down again at the stones in this being's hands and understood that she was being asked to choose.

Her right hand rose slightly, then her left. Thoughts began to race through her mind and she quieted them immediately with the remembrance of the feeling of the table at Valhöll, and the discovery of her own cunning and power. She raised her hands to mimic a gesture of confusion, and then, as quick as she could...she snatched both stones from the outstretched hands in front of her.

Instantly, she snapped awake.

She was standing in the meadow to the side of her cabin, and it was raining...she was soaked through, and it was freezing.

Unn turned slowly towards her cabin and saw The Eye standing in the doorway, watching her, along with Hord, who was holding a heavy wool blanket. When Unn's gaze met The Eye's, they turned to Hord and nodded, indicating that the tea's trance had worn off. Hord trotted out to wrap Unn in the blanket and help her inside.

Once by the fire, Unn nodded to him.

"Go ahead with our plan."

Hord left with the men to begin building the settlement where they would make their home. Unn was quiet for some time, sitting by the fire and weaving. She nodded or shook her head when asked questions but did not seek out conversation for many days.

After several weeks, just as the snow began to melt and the white flowers that Helgi's people called Candlemas flowers (Unn and her children called them fairymaids) began to show, Hord and a few men returned.

Unn went to her brother and thanked him for his hospitality.

Helgi gave her ten horses as a gift and gave Olaf and Bjorn longbows and arrows. Tears came to Unn's eyes when she saw that the bows were carved with images of Ullr, the Norse god of winter and hunting, on skis with a bow in his hands.

"My father gave me my own bow just like this when I was even younger than you two," Helgi said gruffly. "You are well past the time when you should be helping the men hunt. Practice often, as I've shown you."

She bade Helga and Olaf and Bjorn pack up the furs and dried food they had accumulated in their time with Helgi's people.

She kissed Yngvild the Fair goodbye and made her promise to send word west when she was due with her first child by her new husband.

And then she mounted her horse and followed Hord to the settlement he and the wolf men had built, to the west.

Jane closed the book and laid it down carefully next to her bed. She caught her own reflection in the mirror and forced herself to smile. As she did so, a clear, almost audible thought popped into her head.

This isn't the end; this is the true beginning.

Downstairs it was quiet, and Jane had to walk through to an area off the garage to find Howard and Robin.

Robin was wrapped in a blanket, intently focused on Howard, who was speaking quietly, but stopped when he saw Jane.

Jane smiled and went to Robin, kneeling down and kissing the forehead of the baby who had always been an old soul. They always had a part of her heart she suspected had been reserved for the one who would experience too much. Or at least...what Jane had always secretly feared would be too much. Too much struggle, misunderstanding, cruelty, being-on-the-outsideness, and now...way, way too much psychic risk.

Oddly, it felt like it all made sense now, and instead of the desperate protectiveness and low-level anxiety she had always felt about Robin, their safety, their future...now she felt calm, and understanding... and pride.

"This is who you really are, who you're destined to be," Jane said quietly, feeling as if the words were coming of their own volition. "I understand, and I'm here."

Robin grinned, widely and slowly. "That's the spirit, Mom! Now, who's ready to watch me 'shroom out?"

Howard, not smiling, held out a cup.

He looked at Jane and jerked his head to the doorway, where a couch cushion sat. She dutifully went and lowered herself down, outside of the room, in the shadow of the next. An observer, struggling to hold on to her objectivity. Howard stood too, bowing down to give the cup to Robin. "We'll be here, watching and waiting for your return." He then said something in what sounded to Jane like Norse, repeating it in English.

"Your line's past, and its future. The path between worlds."

He gestured to Jane with his head and she scooted over to give him space to sit down as well.

They both watched, their breathing audible, as Robin looked into the cup, and then without hesitating, downed it in one gulp. Jane could hear the slight intake of breath from Howard, but he said nothing. For an instant, she wanted to laugh at him for taking her to task over being worried and casting a pall on the atmosphere.

Robin breathed in and out. "Wow. That's disgusting. Who knew an ancestor cocktail was so gross." They sat for a moment, tapping their hands on their knees. Jane could tell they were trying not to look at the doorway.

"Am I supposed to...just hang out? How long will this take to kick in? Is it like mushrooms?"

Again, Jane could feel the exertion of Howard trying to be calm. "Just...be patient. Relax. Wait."

What felt like an eternity passed.

Robin let out a whistle, tapping their knees. Jane wanted to say, "Don't be nervous," but stayed silent. *This must be them, alone.*

She tried to be motionless, like Howard, and she tried not to sniffle. She noticed that there was a space on the wall where it looked like a clock had been and wondered if Howard had removed it.

Suddenly a thud. Jane's heart leapt to her throat when she saw Robin had dropped to the floor, hard, and Howard's hand shot out to stop her from moving to her child, even though it looked like Robin was convulsing.

She looked into his eyes, and they cautioned her to be silent.

Seconds seemed to drag, and Jane agonized, telling herself to ignore every maternal instinct that screamed, *"Call 911! Go check their breathing! Wake them up!"*

This is the beginning. Not the end.

Jane felt herself shaking her head, no, no, no!

She looked at Howard again, the dull stab of fear, feeling as if it was going through her heart like an actual knife. He shook his head as well, touching a finger to her lips, willing her silently with his eyes to be still. *This can't be right*–Jane argued with herself, against the feeling of *knowing* that this was in fact, the right thing, tears coming to her eyes as she watched Robin shake. A low moan emanated from Robin and the sound broke Jane's resolve. She made to stand, wrenching her arm away from Howard's grasp as he attempted to stop her and pushing him away. But as her foot touched the floor to stand...Robin stilled.

The very air in the room changed.

Suddenly Jane knew they were exactly where the cup of henbane, ashes, and blood was supposed to take Robin...between worlds.

Robin, who Jane could sense, feel, was Robin-but-not-fully-Robin, sat up.

There was no sound, but Jane and Howard's shallow breathing. Jane tore her eyes away from Not-Robin to look down at Howard's fingernails digging into her wrist, and could see the hair standing up on his arms.

Movement.

Not-Robin stood, slowly, unsteadily, drunkenly.

When their face turned, Jane felt the blood drain from her own face and would have had to stop from crying out, if her throat hadn't closed involuntarily.

Robin's eyes, both iris and sclera, were opaque, pale gray, and filmy.

They watched, motionless, as Not-Robin looked around the room, not seeing them, finally coming to stare at the window. They walked to it, looking out, touching the glass almost reverently. Slowly their eyes went over every part of the room, stopping on the backpack laid on the table. They walked to it, carefully reaching out to touch the pin on the front...the black heart, with the teddy bear face, Xs for eyes.

Time seemed to stand still, Not-Robin staring at the image and touching it.

A loop of understanding closed in Jane's mind.

No, not a loop...a sphere.

What seemed like a lifetime passed before they turned, and caught sight of them, sitting in the doorway. They crossed, and slowly knelt, looking first at Jane, then at Howard.

Jane felt her own eyes widening involuntarily in horror at the sight of the opaque gray stare, and it was a stare, eyes almost unblinking, up close.

Not-Robin tilted their head curiously at her...but broke into a smile at the sight of Howard.

"Hvar em ek, gamli vinr?"

The voice was like something from a horror movie. Deep and sotto. Melodious and scratchy.

Tears were filling Howard's eyes and spilling onto his cheeks. He smiled, nothing like Jane had seen since meeting him–a true, happy smile that lit up his face. He sniffed, and his voice was shaky as he responded, quietly.

""Vér erum mörg ár frá heimkynnum, vinr minn."

Not-Robin gave a chilling half laugh, then looked confused, smiled again, touching Howard's face and then his clothes, gently, all in rapid succession.

"Ertu enn á lífi, gamli?" the voice was a whisper this time. Howard simply nodded.

Looking around, above and below, and seeing the room behind and beyond them, they stood slowly and stepped through, walking slowly and continuing to observe the environment.

Howard held Jane's arm, shaking his head when she started to ask what was being said, what was happening.

Not-Robin stopped in front of a large mirror, hanging in the foyer, looking at their reflection. Jane felt Howard tense, and wondered if this was a danger, Not-Robin seeing the image of real Robin.

They stared at the reflection for some time, reaching out to touch it cautiously.

"Leitarðu, barn?" The creepy whisper. Jane could barely hear it. An even more unsettling chuckle came next.

Both Howard and Jane jumped as Not-Robin fell, heavily, to the floor, their head bouncing off the tile like a bowling ball. Jane cried out, but Howard's hand stifled it before the sound left her mouth, his head shaking slowly, his eyes telling her it was part of it, and that Robin would be alright.

More shaking, and Jane began to shake as well. Doubt swirled again. *"You need to call 911! If this is a seizure–you'll never forgive yourself if this kills them–"* she squeezed her eyes shut, willing herself to trust.

A scrabbling noise opened her eyes and she saw Robin–because the energy and mannerisms of Robin were again present–get to their knees and stand, looking around as if searching for something.

As they stepped into the light, Jane felt herself involuntarily draw back in terror. Robin's eyes were now wholly and completely black.

They grabbed a marker from a jar near the telephone on the wall, knocking it to the floor and shattering it. Howard held Jane fast, preventing her from rushing to protect, and, she realized now, hinder.

The cap came off the marker, and Robin ran to the closest wall, marking, scribbling furiously.

Howard and Jane could not see what was being written on the wall, they just sat, silent, waiting. Jane had no idea how much time passed before Robin dropped the marker, and walked to the middle of the room and sat down, cross-legged, on the floor.

She and Howard sat and watched as they sat, staring and silent, for what seemed like an incredibly long time.

The sunlight faded even more and darkness began to shroud the room, but Robin didn't move a muscle.

Jane's legs fell asleep but she stayed motionless as well, only occasionally looking at Howard, whose eyes never left her child.

Finally, a shrug and a groan broke the spell. Jane could feel the atmosphere shift, and the air was once again normal. When they turned, Jane could see white sclera and Robin's golden-brown irises.

She jumped to her feet, rushing to help Robin up and to the couch.

"Fuck, that was weird."

Jane felt relief flood her body and tears burst out of her, tears of relief she didn't realize she was suppressing until she sobbed them out onto Robin's neck.

"Jesus, Mom, I'm fine, it's okay." Robin collapsed onto the couch, eyes closed. "I just need to rest for a minute."

Instantly they were in a deep sleep.

Jane shook them, looking at Howard. "They hit their head pretty hard, they shouldn't sleep!"

"No," he pulled her hand away, gently, touching her shoulder and helping her up. "Let them rest."

He turned and pointed to the wall.

"They've had a big night."

10

The wall was covered, completely covered, in what Jane could only guess were runes. There were a few drawings, which included what looked like a model of the earth, with another globe superimposed over it, a diagram that looked like a house in the middle, and a family tree with maybe fifty areas for names.

She stared, feeling her mouth fall open. Howard was shouting for everyone, and when Abe entered the room, Howard took him by the arm and pointed.

"Mé olemme vasti várt."

"Okay, enough; English, please."

"This is our answer." Howard was excited, and again Jane was astonished at how different he was, just as he had been when Robin/Not Robin was staring at him with those eyes that would freeze the blood of any rational person.

"What does it mean? Is Robin okay?" Lucas, not typically a tender brother, was leaning over Robin with concern. Anne Marie knelt beside the couch on the floor.

"Robin is fine; they're resting. This…" Howard gestured to the crazy looking wall. "Is the result of their efforts."

"It looks like something that would be on a serial killer's wall," Anne Marie wrinkled her nose.

"What does it say?" Jane stood beside Howard, still unable to believe what she had witnessed.

"I think these are notes Robin wanted to get down, in case they forgot." Howard looked at everyone else. "It's normal for someone experiencing *seiðr* to feel they won't remember what they are experiencing, when they do this for the first time, and try to write it all down."

"For the FIRST time?" Jane's eyes widened. "How the fuck do people do this over and over?"

"What was it like?"

"What happened?"

"What did Robin do?"

Jane waved the questions away, and for what felt like the hundredth time fought the urge to laugh as she saw Abe and Howard's faces and realized the influx of young minds into the mix was not something they had been prepared for.

"Just…let's let Howard get through this and tell us what our plan is, there will be time to explain all of that later."

"Will there?" Anne Marie shrugged in the corner. "I mean, if we have killers after us, how do we know we have a 'later?'"

"Well, if we don't," Jane fought to keep her voice calm, "Then we need to focus on the part that might help us first, right?" She turned to Howard, who pointed back to the wall.

"This is Robin telling us how to proceed. First, we need to bring as many allies here as possible. Abe, we need all of Ridgeline here, if we can get them. This is a last stand."

The phrase seemed to have the same effect on all of them. They looked at each other, hit by the weight of the moment.

Abe nodded. "I'll start making calls. Richard," Richard stepped forward. "Go tell the men outside to change shifts. The first watch needs to get some rest."

He gestured to the wall, and to Howard. "This…might work. But it might not."

"What does it say? Come on," Jane waved at her children. "We can't read runes. Please tell us what all this says!"

"It says we can reason with the Brotherhood today," Robin's voice made them all jump, and they turned to see them sitting up on the couch. "But we'll have to survive a fight first. We'll have to defend ourselves. They'll only listen if we survive, and only bargain if we are able to take a very specific captive."

Jane was at their side immediately, holding their hand too tight. Robin laughed.

"Mom, come on, I'm fine." Then a curious tilt of the head. "Did you watch? What was it like?"

"It was fucking terrifying. What was it like for you?"

"Like a dream. A weird dream." Their voice softened and they got up, slowly walking to Howard. Robin's smile and the touch on the shoulder seemed old, friendly, and familiar in way beyond what two people who had just met would have.

"I saw it. Where you came from, where you lived. It was beautiful."

"Yes," Howard said, hoarsely, eyes shining. "It was."

"Were they here? While I was there? Is that how it works?"

"Yes, yes, and…yes, I think so."

Robin nodded, and looked to the wall again, seeming surprised.

"What, what's this language?" They shrugged. "It doesn't matter. I remember." They turned to face the family.

"Everyone here today will need to fire a gun. Will probably need to kill someone. But we must defend ourselves."

They took a breath, and with the presence of a preacher, continued.

"This isn't going to feel right in some ways, but we have to live. And we will, if we band together and decide that we're going to get through. All of us can survive. I don't know if we will, but I know that we can.."

"There's a man with them, he's young, like, Lucas's age, at least, he looks like he is, and he'll be wearing a black hat, like a baseball cap, and a black hunting vest. We must capture him, and he has to be alive, but everyone else, we may have to kill."

Robin looked at her mother. "You've lost enough people for now. There's been enough death in this family. No one needs to die today, if we play it right, but everyone here has to understand…" Their voice rose an octave and it made everyone stand straighter, "it is them, or us. You will not survive if you don't understand and accept that even though we need this one man alive, you'll have to kill someone else today. Or maybe several someones, to protect yourself and the person next to you. Do you all understand?"

Jane knew immediately it was for the benefit of herself and the other siblings that Robin was saying this. The three men in the room had lived long lives, in other eras where violence was common, and she had a distinct feeling they were not strangers to it, even with all of the gentleness shown to her and her children.

Jane had been raised by a tough man, and had brought her children up to defend themselves and do it well, but only as a last resort. All knew how to execute a judo throw, thanks to lessons that Jane was able to provide and take herself, in exchange for writing the gym's blog posts and social media, and they could all shoot a gun. They knew to punch without breaking fingers, but they had been taught to talk their way out of trouble, and apart from a few fights in the tough neighborhoods of their upbringing, all were opposed to violence, in theory.

Could all that be undone in a five-minute pep talk?

Jane began to sweat. Would they be able to do it?

"They understand," said Howard, again seeming as if he'd read her mind.

"They know."

None of the children said a word, but all nodded, as did Robin. They had changed, held themself differently, spoke differently, even gave off a new energy.

"When we get them to pause, to talk to us, they'll come in, and I'll speak to them."

"What?" Jane wondered if any part of this would occur without her feeling more afraid than she had during the last.

"Yes, they're going to want to parley," the word sounded bizarre in Robin's voice, "I'm going to tell them we're all part of the same family, they have nothing to fear from us. I'm going to offer an alternative to wiping us off the face of the earth, that will also solve their dropping birth rate, which is what revitalized this blood feud they have with our family."

"Wait, *what*? What's a blood feud? God, this sounds so Neanderthal. It's insane, I don't understand half of what you're saying." Anne Marie was shaking her head. "I still don't know why we can't get the police involved. Doesn't the, loogahoo, or whatever have its own police? Howard, you said it was an ecosystem all its own..."

"It is," Howard began.

"But they can't get involved," Robin said, almost to themselves, looking to Howard for confirmation.

"This has to be settled between the branches in the blood feud. I saw it all." "The men who killed Renee, our grandmother, Pappy killed them, and then when more came to kill Aunt Kimmy and Mom, he killed them too, which seems like self-defense, and an agreement was struck to let it go. Now Pappy has died and the son of one of the men wants revenge. Kimmy was revenge for one of the men who died, and they want to kill Mom because, well, because she was supposed to have died, and didn't."

Jane stood. "Then let them take me!" She looked around. "If it saves all of you."

The room burst into a cacophony of rejection.

Robin shushed everyone and looked at their mother. "I know what you're thinking; it won't work. This guy and his men, they're beyond that; they want to extinguish all of us. They would kill you and still come after us when the blood price is paid. They believe tamers simply existing is causing the *lugaru* birth rate to drop; but I don't think it is."

"I believe if we can show them *lugaru* who interbreed with tamers are the key to continuing the condition, they'll let up." Robin turned to Howard.

"Is it supported by what you've seen in *lugaru* research? Does the tamer gene support *lugaru* continuation?"

Howard nodded, a surprised look on his face. "I have some research I can pull up-Kimmy's was still in the very early stages–to support you. If they'll listen. They have their own researchers, but many of them are shackled by their religion and small mindedness.

If there are intellectuals among them who will listen to science, we can appeal to them."

"There are no intellectuals in The Brotherhood," Richard spat, "They're gangsters. Worse than that, they're gangsters stuck in the Stone Age."

"That's not true across the board," Howard responded, softly. "I might even be able to get someone here, an objective third party, if we can get them to agree." He turned to Jane and the kids. "We have traditions, and they're serious. No one wants to get involved if it's a blood feud, or will expose them, but if I can make the argument that it's about continuation of the species, someone I know will come. After the fighting is over."

"Call them." Robin's tone was calm, but authoritative. Jane felt a surge of pride and respect, especially when Howard quickly rose and went to the other room.

"We have a cache of weapons here," Richard said quietly, pointing to the stairway that led to the basement. "I'm going to start bringing them up, and we'll look at securing the doors and windows…we have barricades and shutters that will be helpful."

"I'll help." Lucas started to follow him, but Robin raised a hand.

"We have some time; we can save that for later. First, I'd like Mom to read us a story."

Lucas seemed incredulous, and even Anne Marie laughed.

"Are you serious? Do you think that's the best use of time, here, Robin?"

Robin turned to Jane, smiling as if they were talking about going to an amusement park. "The book you're reading, Mom. You're at the part we need to hear now." Robin looked at Lucas and Anne Marie. "The ancestor that began all of this had to fight a battle, too. I think a little family story time might get us in the mood."

Jane went to her room to get the book.

When she came back, Lucas and Anne Marie were cross-legged on the floor, with impatient, uncomfortable expressions on their faces. Robin was sitting on the couch with a space next to them that they patted, with a grin when they saw Jane.

The feeling of *deja-vu*–the guttural, bone-deep feeling of memory of the times when they were all small, and gathered similarly, waiting for her to bring the copy of *Watership Down*, or *Lord of the Rings*, or any number of books that she read to them–it was like a wave, pushing her down, then buoying her up.

She sat, looking at their faces, wondering if this was going to be the last time they sat like this. Robin smiled, reaching over, like Regular Robin, pulling Jane's hair out from where it was caught in her sweatshirt collar. "It's okay, Mom. It's all going to be okay. Just read it."

"Go to the part about the Sunset War. After they reach their new home, by the sea."

Unn and her people reached their new settlement after two days of travel. When they arrived on the second evening, Unn could see fires from inside the palisade, which jutted out from a section of cleared forest. Two longhouses were visible, only just though, because trees had been left growing in and around them.

Hord pointed out the sentries in treehouses, similar to her brother Helgi's, and said that from them you could see the coast for miles.

He explained that a second set of treehouses were further back in the woods, as a retreat, and that the cattle were being grazed in a pasture to the north, with the forest providing a natural fence.

"This is the best of the land," he said. They sat on horseback, listening to the crash of the sea against the rocks that lined the shore at the bottom of the escarpment directly under them. "There is room beyond for growth, but for now..." his pause told Unn that he understood what was coming, "...this will be our best defense."

After everyone had settled in, that first night, after they had eaten at the table in the longhouse that ran its length, Unn stood.

"Sleep well," she said. "Tomorrow we begin a new way of life."

The men and Helga and the children looked at each other, only Hord–who was Unn's closest counsel in all things, along with The Eye–seemed to understand what this meant.

"We will wake early," Unn said, "and set about the tasks of building our home here, and we will train." She looked with particular meaning at Olaf and Bjorn, and Helga. "We have very good natural defenses here, and if we keep our wits and skills sharp, this can be a haven for generations."

"The sheep and cattle we've procured are one line to prosperity, and the seeds I've brought from Írland will be another." Unn's look became serious. "We will eventually have a harbor that will give us the sea, but without the ability to protect ourselves, none of this amounts to anything." That was all she said, and after the food was gone and the ale drunk, and the table cleared and stood on its end for the night, all retired to their sleeping corners, with three men going for the first watch.

In the morning, Unn woke Helga, Bjorn, and Olaf early. The men were already outside, and after Bjorn and Olaf helped see to the animals, they met their mother and grandmother in a clearing behind the longhouse.

Hord and the man called Ulf were there, with swords and the boys' bows and arrows.

"First," Unn said, "You'll train with the sword."

Each boy looked tentatively to his mother as he was handed a sword–they had only practiced with wooden ones until now–and when Ulf raised his and struck the first time...each boy fell to the ground in turn. Instead of barking instructions and swinging slowly, as he had done before, Ulf immediately stabbed at the ground, causing his charge to roll quickly and scramble to his feet.

Unn reached out to touch Helga's arm as she started, and shook her head when Helga opened her mouth to protest.

In a glance that was so quick it could not be seen by most, Ulf looked to Unn as Olaf dropped his guard and Unn nodded, equally imperceptibly. Ulf struck the boy to the ground and raised his arms again, as if to strike.

Unn squeezed Helga's wrist as she saw the boy's mother clench her fist.

Olaf swung clear, jumped to his feet, and almost caught Ulf with a two-handed swing aimed for his midsection. Ulf smiled briefly and then resumed his attack.

The same was repeated with Bjorn, and when Ulf was done with them both, each boy was covered in mud and bleeding from either the nose or mouth.

Ulf took the swords and gestured to their bows and arrows. "Pick them up."

He pointed at a target, painted on a bale of hay, and then gestured at the path that had been cut through the woods, circling past the pasture, around the second settlement, and then back to the main longhouse courtyard.

"Race the path, and the first one to get back and hit the bullseye wins."

Both boys looked at each other, then scrambled for their bows and quivers and took off, hooting the battle call of the wolf men.

When they were out of earshot, Helga began to speak but Unn quieted her by handing her one of the boys' swords.

"Now it's your turn, daughter."

For the entire time the boys were gone, Unn swung the sword at her gentle daughter in law, pushing against her weak defense, fighting the urge to correct her and simply testing her strength.

Helga tripped on her skirts, and at one point, when Unn struck the sword from her hands, its blade nicked her forearm.

Instead of stopping the attack Unn put the tip of her sword to Helga's throat, noticing the fear and then the anger that joined the defeat on the woman's face. After a moment, Unn helped her to her feet, and looked her in the eyes.

"You will get better," she said softly. "Wear pants tomorrow."

Helga had not been raised by a shieldmaiden mother, or allowed to train and roughhouse with her brothers, Unn reminded herself. She also had a fear on her that had sunk its teeth in at the death of Thorstein, and Unn knew that if it was not removed, all the training in the world would be useless.

The boys came running back. Olaf was in the lead but Bjorn already had his arrow to the string and when Olaf paused to reach for his, Bjorn knocked him aside and took aim. It missed, but in the time it took Olaf to rise from the ground and nock his arrow, Bjorn was able to take a second shot and this one hit its mark.

He exclaimed, and received laughs and back claps from both Ulf and Hord as reward. Unn could feel Helga's anger as she watched Olaf's shoulders sag with disappointment, and Helga said, under her breath and only to Unn, "He won only by cheating."

Unn corrected her. "There is no such thing as cheating in a battle."

Both boys were tired, bloody, and eager for more.

All day they shadowed Ulf and Hord, bringing logs to the growing palisade around their settlement, improving their horsemanship, and getting used to the feel of the short swords and daggers that they would now carry with them.

Unn and Helga made bread, venison stew with meat hunted by the men and roots found in the forest, and at the end of the day, all gathered around the long table and ate their fill of good food, and drank their fill of the mead Unn had made while at her brother's.

Unn stood, before going to bed, and raised her horn. Everyone else did as well.

"This is our life now. We will work the fields and the livestock, we will train to be the best fighters we can be...and we will close our days with each other, and the pleasures food and drink can offer us."

And in her heart, each night, Unn closed her eyes after she said this and felt again the rush of love and understanding she had felt at each death in her vision of Valhöll.

The next morning, they did it all again.

And again, and again.

Hord and Unn rode the escarpment, planning for the harbor. They rode the perimeter of the settlement, and Unn ordered tree house guard posts at the first point where visitors would become visible.

Pits were dug that could house archers, or serve as hiding places. Olaf and Bjorn practiced shooting and then running to each ditch.

A high field that would give them the best advantage over an enemy approaching was chosen.

Certain parts of the surrounding forest were cleared, certain parts were left wild, and other parts had narrow paths cut into them, and gates built to hide them, covered with brush and short trees.

The days grew warmer and warmer, until they were in a sweet summer, filled with berries and rabbit meat, and late-night games and laughing. Wine brewed with fruit, knorrs being built to put out into the sea from the newly built harbor, hidden to anyone approaching from the south by the jut of the escarpment directly west of their settlement, now a series of huts and three longhouses.

They had built more guard houses to the east, and the wolf men had encountered travelers from the tribes even further north, trading with them, but always keeping their own counsel about their numbers, and about their leader, a woman who all of them thought of as their chieftain.

"We are as prepared for our enemy as we can be," Unn said at dinner one night, looking at the wolf men, her child who was an Eye, her daughter-in-law Helga, and the boys Bjorn and Olaf, who were tanned brown, growing more muscular and faster by the day, and who now carried themselves a little less as children.

'This is a good way to live," she continued. "Enjoying the fruits of our work, but also remaining vigilant, and ready to do battle."

Helga had done well, learning to wrestle, and even liking it a little. She could defend herself reasonably well, and she had begun to ride more and weave less. One of the wolf men, Gurund, had always been fond of her, but she had never looked at him more than once or twice. Now, she flirted with him, laughed at his jokes, and Unn's heart lightened a little bit more.

When the day finally came, Unn was in the fields, helping the Eye harvest oats.

The Eye stood, slowly, and said, "Did you hear that?"

Unn had heard nothing, but also stood. The hair on the back of her neck was raised. She dusted off her hands. "Go find Helga and tell her to be ready."

By the time Unn had made her way to the guard house nearest the palisade, she heard it; a wolf's howl.

A horn would let attackers know that they had been seen, so it had been decided that the wolf men would howl as a warning and run in wolf form– many times faster than a man–should enemies appear.

Unn could see a wolf running towards her at full speed as she stepped out of the gate. She nodded to the guard who sent a runner to assemble everyone. Unn's leather jerkin and gloves were in the guardhouse, along with everyone else's, and as she stepped inside and began pulling off her apron and blouse, the rest of the camp came in as well.

They pulled weapons off walls in silence, the strongest left the few helmets for others, and the wooden shields lined by the door were picked up.

The black wolf, Hord, changed into man form in the courtyard. As he stood, naked, he pointed towards the south.

"At least a hundred men," he said breathlessly. "Two dozen or more mounted. We have to hurry to make it–they're going at a brisk pace."

They began to march, double time. Unn felt her legs beginning to shake, even before they had gone a quarter of the way.

Her vision became clear, her hearing sharp, and she resisted the urge to look behind to the house where Helga had stayed, resisted the inclination to wonder if the children were armed well and wearing the leathers, chain mail and helmets she had set aside for them. They had all trained for this, everyone was ready. All was as it was meant to be.

She could see the troop of men pushing into the mouth of the valley that she and Hord had chosen as a battleground and prepared for this purpose. "We are meeting on my ground," she reminded herself. 'We have made this place ready to our advantage.'

When she stopped, the rest of them stopped. Unn climbed atop a boulder, flattened at the top, that surveyed the valley, and as soon as she did, the people following her fanned out.

She could hear the cry of the men below them as they saw them. Unn turned to face the men and her children.

"Do you see the whip bearers behind the last row? Do you hear that sound?" Amidst the shouts, the crack of whips could be heard. Unn looked at every face as they understood what it meant.

"They are conscripts–forced to this fight. He only has slaves. I..." Unn felt the salt of tears burning her throat. "I have brothers."

A howl rose.

"We know what to do, but each one of us must still fight their part as they see fit. As for me, this is how I will do it!"

Unn turned to face her attackers again, and threw her wooden shield in their direction, down the hill, and raised her sword with a shout. A shout that only deepened as she turned her face to the sky, as if she were declaring to the gods that even if they were against her...she did not care.

The shouting behind her increased, and from the sides of her vision, Unn could see every man beside her throw his shield down the hill as she had. They screamed at the sky as well, they beat their chests with their swords, and Unn laughed like a child.

Now her arms were shaking as well, but she jumped from the boulder and gave place to The Eye, wearing no armor, carrying no weapon, clad only in a white robe, turned so that the hood was hanging down in front.

Ten wolf men, in man form, slid naked down the hill. A cry came up from the attackers and arrows flew...landing at least 50 feet from them.

The Eye stood, looking first to the approaching attackers, and then down to the men below them.

Then The Eye slowly raised the hood so that it covered their face, and lifted hands skyward, calling on Odin to change the warriors into wolves and to make Unn invincible if he knew her cause was just.

They had rehearsed it many times. The men below them began to advance, naked, shouting the same prayer.

Unn raised her sword, waiting for the men to reach the point where they would be audible to the attackers, where the words of their cry to Odin to turn them into wolves would be heard by those coming against them, who were following the son of the man who had felt entitled to her and who was not satisfied with gaining her husband's kingdom.

She had never seen Turg, the third son of Earl Einar, but there was a man with a silver helm in the front, eyes staring ahead, head unmoving.

He was flanked by two spearmen, and Unn knew without being told that this was the man who would be happy with nothing less than her head.

Ejgil of the wolf men was the first to take an arrow and fall. Unn gasped. The rest of them continued forward, until they reached the point where their voices could be heard.

Then they shifted into wolves in front of Turg and his men.

"Hold," Unn said, keeping her sword aloft until she could see the faces of the men in the front line and hear screams of terror.

"Now!!"

They all slid to the bottom of the hill, save for a line of men who would guard a retreat, if necessary.

As Turg's men reached the wolf men in the front line, arrows fell upon them from the forest to the west. Almost at the same time, arrows flew from the forest to the east.

In the chaos of Turg's taskmasters whipping the terrified recruits into a charge and foot soldiers and mounted mercenaries reeling from side to side, trying to see the hidden archers in the woods, Unn willed herself not to look and make sure that her son and grandson were not visible in the tree stands where they shot from. No more arrows came, and as men were dispatched to each side to engage, she screamed at the top of her lungs to her small army to take advantage of the winnowed numbers.

"Forward!!"

Wolves tore into legs, swords swung, Unn heard something–ax? Knife? --fly past her head.

She felt her own panicked breathing and willed it to slow, parrying a soldier's sword aimed toward her gut.

The force of the thrust and the blow that he threw to her face stunned her, and she had an instant realization that no man who had trained with her had showed such force.

The clang of metal and grunts and screams filled the air.

Unn knocked her opponent's sword from his lax grip and slashed his neck. He fell to the ground gushing blood, just in time for her to avoid having her head severed by an axe swing. She stumbled, falling backwards, her breath leaving her in a gasp. The soldier swung again and she dodged, kicking at his knee and felling him, scrabbling for her axe and striking him in the chest.

He rose, bellowing like a moose, and grabbed her. Unn screamed, elbowing his neck where it was exposed and then aiming for his nose. He punched her and she reeled to the ground, stars blurring her vision, and again she realized that she had only tasted a portion of men's strength before now–even from her husband, who she had thought the most brutal of his kind.

The man raised his axe for the death blow and Unn had a flash of her father, her children–then he was gone. Hord stepped into her field of vision, shouting at her.

"Get to your feet!!"

She staggered up, unable to see her sword or axe anywhere. Men were everywhere, muddy, almost indiscernible from each other, blood was flying, horses' cries and soldiers' shouts rang amidst the constant, overwhelming clang of metal against metal.

Suddenly Unn heard her name. When she turned, she knew that the man she saw could be no one else but Turg.

The look on his face showed that he knew who she was—she was the only woman on the field, after all—and his expression was one of pure hate. Different from the bloodlust and defensive terror she saw on the visages around her...a consumed look.

For a split second she thought of Thorstein, and what he would be like if she had been killed and her murderer known to him. He would have entertained no thought of her guilt or complicity, she knew. He would be ravaged with grief and bent on revenge.

Just like this man who was now spurring his horse towards her.

She scanned the muddy ground again and still saw no axe or sword. Her knife was gone. Instinct took over, and she could almost hear her father's voice—she would swear that she did, in later years—urging her to rush the horse.

She did, squatting down just as she met them and Turg's sword arm raised. The horse reared and Unn jumped just underneath and to the side as it did, narrowly avoiding its hooves and grasping at Turg's foot, yanking it from the stirrup.

He turned to swing at her but fell from the saddle, landing hard in the mud. She grabbed at his sword arm, tucking it and leaping across his chest in a wrestling hold that she had used to defeat her brothers time and again as a girl.

Turg had evidently wrestled his brothers, as well. He rolled, the correct answer to her hold, and punched her full in the face with his free hand, causing her to gasp and her grip to falter. Before he could completely loosen his arm, however, she swung her knee into his armpit, kicking up and bringing her elbow up under his chin, hard enough to daze him, and when she swung her elbow again, across his jaw this time, she felt his body soften.

That was all she needed to lean over, reach the knife hilt she saw in his belt, and slice his own blade across his throat.

Blood gushed in a spurt, hot onto her chest, spilling onto the ground all around them, slicking her hands, their clothes, and filling her nostrils with a heavy, metallic scent. Resisting the urge to push away, she cut him again, the blade struggling to find solid flesh in the pulsing waves of blood.

His eyes glazed and he fell back. Unn struggled to her knees and then her feet.

The battle raged on. Frantically she looked around and pried an axe from the hand of a dead man, and a lance from the hand of another.

She vomited when his head came loose, but straightened immediately, wiping her sleeve across her mouth and stabbing the lance's point into Turg's open throat.

Lifting it aloft—and staggering to balance its surprising weight— she screamed hoarsely, blood spraying from her split lip.

"Turg is dead! Your master is dead!"

Men from both sides turned to behold the grisly sight of Turg's head held up, and the fights that were making up the battle began to cease, slowly, as several of his men began to run or ride away.

"Take this!" Unn shouted to one of her men, and she grabbed the reins of Turg's horse, putting her own foot in the stirrup, and jumping to mount. She kicked her heels and took off towards the settlement, hearing Hord's voice behind her, shouting orders to her men to let none of Turg's men escape.

An arrow whizzed past her and a chill of fear almost caused her to turn the horse, but she didn't. She rode hard until the walls of the encampment were in sight, and when she saw fighting in the courtyard she urged the horse even harder, swinging her leg over the top to jump from the saddle before the animal came to a stop.

Hord, in wolf form, shot past her, snarling and tearing at the arm—and then the throat—of the man about to strike a death blow to a bleeding Olaf.

Unn ran to another man, raining down blows on the door of the longhouse where The Eye was bolted inside. She tackled him, fighting him for control of his ax until the door swung open and an arrow flew through the doorway and went deep into his chest. The Eye raised the bow again but when Unn saw where it was aimed, she raised her hand to stop her child from shooting.

Helga was holding up a sword, deflecting blows from a short man almost exactly her height.

"Mother–"

"Wait, wait one moment..."

Helga took a gash to the arm before knocking the man's sword away from him and slashing him back. It was not a serious wound, but Unn went closer, picking up his sword, holding it at the ready, but willing her daughter-in-law to defend herself.

Helga's attacker charged her, grabbing for her sword and knocking them both to the ground in the process. Unn watched him punch her directly in the face, her cries causing Hord the wolf to turn, but Unn called to him and shook her head.

She could see the man did not have the advantage.

"He is weak, Helga! Kill him!"

Olaf was getting to his feet and staggered towards his mother, but Unn could see that Helga–after taking another blow to the face–was struggling to reach her calf, where a knife was sheathed.

As the man raised up Helga stabbed him, hesitantly at first, but as he shifted and slouched away from her, her cries of pain became shrieks of anger, and Olaf slowed to a shuffle and watched as his mother straddled her attacker and stabbed him again and again, his blood splattering her face and chest as she continued to scream.

When she finally slumped off him, exhausted, Olaf went to help her up, and as Helga rose, she caught Unn's eye. She would be forever changed, Unn thought, but unlike the change that had overtaken her after Thor's death, this one brought a part of her forward.

The fight had broken her nose and knocked a tooth loose, but Helga's charm only increased in the following years. Her countenance happier and her stride more confident, she once again looked at men who looked at her and chose one every now and then as a companion. In her later years she gave birth to a daughter that Unn loved and counted among her grandchildren...but she never let a man live in her home, and if anyone ever asked if she was married, she always said yes...to Thorstein Olafson.

Twenty of Unn's men were lost in the battle, a hard loss, but none of those who came to kill them were left to travel home in the boats that Unn and her people eventually found down the coast.

Bjorn was found in the forest, slowed by an arrow in his leg that caused all of them to worry for a good amount of time. The Eye nursed him back to full health, along with the others who were wounded, and within a short amount of time even the limp it caused had disappeared. Many years later while visiting his Uncle Helgi, he found a wife and built a home...although he and his family came back yearly, with his sister Yngvild the Fair and her husband and children, to celebrate midsummer and pay respects to their mother.

Olaf had also been wounded, with some cuts to his face and side that were sewn up and left scars that he joked in later life made him look more fearsome than he was.

"The only battle I ever fought was at twelve years old," he liked to say in his old age, "And its hero was my grandmother. The gods decided I deserved a life of peace, after that."

He married a girl he met in the north, on a trading expedition with the tribes who lived in the remote northern regions. She was slightly taller than him and a ferocious fighter who had won renown as a warrior with her people...sometimes against the Norse.

Unn named him as her successor, and one of the reasons she cited for doing so was his success in winning a wife that he had to convert from hating his kind.

"Keeping peace with anyone else will be an easy task compared to that feat," she would laugh.

Olaf and his wife, and the wolf men and the others expanded the reach of the settlement year by year, making families and growing crops, raising cattle and children in the shadow of the forest, by the sound of the waves of the sea.

As Unn grew older she wrote of her experiences, with the help of The Eye, who took down all that happened as Unn remembered it, and all that they learned of the wolf men as they lived side by side, year after year, sharing stories of their lives and how they came to discover that they were what they were.

Some of the mere men who had fought and lived with her moved on, to other lands...but not one of the wolf men left.

In the long winter nights, when they would gather in one longhouse and tell stories and drink, each of them admitted in turn that the calm they felt with Unn was nothing they had felt before, and that they worried that when Unn was gone they would become wild again.

Because long life was a feature of their affliction; decades had passed and none of them looked a day older than they had when they left Dyflin, and all of them had admitted to living for many years before coming into Olaf the White's company.

"You must do your best," Unn would say. "And remember this time. When all else fails, remember how you felt, remember what it was like to be calm. You will find it again. I know it."

The Eye suggested that maybe there were others who had the ability to calm turnskins' impulses to change, the way that Unn did, and wondered aloud if once she were gone, the band of wolf men— leu garulf, as they now called themselves, a word that one of their number said was used in his homeland to describe their kind—should devise a way to search the world for others who had the gift.

They all agreed, and a plan was made to disperse around the world to search after the death of Unn...along with a pact that they remain in contact and support each other always.

"Your strength is not me," Unn said, repeatedly, in her last days, "It is that you are together and understand each other. This world will not understand you...you must make your own world within this one, and you must protect each other. Promise me."

Each one of them did promise her.

As it became clearer that Unn's strength was failing, the wolf man Hord stayed in wolf form more and more. He lay at Unn's feet or on her bed, warming her as she became more and more frail.

It was his howl that woke the house in the early hours of one winter morning, telling all, wordlessly, that she had died. She was deeply mourned. Her burial feast drew kin and friends from far and wide, and the whole of the village that had grown around the settlement keenly felt her loss.

After some time, the leu garulf came together and prepared for their dispersal. The great-great granddaughter of Unn, called Unna, shared not just her great-great grandmother's name, but also her ability to soothe the tendencies of the wolf men, proving the belief of The Eye that it was a trait not unique to Unn.

Some of the group decided to stay, for this reason, but most kept to the original agreement to go out into the world and find others. They resolved to meet again in five years and share what they had learned.

Unn's great-grandson, Ruaidhrí mac Auley–Auley being the name Olaf was called by his northern kinsman–the father of Unna, built a stone tower as a memorial for his great-grandmother and a testament to the battle that was fought in the valley beneath their village, called The Sunset War by those who were there, because of the eerie light that had illuminated the valley as the moon passed over the sun in midday, an omen all had taken to be a sign from the gods. He embraced each wolf man as they left the gates, telling them that the family of Unn would always be grateful to those who fought alongside her and made their lives possible.

The wolf man Hord did not change back into human form to bid his brothers goodbye.

He stayed by the side of The Eye for years as a wolf.

He went along when The Eye found life without Unn in the village unbearable and retreated to a hut deep in the forest.

Olaf-Auley, Ruaidhrí, and young Unna came to the hut often, bringing food and writing utensils. The Eye spent time walking in the woods, copying the discoveries that the Eye and Unn had made about the wolf men and written down, so that there was more than one book of each volume. The wolf men themselves came from time to time, both to visit, and to tell some remembered bit of their early lives, or experience that might be useful to remember.

The wolf Hord never sat with them, or anyone, as a man.

Villagers would come, seeking remedies for ills, or answers to questions, and The Eye would talk with them, make poultices and teas, listen to their concerns and their dreams, and share whatever visions or wisdom were revealed.

One rainy spring day Unna came to the hut, and found The Eye, lying dead, eyes open, and the wolf Hord gone.

The Eye was buried next to Unn, and the burial feast lasted three days. Unna Ruaidhrísdottir brought all of the copies of the books that The Eye had copied into the village, and took over their upkeep.

When the next five-year mark hit, the wolf men returned to Faol Srath–the name their northern neighbors had given their settlement, although the Norse among them called it Ullfur--Unna presented each group with copies of what was their only known history, pieced together from accounts given by each leu garulf, and observations of The Eye about the characteristics of both the wolf men and the women who were tamers of the worst of their impulses.

"It is my intent that this town stay a sanctuary for you until the end of time," Unna said. "But in the case that it does not...you must take these with you, and meet regularly, to fill them with what you learn about your kind in the world. These books will be your true home...do not let it be destroyed."

This time, the man Hord appeared, in his human form. He embraced his wolf brothers, mourned those that did not reappear, and read the updates that had been made to their books.

This book was begun by The Eye, and until it was finished by Unna's descendant Oona Mac Auley, the children of Unn lived in the town Ullfur, which spread its boundaries into the sea and onto a neighboring island after some time.

The leu garulf now wander the world, seeking answers and more of their kind, and true to their promise to their tamer, Unn the Deep-Minded, they hold these volumes as their legacy for those that come after.

The spell of the story was broken by the sound of Richard clattering up the stairs.

Robin patted Jane's shoulder and looked to their siblings, all quiet, deep in thought, digesting what Jane had just read.

"These are the people we come from. The things they faced. There's more, so much more. I only saw and felt a part of it, and I'm excited to learn more, read more, and we can do that after this is over. But we have to get through this."

Robin slid to the floor, looking at each of them. "I love all of you. I know we can do this."

"I love you all too."

"I love you guys."

Each of them repeated the sentiment, grabbing hands, hugging, and then standing to go down the stairs and help Richard, who was putting crates on the sturdy dining room table.

"Everyone be careful; some of these are already loaded. I don't know what your experience level is with guns, but there's more down there. Help me, but watch out."

This can't be happening. Jane felt the course of emotion run through her again. Watching her children pick up guns was unreal. Watching them receive directions from Richard on how to fire each one, where the safety was, etc., felt like a dream. A terrible dream that had started with Kimmy's death, and simply gotten worse.

She took the book back to her room. Sitting on the bed, she told herself what she did every time something difficult had been in front of her, when she sat in the middle of a hard situation.

Picture yourself on the other side.

Her grandfather's words, for every instance. *It's like you're a time traveler; you just have to see yourself on the other side. See yourself laughing about it, glad you got through it.*

She couldn't picture herself laughing about this. But she could see them on the other side. Stronger. Maybe more jaded, but alive. She could see all of them.

Something popped outside. The sound a firecracker makes, then another.

Suddenly the sound of breaking glass and a scream, from Anne Marie. Before Jane could draw a breath, another pop came, the sound of the window behind her breaking, the mirror exploding in front of her eyes. She dropped to the ground.

It's happening...it's happening...it's happening...

Jane crawled to the door and ran down the stairs.

Richard and Lucas were holding what looked like a metal hurricane shutter to one of the enormous windows, Howard hammering it to the wall. Several of the others had been covered, and Robin and Anne Marie were standing next to the table, also holding guns, pistols.

"Jesus," Jane waved them towards the room where she and Howard had watched Robin's transformation. "Get in there; it's an inner room, no windows." She grabbed a 9-millimeter from the table and checked the clip, sliding a round into the chamber.

Lucas laughed. "Damn, Mom, like a gangst..." Another hail of bullets rattled the windows, making Anne Marie shriek again.

"Stop that, goddammit, Anne Marie!" Jane looked around. No bullets had reached them, thanks to the window covering efforts of Richard and the others. She waved them away.

"Get to the center, where's..." a sudden moment of panic. "Where's Abe?"

"He's out with the guard change," Howard's voice was somber.

"We have to get him in!" Jane started towards the door, and Howard grabbed her.

"He wants you in here. Get to the center, in front of that door, in front of the kids."

Lucas stepped around her. "If you think I'm letting my mom stand in front of me in a gunfight, you're crazy."

Exasperated, Jane sighed as he gestured with his head. "Mom, get in the room."

"I need to help them; we need as many eyes on the outside as possible." Jane pointed where Howard and Richard were standing, aiming rifles through slits in the shutters, looking at the walkways leading to the house, illuminated by flood lights. Jane could see through the cracks around the metal covering the windows.

"We can handle that." Lucas went to the door. Jane pointed to the back.

"I'm covering the back door."

Jane pulled her cell phone out, calling Howard's name as she dialed Abe's number. When he answered, his voice was breathless and whispered.

"Yes, Jane, are you okay?"

"We're fine, Dad," the word caught in her throat. "Please, get in here if you can, but if you can't, tell them we need to parley. Tell their leader..."

She could hear the next rain of bullets in stereo, both through the phone and outside, and Abe's shouts. Her heart in her mouth, she wondered if her impulsiveness had killed him, distracted him into getting shot. But she heard his shouts to the other men, and then squelching and tearing, and growls.

She put the phone down, watching through the slit, gun barrel aimed through it, fighting tears as she listened to what sounded like a dog fight through the speaker, unable to hang up and sever the connection.

"Mom, what's happening?"

"Anne Marie," Jane sobbed, listening to her father fight, as a wolf, through the phone on the floor. "Get back in the room, take another gun, and if anyone gets through this window and me, shut yourself in. Shoot anyone who comes through the door that isn't one of us, don't stop shooting until the bullets are gone."

Jane gasped. A man in black came through the hedge and toward the window, crouched as he approached, gun aimed towards the house. He wasn't wearing a vest, just a button-up black shirt and pants. No hat. It wasn't who they needed. For a moment she froze; should she shout a warning? Was this the only way? And then her finger squeezed the trigger and the report and recoil of the gun made her shout, even as it missed him. He fired and she screamed when the bullet hit the shutter just above her head and he kept moving forward. This time, she aimed lower, pulled the trigger again and saw the spray behind his head as it rocked back and he fell.

It was that quick. That easy.

I just killed a man.

Guns went off elsewhere in the house, and Jane had to force herself not to look, to keep her eyes on her patch of ground, to defend against anyone coming through. Her phone was still lying on the floor beside her, and she could still hear growls, snarls, and yelps. She heard Anne Marie shriek behind her and turned, almost involuntarily, and saw the door buckling under an enormous crash at the same moment she heard it.

There was a blinding light behind it, and the gunning of an engine. Jane panicked.

They're driving through the door!

Lucas and Richard were firing their rifles through the buckled sides and the door eased backwards as the truck that had barreled into it pulled back.

Richard's rifle clicked, empty, and he threw it to the side. Pulling his sweater over his head, in an instant he was a wolf, slipping and scrabbling on the tile before kicking his pants and shoes off of his back legs and leaping through the gap, snarling. Lucas's face went white as he watched, but he quickly returned to firing, and Jane could hear truck tires spinning.

She turned to slam the door of the room where Anne Marie and Robin were, and Robin held up a hand to halt her, momentarily. "Remember, Mom, black hat, black vest. He's our chance."

Jane nodded and pointed at the guns. "Don't let anyone but one of us through this door." And then she slammed it shut, pulling the table in front of it.

"Lucas! Fire at the lights!" She was running to the door, Lucas still shooting through it. The truck reversed, revved and rammed towards them and Lucas hit the header light flooding the entryway, then each of the headlights, shrouding the entryway in darkness again.

"Mom, the driver, it's him! Help me get him…"

Before her *"No!"* could get out of her mouth, Lucas was through the door and a gunshot rang out. Jane heard his cry and screamed, running to the door and sliding to the floor to go under and through the mangled door and outside.

Lucas was standing up, but there was blood leaking from his collarbone. Jane saw the driver, the black hat, black vest–and her immediate reflex was to aim. Lucas's shot rang out first, fired from his right hand at almost point-blank range, and the driver shouted. The passenger raised his gun, aiming at Lucas and Jane felt herself shoot before her mind had followed through. He slumped forward, lifeless, and Jane jumped to the hood of the truck, scrambling over to where Lucas and the driver were struggling for Lucas's gun.

Jane felt her hand tighten, almost of its own accord, but Robin's words rang out in her mind.

We have to take him alive.

She turned the gun around and as soon as the back of his head was exposed, she swung it with all her strength. He swore and she swung harder, and then swung again, yelling and willing it to knock him out.

The third time she hit him, he slumped. Lucas jumped up and immediately grabbed his arms, groaning in pain when he realized how badly he was injured.

"I'll get this arm–just get back inside!" Jane and Lucas dragged the unconscious young man over the driveway and pulled him through the door.

Jane tried not to panic as she looked at Lucas's pale face, shouting at Anne Marie to get rope, chain, anything they could get around this kid's neck before he woke up. Because she knew, somehow, that his waking defensive instinct would be to turn. And if he did, they would be in trouble.

Jane heard the rumble of vehicles, more gunfire, and wondered if it was allies, from Ridgeline, or more of the Brotherhood. Lucas was helping her hold their captive, and Jane was fixated on her son's collarbone. Blood was slowly creeping across his shirt and she fought the urge to drop the limp man and grab Lucas and run. Run where? Anne Marie was fumbling in the garage, and Jane heard the rattle of her tossing things as she looked. She dragged Black Hat Boy to the living room, and then to the inner pantry where Robin was. Pushing the table aside she shouted, "It's Mom," before swinging open the door and dragging the young man inside with her.

"Give it here," she took the length of rope Anne Marie brought. "Help me get it around his neck–tight. Lucas, do you have a knife on you?" He always did. Jane could see he was using his non-dominant hand and her heart clenched, trying to gauge if the stain on the front of his shirt had grown. He saw her eyes and snapped, "I'm fine, stop looking at me like that." But Jane could tell his voice was weak.

"Anne Marie get his knife–cut another length off of this."

Together, at Jane's direction, they bound the boy's hands behind him and put the rope around his head, noose-like, tying it to the knob of the door behind them, that led to the garage. "Quick!"

Jane looked out at her phone on the floor, trying not to picture what was happening outside, trying not to feel the increasingly desperate terror of what would happen to them if Abe, or Richard, or Howard…or all three of them…were killed.

"If he wakes up and turns, this is going to be a fight none of us want, trust me."

They had barely secured the knot when his eyes opened and he sprang to consciousness, shouting and flailing. All of them backed away, and it was only then Robin and Anne Marie noticed Lucas's shoulder.

"Oh my God…Luc…you're bleeding!"

Jane grabbed at the young man, patting his pockets as he swore at her. Lucas had shot his wrist–it was bloody and bent–but other than that and the bloody scalp Jane had given him, he seemed unhurt. Jane pulled a phone from his pants.

"You bitch! Let me go! Get your fucking hands off me, you tamer piece of shit!"

They all gaped at him, as Jane tapped the phone to life and held it up.

"Code, please."

"Fuck you."

Anne Marie hit the bound man with a force that shocked Jane, and she fought the urge to scold her, realizing the irony of the impulse and also feeling impressed by her daughter. Jane tapped the phone again. "Turn him over."

Anne Marie rolled the prisoner to his back and Jane grabbed a finger–from the broken wrist hand–and put it over the Touch ID on the screen. He screamed in pain and the phone unlocked. She hit the call button, and the first name—five missed calls--read, "Tată." She held it up.

"Who is this? The person in charge? Who is Tată?"

A silent, surly stare was the young man's only response.

"It's Romanian. For "father"." They all turned to see Howard.

Jane turned to him. "Is his father in charge of the Brotherhood?"

Even before Howard's reply Jane could see by the boy's face she had guessed correctly. She hit the number.

"Don't you do that! You fucking–"

"Shut him up," Jane nodded at Anne Marie, who punched the young man squarely in the mouth for a second time. Her daughter evidently had a side this conflict had released, Jane thought with concern...and a little pride. She grabbed a dish towel from the bench behind them, shoving it into his mouth.

Two rings.

"Și e o țeapă pentru toată lumea! Ce naiba se întâmpla?"

"This is going to have to be in English," Jane said, making her voice calm. "I'm looking at your son and hoping you love him enough to cease this madness and come talk to me."

There was a long silence at the other end before the voice spoke again. It was also calm, but the anger was palpable.

"I'm not the one who started this. What's happening right now wasn't my idea. I'll try to stop it, but I'll tell you right now I don't like being threatened.

Jane felt a surge of rage. "And I don't like being shot at, and I like it even less when my children are shot at, and my family members killed. Stop them now or he'll die badly. Call when you're close, I'll keep his phone on; I'm assuming you can track his location if it's true you didn't send him here."

She hung up.

Lucas chuckled. "Mom was born to do this shi…" His voice faded as his face paled and he would have fallen to the floor if Robin and Anne Marie hadn't caught him.

"Lay him down," Jane said, her eyes never leaving their captive. "Robin, get one of those dish towels and put pressure on it. Anne Marie…search how to take care of a bullet wound."

11

"Trust not him whose father, brother or other kin you have slain no matter how young he be, for often grows the wolf in the child."
                                                    ~ Völsunga Saga, c.21

Howard ran back out, to try and spread the word that they had the leader, as Jane wondered if the voice on the phone called someone who was there.

However the message was relayed, the shooting and the shouting stopped. They all looked at each other, and Jane stood to go to the door and see if she could tell what was happening. Lucas had come around, and was cursing at his siblings, who were pouring vodka they'd found in a cupboard onto his wound. Mercifully there was nothing to dig out; the bullet had ricocheted off his collarbone. They fashioned a bandage out of paper towels, packing tape from the junk drawer, and a potholder. Jane glanced at their prisoner, who glared at her and mumbled something through the dish towel.

She went through the door cautiously and felt a surge of relief when she heard Richard's voice as he came through the door, naked and muddy, carrying his clothes.

"Oh my God," Anne Marie shook her head. "Way too much comfort with nudity in this group."

"Did you do this?" Richard looked at Jane and waved toward the door. "They're saying they were told to wait for a parley..."

Abe came through next and Jane rushed to embrace him, even though he too, was naked and muddy.

"It's stopped, for now. I'm assuming we have..."

Jane pointed to the pantry, where Anne Marie and Robin were stepping through and greeting everyone with relief.

"He's in there."

Abe stepped through and looked.

"Do you know who he is?" Jane asked.

"His name is Andreas Vaulni. He's the son of the leader of the Brotherhood."

Jane looked outside nervously. "I can't see a thing; what happened? Did the Ridgeliners make it?"

"Yes. There's a…line, we'll call it. Someone called out to the Brotherhood to stop. I'm assuming—"

"I called his father."

Heads swiveled.

"He'll call when he's close. He's coming in to talk."

"Alexander Vaulni likely owns a jet, or at the very least a helicopter, but unless he's somewhere nearby, orchestrating this, or somewhere else, he's coming from Seattle. We have a couple of hours to wait." Howard laid his gun on the table.

Jane was trying to lower her adrenaline, looking at their captive. "The Brotherhood boss lives in Seattle? They really are the posh *lugaru*, aren't they?"

"We need to use this time to formulate what is going to happen," Howard went to the sink and filled a glass with water, an almost comically practical act, Jane thought, after a firefight.

"There's no formulating; we will tell him to leave us the fuck alone and we won't behead this brat."

"Mom," Robin held up their hands. "I will handle this. It needs to be addressed in a particular way; Howard is right."

What a difference a seiðr makes, Jane thought, remembering that only a few days ago this child of hers was too anxious to make their own doctor appointment. Now they were issuing directives as if they'd done it all their life.

Jane took a deep breath and laid down her gun as well. She suddenly felt sick to her stomach, thinking of the body just behind them, outside in the bushes. The one in the truck outside.

She sat at the table. Robin was asking Howard about his contact, who he said was en route. He made a call, speaking French, and with her high school vocabulary Jane could pick out the words "Brotherhood," "head," and the phrase "arriving soon."

After ending the conversation, he informed the group it would be another day, at the soonest, before a meeting would be possible with the scientist who could confirm Robin's vision, and only in the event it was on neutral ground, with a limited number of participants. Howard suggested Boise, with him and Robin going.

"I'm going as well," Jane insisted, and shook her head as the protests began. "No, I'm winning this one. I'm going."

Anne Marie was looking outside. "We need to get this door back up."

"The truce will hold," Abe sounded calm and confident. "At least until whatever happens here happens."

"Let me guess," Lucas's voice was weak, from the couch where he was stretched out. "Werewolf code of conduct."

"They don't like that word," Jane said softly, suddenly feeling very tired.

"How long do you think we'll have? Do you think we should rest?"

"I do," Abe said, decisively, indicating the stairs. "It will be a few hours, like Howard said, but we need to use that time to our advantage, and if this doesn't go well, we may need to fight again."

Everyone seemed to wilt at this, and they all looked at each other.

"He's right," Jane said softly. "Let Lucas sleep here on the couch. Everyone else, go grab a few hours of sleep." She looked at her father. "The men from Ridgeline are guarding the house, right?"

Abe shrugged. "If we can't trust Vaulni not to rush us with his kid in here, it won't matter where we are in the house if he does it. We're surrounded and we will be vastly outgunned."

Jane's blood ran cold. She had not been past the still blocked front door– which was only propped up now, still off its hinges, and so the depth of their situation hadn't been visible to her.

Robin and Anne Marie went upstairs, Abe sent Richard as well and told Howard he would take the first watch if he could be relieved in an hour.

"Can you call one of the men in?" Jane felt concern for him. "You should get rest too."

Abe stood, staring at the young man tied to a door by his neck in their pantry.

"I trust everyone on this place with my life, and with your lives. But this," he jutted his chin towards Andreas Vaulni, whose hateful dark eyes seemed to seethe with rage. "I trust to no one else." He looked at Jane meaningfully. "Watch what you say in front of him."

Howard nodded to her and went upstairs.

Tired, but feeling as if she should stay with her father, Jane pulled out a chair and sat, looking at Andreas as well.

An impulse came over her, as she looked into his hate-filled eyes, and she stood, walking closer.

There had been no time, during all of the revelations of the past few days–had it really only been days?--to sit with the part about her new-found identity.

Tamer.

Was it only a passive gift?

Andreas Vaulni began to squirm, and the hate in his eyes changed, ever so slightly…to fear.

Could she…was it possible to…

He screamed through the dish towel.

Jane remembered all of the times she had sat, meditating, willing love and light to her children. Imagining the positive energy emanating from her, from the center of her being, and floating to them, bathing them in peace.

Now she visualized a different type of "peace" coming from her heart, snaking toward and around the Vaulni on the floor…one that wrapped him like a rope, squeezing power out of him.

"Jane, stop." Her father's voice brought her back. She turned to look at him, and he shook his head. "Don't do that."

She stepped back, taking a seat next to Abe.

"So they're Romanian."

"The Vaulni brothers lived there for many years before coming to America. Alexander Vaulni was born in Hungary, about 400 years ago. This one here, well, he's about your age, Jane."

The young man said something through the dish towel and kicked his feet angrily.

"The rumor," Abe leaned forward meaningfully, "Was that Amadeo Vaulni, this asshole's biological father, ripped out this boy's mother's throat. Probably in a jealous rage. So, I guess killing women runs in the family."

Again, the kicking and rageful mumbling.

"Are you sure you're going to be okay sitting up with him?"

"I'll be fine." Abe seemed not quite fine, but Jane's eyes were shutting on their own, and even the thought of having one of The Brotherhood, the group that now was clearly behind her aunt's death, mere feet away could not keep them open.

She went to the small loveseat across from Lucas, moved it so she faced him more fully, then laid down and was immediately asleep.

It seemed like only minutes had passed when she sprang awake, shocked into consciousness by a dream where the roof had flown off of the house.

She immediately turned to the table, and the pantry.

Howard sat in the chair where Abe had been when she went to sleep. Jane grabbed her phone. She had been sleeping for three hours. She stood, slowly, and bent over Lucas to look at his bandage before walking to the kitchen.

"How's our guest?" she asked Howard, gazing into the pantry. Andreas Vaulni wasn't asleep. His dark brown eyes stared into Howard's obsidian ones, and even in the seriousness of their situation Jane had to shake her head.

That's a staring contest that could go until the end of time.

She was just about to ask if she should make coffee when she was interrupted by a loud rumble, and a floodlight sweeping through the house.

"I think our other guest is here." Howard said.

It was only a matter of minutes before Anne Marie, Robin, and Richard all came down the stairs. Everyone but Abe rushed to peek through the cracks in the shutters, only seeing the black outline of the helicopter as it landed, 25 yards or so from the house. It was on a flat plain Jane could now see housed several trucks and what looked like bloodstains in the snow.

They all looked at each other, a telepathic sorting quickly taking place about who would do what, who would stand where, and who would protect whom. Lucas struggled to his feet, Richard finished putting on his clothes.

Howard looked at Robin, who sat down silently next to him at the table.

Anne Marie came to Jane's side.

Lucas, groaning, picked up his gun and stood by his grandfather.

And they all waited.

They could hear voices, they saw flashlights. Two burly men pulled the demolished door all the way off its frame, and Jane heard every gun in the room click, saw all of her family tense, and raise their weapons.

Only she and Robin left their hands down.

"Sir, wait..." One of the hefty shadows stepped into the foyer, holding a firearm and peering at them. The other did as well, shining a flashlight into all of their faces.

A dark figure wearing an overcoat stepped through as well. Tall, slender. He walked past the two bodyguards, waving off their warnings.

"Can someone turn on some lights?"

Abe reached over to the wall near where he stood and flipped a switch.

The overhead dining room lights came on, and they all blinked.

Alexander Vaulni was handsome, dark-haired, age-wise appearing to be about thirty-five or forty, and impeccably dressed–something Jane found almost hilarious as she looked around at all of them. He looked at each face with barely concealed contempt.

"Where is my son?" he asked quietly, each word a clipped, accented syllable.

As if on cue, the young man in the pantry gave a muffled yowl.

"I am taking him out of this dump, right now."

"Mr. Vaulni," Robin's quiet voice was barely audible. "Could we sit and talk first?"

Vaulni blinked, looking at the table as if he couldn't believe Robin's audacity in addressing him.

"Are you the...seer? Are you going to read my palm?"

His gray-blue eyes landed on Jane. "And you...you're Mommy? Was it you who called me?" His nostrils flared slightly as if he was smelling something unpleasant and his brow furrowed as he looked her up and down. "You're the tamer."

"Yes, to all of those." Jane suddenly felt the fullness of the realization of who she was standing in front of. "And you're the man responsible for the death of my mother, and the woman who raised me after you took her." Her hand gripped the gun in her hand tighter and she felt it rising, until it was pointed at Alexander Vaulni's face.

"How can one person deal one family so much pain? What kind of evil drives something like that?" Everywhere around her, her family was speaking her name while holding up their hands. Vaulni himself smiled, holding her gaze with otherworldly calm.

"My father gave the order to kill your mother, yes. This other one...that was my son, and it was against my instructions. He's also the one intent on killing you." He gestured around the room, "And the rest of this...happy family."

"Mom," Robin's voice was strong. "Put the gun down. We have to talk with him."

"Yes, put the gun down, Mom," Vaulni held her gaze as he shrugged off his coat, black wool, which he handed to one of his guards and waved the man to put away his gun. "I'm very curious to hear what your little magician has to say." He walked to the table, pulled a chair out, looked down at it for a moment and made a face before he sat down.

Jane looked at her father, and then at Richard. Both of their faces were stone. Both of them looking at the man who was, if not responsible for Kimmy's death, at least indirectly involved, both knowing the boy who effectively pulled the trigger was mere feet away. All of the other children moved towards Jane, only Howard and Robin sitting at the table with Vaulni.

"I saw something today," Robin said. "I saw between worlds. I saw with the eyes of a common ancestor of ours."

Vaulni snorted. "The Brotherhood doesn't practice black arts. This doesn't hold any power with me."

"I don't practice black arts either," Robin shrugged. "I just took some mushrooms and henbane with some ashes in it, and I was able to see what started the blood feud."

"That's not a secret," Vaulni said. "The blood feud started with tamers, working with humans to eradicate us. Transfixing us, trapping us, leading us to our death. Generations of *lugaru* murdered, almost exterminated completely, besmirched by a campaign of lies—"

"They weren't all lies." Abe interrupted. "There was murder on both sides, you know this! You killing innocent women now doesn't atone for---"

"Innocent?" Vaulni laughed. "You mean innocent like Renee Roubideaux?" Jane took a step forward in anger. Anne Marie grabbed her arm.

Vaulni saw it, turning his full attention to Jane.

"I'll give you the benefit of the doubt, since you were probably raised by Agricole, yes? Who, no doubt, talked of his sainted daughter?" He shook his head. "She was a maniacally jealous drug addict. Your father misjudged her, trusted her, told her what he was.

And then, she talked. She was so angry at your father for not putting up with her bullshit that she threatened to tell the world what he was. What all of us were. She called a journalist–"

Abe lunged at him, a terrifying snarl coming from his throat, and a shudder ran across his skin, an almost-change. A momentary loss of control. Lucas and Howard jumped to restrain him, but Vaulni laughed, not even blinking.

He went on.

"She called a journalist, and when they wouldn't listen, she went down to the news station. They didn't believe it of course, but it set off a chain of events that resulted in my father ordering a car accident."

Silence fell on the room. Until he continued.

"My father was the leader of the Brotherhood, yes, but back then he was also a security director for the Old Order. That was the capacity he killed your mother in, Tamer. Not as some rogue actor, but as an official carrying out a sentence." He looked around, landing on Howard. "All of you are surprised by this? Even you, Doctor of *lugaru* history?" Howard's silence and shocked expression were answer enough. Vaulni nodded and continued.

"My father orchestrated the accident. Killed your mother. And when he learned there was a sister, he sent me to Agricole's home, to kill her. Agricole was packing everyone up to flee. The sister, Kim, wasn't there, but you were."

"The council hadn't said anything about the rest of the family, but Agricole knew it was heavily influenced by the Brotherhood at that time, and that you and your aunt would be on their radar. Hence his desire to move and cover your tracks. He was going to change everyone's last name, he assured me. No one would ever know who you were."

"Your grandfather, what a fighter. He killed three men, one of them my cousin, Felix, another my brother, Amadeo. And when he got to me, I honestly thought I would die there too, but he turned back into a man and asked me to do the same. He had an offer."

"He said he existed outside of our world and our rules. That we had already punished his daughter, and if I would let his other daughter and his granddaughter live, they would never tame a turnskin. Never exert power in our world. He said he wouldn't even tell either of you what you were."

Vaulni leaned onto the table, staring at Jane.

"Think what you like about me, but I am a reasonable man. I have my beliefs, and they include the one that tamers may be responsible for our demise. I believe it's already happening. There are only a fraction of turnskins born now, compared to the past."

Something flickered in his eyes.

"But I have never believed that we needed to kill innocents. And I believe in the old ways of respect and honor, as well. I made a blood pact with Agricole Roubideaux that day, and I kept it."

Here he turned and pointed to Abe. "You let yourself be discovered by Kimbell Roubideaux. You let her stay when she came here." He shrugged.

"She violated the agreement."

"The agreement died with Pappy," Robin said slowly. "We can't be held to it after his death. You're rationalizing your son's behavior. He's the one who discovered Kimmy was here, and who misunderstood her work–she was going to publish findings to the Council that outlined how to bolster the dwindling birthrates of *lugaru*. Tamer DNA is part of it–we can show you the research and Howard is bringing in a scientist who can interpret it for you–an objective scientist with no ties to either camp."

His face was motionless, but Jane could sense Vaulni's mental wheels turning.

Robin went on.

"The future won't be the same. To keep existing, *lugaru* must evolve. They must change. And tamers will help with that–I've seen it. There's a change coming to the world, as well. Our kind will have a battle, with some humans, with some on our side, but after the destruction, there's a chance for paradise."

Still silent, but Jane saw the tiniest furrow in his brow. Suddenly something became clear to her.

"You're losing control," she said, quietly. Vaulni's eyes snapped to her angrily, then glanced at the door of the room where he knew his son was tied up.

"Yes, he can hear us," Jane walked towards the door. She could see Vaulni's son, desperately trying to work the dish towel out of his mouth, eyes burning with rage. "But that's okay. He's the one who believes he'll take control from you. It's not a secret." She waved towards the door. "All of these men followed him here. Maybe thinking you gave the order, but...maybe not. Maybe just following him."

Vaulni stared at her, hard. He turned to Robin.

"You said you knew why the blood feud was carried on. Tell me, fortune teller. Why?"

"Andreas is Amadeo's son, that you took to raise. He discovered your compromise, and believes it was weak, and that it's his duty to avenge his father. Even though all of it should technically have ended when our grandfather died."

Robin stood, and Vaulni's men instinctively reacted. A shake of his head, and they relaxed.

Robin went to the wall, to the family tree, and pointed.

"Your brother," Robin said quietly, "Is one of our common ancestors. He was Pappy's father."

They looked at Vaulni. "Did he know?" The silence was deafening, and prolonged.

"I don't know," he finally said, and there was the slightest hint of emotion in his voice. "I did not."

All of them looked around, at each other, at Vaulni, at his seething son on the floor of the pantry. Questions swirled around the room as they all digested the revelation that Jane and her children were also Vaulnis.

Alexander Vaulni shook a finger at Abe, and quietly chuckled. "You've got a good one here, Abraham. You must be proud." He shrugged. "So, even if this is true—and I'm not taking your word for it—I'm guessing you're not in a forgiving mood. And if I'm not able to control my son, and I'm not willing to leave here without him, alive, where does that leave us?"

"I know you love him." Robin's voice was soft. "I know that you want to save his life right now. And I'm telling you the only way he lives is if we do. I can see it as clear as day; if he kills another member of our family, his death quickly follows."

Another faint, almost imperceptible tell…a twitch at the side of Vaulni's mouth.

"Is that a threat?"

"No," Robin shook their head. "Just a warning. An outcome from his act. I saw it. As clearly as I am seeing you."

Alexander Vaulni sat and stared at Jane's third child for a long time.

"You know, young one. I'm four hundred and thirty years old."

"My grandfather, when I met him, was about the age I am now. He told me a story that his grandfather told him. About our people being driven out of their homes and into a region inhabited by strangers."

"Before this displacement, they changed at will. They lived as they wanted, long, long lives filled with wildness and abandon. But afterwards, they had to conform. They had to tame their true natures. Their lives grew short. Dull. They became farmers. They forgot how they came to be, why they were different from mere men…they forgot that they were children of gods."

Vaulni changed his gaze to Jane again. "You have probably learned some tamer history by now. But do you know the stories of the *lugaru*? Do you know of the other turnskins? Do you know we were brought to the brink of extinction, and that tamers played a part? You have been told you are a complement to us. But others see you as a curse."

He sniffed, an affectation that made him look like a bad television movie villain. "I won't listen to tarot card readings or drugged visions, but," he looked at Howard. "If there is evidence–scientific evidence– that the dying out can be reversed, I'll listen."

Howard nodded, and then stepped towards Vaulni.

"*Alexandru...*" his voice was oddly friendly, and Jane saw it again, the faintest flicker of emotion on Vaulni's face. "You know the Brotherhood beliefs aren't rooted in fact, but fear. Superstition. You know it. And I know you. You're a man of reason. And heart."

"Stop," Vaulni held up a hand, the word "heart" seeming to anger him. "This isn't a conversation to be had here, but I said I would listen."

After a long, silent moment, he sighed. "And I will do everything in my power to make the boy understand that the blood feud is over. That's all I can pledge."

"Here is my pledge," Abe leaned forward. "The council already knows about this incursion. You might think because we aren't wealthy like you that we don't have influence, but that isn't true. You bring more risk of exposure through acts like this than anything this family has brought about, and your days will be numbered if it continues."

"The time of my family being fractured is over. The time of separation from my daughter and her children is over. They are fully part of us now. The council may listen to your son's reasoning about Kimmy's killing as payment for a blood feud, but it is over now. Anything else will bring consequences from the international council, and you know it."

"Yes, and I have the little magician's curse as well. I get it." Vaulni stood. "Now I'm taking my son and my men, and I'm leaving." He turned and looked at Richard, who Jane was just now seeing was gripping his gun and staring at the door of the pantry where Kimmy's killer was.

"Do we have an understanding?"

Silence.

Jane moved to her brother and touched his shoulder. "Think about what Kimmy would want, Richard. I know it's hard, I know it's awful, but," she smiled through tears. "I can't lose a brother I just found. These kids deserve all the family they can get. Please."

Richard said nothing, but looked into Jane's eyes for what felt like a lifetime to her, and then glanced at her children, who were laser focused on their newly discovered uncle. Slowly, he released his grip on the gun and allowed Jane to take it. He turned his back as Vaulni called to his men and motioned to the pantry.

"Collect him, and let's go." He stood and nodded to Howard. "Send me a pin for the meeting, and I'll see you and your scientist tomorrow."

The men hauled Andreas out and Vaulni held up a hand as one of them reached for the dish towel in his mouth.

"Let's untie him in the chopper. Maybe leave that gag in for a bit."

Vaulni swept up his coat, glanced around the room, and then left, but not before sniffing again and making an unpleasant face.

And just like that...they were gone.

They all stood, looking dumbly at each other, until Jane pointed to Lucas.

"Dad," she used the word on purpose, and his expression when he heard it made her grin. "is the doctor from Ridgeline here, by any chance? Lucas was shot."

Immediately everyone sprang to life, with Lucas waving them away until he was taken to the couch again.

Jane stood, staring at her hand with a gun in it.

"We all need therapy now." Anne Marie sank down at the table and Robin laughed.

Jane sat at Lucas's side, staring at her father. "Did you know all of that?" He shook his head.

"Not all of it. Some. I'm sorry I didn't tell you about your mother. It just didn't seem necess--"

"It's okay. Let's just clean up and try to get some normalcy. We have the rest of our lives, or mine I guess, to talk about the rest."

"Hey," Anne Marie was looking through the cupboard. "Can we make cookies or something?"

Jane stared at her for a moment, then shook her head, chuckling at the bizarreness of it all, the surreality. If nothing else she thought she understood about the world had been correct, at least one thing was stable; her children's resilience and their appetite.

At least the worst is over, she thought, as she nodded at Anne Marie and stood.

"Fuck yeah...let's make cookies."

And then...it all exploded.

12

I don't have many friends…my mother and my siblings are my friends.

I live with Anne Marie, and we're so close in age that most people think we're twins–I sometimes feel as if we are twins, and I just got left behind in the womb for another year. I'm slow, physically slow, and that would make sense. My mother likes to laugh and say I move like an elderly, drunken snail crawling through frozen molasses.

It was partially my slowness that prompted my mom to take me to the doctor when I was around seven, to see if there was something causing it. The doctor said, yes, something was causing it.

Autism.

I think she knew something was different but feared me being labeled. Eventually, I guess she became more fearful of what would happen if I wasn't. I didn't want to be labeled, either, but it did make sense. When the doctor expressed surprise and offered encouragement because I was so verbal, my mother laughed and said, "Well, look at the rest of the kids. We're chatterboxes. So chatty that even the autistic one can't get away with not talking." She deals with hard things by joking about them. It's not the worst thing in the world, but it's also not the most gentle parenting technique.

When my father would rage, we would laugh behind his back. It made it better; it made it bearable. When my mother left him and he went on a campaign of hate and destruction, it was harder to laugh, but we still did. He reduced us to a run-down garage apartment and meals from the food pantry while my mom worked multiple jobs, but we laughed about that too. And it made it bearable.

But the older we all got, the less I found to laugh about.

As a teenager, I read an article about autism after my diagnosis that said autistic people may struggle with humor. It made me feel like I didn't even fit in with the group that was supposed to explain some of my differences.

Around the same time my peers, people at school, were all talking about who they liked. Who they wanted to kiss, or do more with... and I didn't have anyone I thought those things about.

I searched "not interested in sex" and found a bunch of advice for menopausal women, and men with dropping testosterone levels...not thirteen-year-olds.

But I did find a video about being asexual and that made sense. Then I found one about being non-binary, and finally I felt like we were getting somewhere with the labeling stuff.

I remember my mom's face when I announced that I was non-binary, and asexual. At first, I thought it was disappointment but then, as I listened to her concerns...*You're not interested in anyone? You might change your mind...you might be a late bloomer..."* I realized it was fear.

Fear born out of love. Fear of me not having enough love.

She was afraid for me to be too different. I was already on the outside, and now, each successive discovery about myself put me even further out there.

I knew she thought of me as a baby bird–not the most empowering or complimentary visual–so when I looked for a name that could be gender-neutral, I asked to be called Robin. Maybe to soften the blow of tossing the old name, the one she gave me, out.

Knowing it made her afraid, for there to be so many differences making life a challenge for me, I held back telling her that there was something else.

I could see things.

I told her some, when it was too scary to keep to myself. I knew when our family dog was ill that it would be the end. I knew my brother had stolen our neighbor's bike, and where he had hidden it, and I was so terrified he would go to jail that I snitched.

I didn't tell her a lot, though. And I found that I could turn it down, to a certain degree.

I knew the fear she felt had to do with how the world would treat me. I knew that her love for me, a love so deep it hurt, because I could physically feel it sometimes, would distract her from enjoying her own life, once she got it on track, after the years tangling with my father were over and she began to climb out of the financial and psychological hole it put her in.

I didn't tell her about the times when the world wasn't kind. She knew about some of them, and if she had known about others, she might have done time.

It was comforting enough to know what she would have done, if she'd known.

What is the difference between loneliness and solitude? Is solitude when you choose it, and loneliness when you don't? I guess I made peace with feeling alone, after years of trying and trying to make friends, and seeming to succeed, only to find out that no one seemed to think of me as the friend I considered them.

Maybe my first magic trick was turning loneliness into solitude.

There were times I still wondered, though, if other people ached as deeply as I did to feel connected.

I loved being a kid with my siblings. I miss it. I miss living together, laughing together, figuring out all of our things…together. I know Anne Marie will always let me live with her, she's told me so, but I have wished it wasn't an acquiescence to my oddity. I have wished it wasn't something I've heard her say to my mom as a reassurance.

I've wished for a return to that time before, and I've even wished, weirdly enough, that we were more like animals, living in a pack, all together, for the rest of our lives.

And look…we are, in fact, animals in a way.

The phone call telling us that Kimmy had died, the urgency to get her home, the secrecy, the crazy reveal from our *grandfather*--that was a trip--all of it is like a blur now, and all the pain from before is a blur too…and I think of all of it as BS now…Before *Seiðr*.

I saw and felt so much. More than I ever thought was possible to see and feel. Instantly, I understood. I saw through The Eye's vision, I saw the sea from the hill and the little hut where The Eye felt at home—where they turned loneliness into solitude. I saw Hord, I saw such love and friendship in his eyes and felt his loyalty in the middle of my bones, like ancestral marrow, giving me health and strength. I saw Unn the Deep-Minded and felt the same love-fear that my mom feels when she looks at me, and I knew then that I was never really alone. Through years and generations my family looks at me and feels me and now I feel them. We are all connected, they are always talking to me, and they always love me…always want to help me solve the puzzle, slip out of the trap, live another day, and laugh at it all.

When I came out of the henbane fog, I could see my mother look at me differently. I felt less fear. I saw pride in her eyes and it made me happy.

I explained what I could, and as I watched my family fight, I felt pride too, and relief, it was going to go the best way possible, and no one needed to die. That was the overarching prayer, if you could call it that, that I kept whispering to the ancestors and the "gods" I felt. If any of what I have could be called magic, let me use it to keep my family safe—I can't lose any of them, not even the ones I just met. I can't imagine life without any of them, but the ancestors whispered back that you never really lose anyone, in fact you find more, silly goose, haven't you just seen that?

But I felt it, deep in my cells, that we could live. We could succeed. I pictured it, taking the son, reasoning with the father, and after the dust cleared, I watched it happen in front of me.

I watched my mother face off with Alexander Vaulni, the man that I had seen in my vision as a dark figure, lit by a full moon, taking her hand over a table and making peace. There was no touch of hands as the battle ended, but an accord was struck, and Vaulni left with his son still bound and gagged.

The feeling I had was one of an unsettled peace—the feeling you have when something almost feels too good to be true—and I wondered to myself if we could really trust that Vaulni could keep his son in check. I had looked into Andreas's eyes when he was tied up with Anne Marie and me in the pantry, and I could see so much hate, and not just hate, but resolve. The certainty alone that could carry a thirst for vengeance past reason because it had taken hold in his mind as justice.

Does a true believer give up a quest for justice?

I knew I had no choice but to trust, though. It was what I had seen, it was what we had to say, and it had worked. We had peace. The Vaulnis and their men had gone through the door. I had almost succeeded in putting the uneasy feeling aside when Richard suddenly tore off his shirt and sprang to the open doorway after them, changing into a huge gray wolf as he did so.

It happened so fast, and was so unexpected, that I couldn't move, or speak.

Like an elderly, drunken snail, through frozen molasses.

I looked up and saw my mom's face, shocked and still as well, for enough time for Richard-as-a-wolf to leap outside and disappear into the yard, illuminated by spotlights from the Vaulni helicopter.

All of us seemed to burst into action at the same time. I could hear Abe shouting as he ran, my mom too, and Howard pushed me aside and ran outside as well.

Cooi jumped over my feet, and I could hear his toenails scrambling on the hard floor even over his barking. I screamed his name and ran after all of them, feeling my siblings' hands grabbing at my arms, pulling me back, jumping at the sound of shots being fired, halting momentarily and then running for the door and then the yard when I heard my mother scream.

It was a terrible sound.

By the time she had called me to tell me about my Aunt Kimmy dying, she had known for a day. I don't know what happened or how she looked or sounded when she found out about that, but I knew it was hard. Kimmy was like her mother; she was like our grandmother… we were all devastated, but I had worried the most about my mom.

She's lost so many people—her mother and her grandfather to death, man after man to stupidity and self-preservation…so much loss.

But this…it was a wail that I'd never heard anything like. I never want to hear it again…it was a scream that pulled the hearer into the pain.

I could see her, kneeling beside Richard, who was now in his human form, lifeless.

Alexander Vaulni was on his knees too, holding the limp body of his son, whose throat had been ripped out.

And Cooi…Cooi was dead too. Next to Richard. My mom laid her head on her coyote-dog's body and screamed again, going from her dog to her brother, wailing a heartbroken cry.

I stumbled to her, putting my hand on her shoulder. I could feel and hear my siblings around us, screaming, crying, kneeling around my mother, shouting at Vaulni, whose men had guns aimed at all of us.

Abe, my grandfather, was staring at Richard's body, his hands cradling the bloody head where a Brotherhood bullet had gone through it, tears streaming down his face in disbelief.

For a moment, my mind stopped on the thought that my vision was wrong, and we were all about to die.

"No one needs to die…" I had heard it, clear as day. How could I have been wrong?

Or was I wrong? No one *needed* to die, and we were safe, Richard could have lived…

…but he didn't want to…

I looked at his body, his wide staring eyes, a person who had been alive with us in the room a minute before, and could feel his spirit still there, lingering.

I'm sorry.

I heard it whispered over and over, and couldn't tell at first if it was him, or someone…something…else, but it repeated.

I'm sorry…it was too much…

And I knew. I understood. It was too much to ask. And it was too much to live with.

We all loved Kimmy, and it did feel as if letting the man who killed her walk out the door was a betrayal in a sense, but the desire to keep everyone else we loved alive overrode it.

But not for Richard.

I knew he was sorry. I knew he didn't want to endanger us, and I also knew he had reached a knowledge that there is a point where you cannot compromise. And he not only believed we would be spared retribution if Andreas died, but we would also be kept safe from him when he would, inevitably, break his agreement.

He would never have given up. You were blinded by wanting everyone to live, but it's okay...this is my part.

That was how I learned that my sight is not foolproof, and that my desires can overshadow things. So much to learn.

And as I looked at Alexander Vaulni, I wondered if I would get the chance to.

He stared at his son, tears streaming down his face. He tried to speak and choked, and then screamed in rage.

"We had an agreement! This did not need to happen!"

He turned his frantic, angry glare on Abe, and then on my mother.

His men cocked their pistols, almost simultaneously.

In the split second that Vaulni's eyes landed on my mother, sobbing, I saw and I felt, and I realized. I remembered the whole of the vision.

I watched his face change as he looked at her, her arm around her dead dog, her head laying on her dead brother.

She raised up and lifted her eyes to his, and I could see her face too. No defiance, no anger. Just an immense sadness, blood staining her cheek.

For what seemed like an eternity, they looked at each other.

What makes us who we are? Is it our sense of humor? Is it our preferences, the things we like and love?

Is it our losses?

Her eyes moved down, almost imperceptibly, to Vaulni's dead son, the man who had killed Kimmy, and then back to Vaulni. I could see it, and he could as well, the empathy, even in the midst of her sadness. She saw someone who had lost a child–not a good person, but their child, nonetheless. She could see the grief cracking the face that had been so haughty just minutes before. She felt his pain. She felt not just this moment of his pain, but the pain of hundreds of years, pain from a past that was infinitely brutal.

In that moment, I saw clearly what makes my mother who she is. And it was beautiful.

Alexander Vaulni saw it too. Just a glimpse, clouded by pain and grief, but he saw it.

I've watched my mother, my whole life, move through loss and triumph, loss and gain, loss and defeat, loss and lessons. A repeating cycle like an individual calendar, that always, always, results in strength, even if she doesn't see it, even if she doesn't feel it right away.

I've watched life beat her down, over and over, and I've watched so much get stripped away.

What always comes back after every disappointment is her laugh, and what gets honed is her wisdom, her strength.

And her love.

When I saw Unn, in my vision, and when I saw the stream of successive mothers throughout our family line, I saw the same thing, over and over and over...a woman navigating loss and win like she was piloting a ship over rough waters, coming closer and closer to total obliteration with each storm, and laughing into the wind each time she won, until the final passage took her to the end.

In the space of minutes, Alexander Vaulni had seen my mother at her strongest, only made that way by circumstances we could never have experienced before, and then he saw how deeply she loved, how deeply she grieved those she loved, and felt how powerful her spirit–tamer or no–was.

One of Vaulni's men asked him something, in a language I didn't understand, but I knew what the question was. *What do you want us to do?*

He kept staring at my mother, as if he was seeing her for the first time. All of us were frozen, waiting to see if he gave the order for us to die, and finally he said, "This is over. We have a peace, and we are keeping it. I want you to help me get my son home. Get the men who died here and bring them too."

And just like that, they were gone. The helicopter lifted and we were left, a family sobbing in the snow.

As Vaulni left, leaving us in the dark with a doorless home, and as we carried Richard's body and Cooi inside, I thought to myself that all the lonely years, feeling like an outsider, weren't wasted at all. Even in the throes of grief, I knew in that moment that it all makes us who we are.

Loss followed by gain. Loss followed by fun. Loss followed by triumph. Loss followed by love.

My sight was improved by the *seiðr* and with every moment that goes by I feel more and more comfortable calling myself a Seer. More and more comfortable with the understanding that I'm also developing myself, and this gift that finally feels like a gift.

This is what it feels like when a feeling you've had, not even well-articulated enough to be called a dream, finally comes true.

And if *Ragnarök* is truly coming, I'm going to spend every moment savoring this time, and using it to find a way to help my family survive it.

The End

About the Author

Jill Farr lives and writes in the Pacific Northwest. To contact her team for readings, book signings, and other queries, visit jillfarr.com